I'M NOT IN LOVE

(I PROMISE)

LAUREN GREENE

ALSO BY LAUREN GREENE

<u>VENGEFUL HEARTS</u>

Dark Romance Series

Book 1 - I'm Not in Love (I Promise)

Book 2 - Bulletproof Love (*Preorder coming soon*)

<u>PALM COVE</u>

Small Town Interconnected Standalones

Book 1 - Fight For It

Book 2 - Fight For Her

Book 3 - Fight For Us

<u>GREYRIDGE</u>

Small Town Holiday Themed Novellas

Book 1 - Holiday Heartstrings

Book 2 - Holiday Hook-Up

For the ones who never outgrew their emo phase - this one's for your little black hearts.

(It's never been a phase)

AUTHOR'S NOTE

Hey loves! Before you dive into Damon and Blake's story, I want to be upfront with you about the content. This book is definitely intended for mature readers (18+) only, and I want you to be able to make an informed decision about whether it's right for you.

This story contains themes of:

VIOLENCE & CRIME
- Organized crime and criminal activities
- Gun violence and weapons
- Murder, gore, and mutilation
- Human/sex trafficking
- Stalking and kidnapping
- Physical violence
- Death (including parent and sibling)

PSYCHOLOGICAL & EMOTIONAL
- Manipulation and dubious consent

• Panic attacks
• Substance use and drugging

SEXUAL CONTENT (All scenes between consenting adults 18+)
• Explicit sexual content including oral sex and other intimate acts
• BDSM themes including dominance/submission, edging, and punishment
• Impact play and rough encounters
• Exhibitionism and voyeurism
• Various kink elements including primal play, mask play, knife play, and somnophilia
• Both gentle (praise, aftercare) and intense (degradation) elements

This isn't a complete list of everything you might encounter in the book, but I wanted to give you a good idea of what to expect. Your comfort and safety while reading means everything to me, so please make sure to check in with yourself and practice self-care while reading. If you have specific concerns or triggers you're worried about, please don't hesitate to reach out to me on social media – I'm always happy to provide more detailed content information.

Take care of yourselves!
Lauren

SPOTIFY PLAYLIST

PROLOGUE

Choosing to give my life for love is my proudest moment.
Choosing to die for her, my greatest achievement.
Fog lifts, giving way for clear resolve.
This is for her.
My angel. Lips like red roses, hair dark as night, eyes of pewter
in pale moonlight.
The highway, driven for years, suddenly an open road.
I'm cruising toward my own demise.
Bullets for kisses.
Blood for a smile.
In the end, it's you and me, baby.
Walking alone, hand in hand, endless miles.

CHAPTER ONE

DAMON

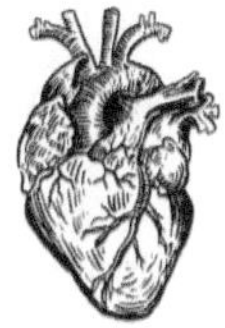

My knees crack as I crouch lower, hiding in the shadows cast by the home we're surveilling. The job is simple—I case the property and take photos of anyone coming and going, Jasper plays the invited guest, and Leon hangs back around the corner keeping tabs on cameras, ready at the wheel in case shit goes south. Knowing Jasper like I do, shit is bound to go down that way.

The time-worn brick colonial stands before me, it's weathered white trim and paint-flaked windows beckoning me to peek inside. If Leon hadn't specifically asked me to stay at least twenty feet from the place, I'd be flush against the house, watching Jasper's back through the windows.

"This is the worst," Jasper gripes. He hasn't stopped whining into my earpiece since we arrived thirty minutes ago. He drones on about something or another, but my focus shifts abruptly as a dim light flicks on in a lower bedroom. My breath catches in my throat and I'm momentarily stunned by a living, breathing angel.

Crimson lips, jet black hair, creamy skin, curves silhouetted against charcoal-gray lighting.

I sink deeper onto my knees, hiding further behind the half wall where I set up my gear, and study her.

A light breeze rattles branches nearby. They sway ominously, casting shadows across the perfectly preened lawn. Moisture from this morning's rain shower saturates the thick denim of my jeans, sending a chill through my bones. I can barely feel it over the telltale signs beginning to manifest within my body.

I've worked on pushing those familiar urges down deep for years. The thumping heartbeat. The quickening breath. The trembling limbs. The primal need that pulls me to abandon everything and go after what I want. Forget about the where or when. That never mattered, not when instinct takes over. All thoughts converge into a singular focus—a burning desire that overtakes my ability to think rationally.

My angel bobs her head, swaying rhythmically around her bedroom. Her lips move and expression shifts in intensity. Whatever she's singing along to isn't a happy ballad. She looks ready to draw blood. I'm instantly intrigued. *What's wrong and how can I make it better?*

I crane my neck to get a better look, knowing another few inches won't help. Even my slew of surveillance equipment can't get me a clear enough view. I hate that shit anyway. I prefer to use my own two eyes and sharp reflexes. The equipment just gets in the way, despite Leon insisting I bring it. The only thing I will use is my camera, now that I have a masterpiece to photograph.

"If I get offered another mini quiche, I'm going to hurl. Please tell me you got what you need, D," Jasper gripes again.

I curse under my breath and break my gaze away from the

window to check the entrance. "Not yet. No one has come in or out since I set up. Confirm, Leon?"

Leon rumbles a gruff, "Confirmed." He hates being interrupted while he's in tech mode.

We were lucky to get the intel about this party. All we could wring out of that waste of space guy in Palm Cove was a town, *Willowbrook*, and a nickname. *Sweeper*. I can't forget about the fun time Jasper had toying with the guy before ending his pathetic life. Entertaining Jasper isn't easy.

Once we left Florida, it took us over a month to piece any more information together. We could thank Leon and his genius hacking skills for finally gleaning tonight's nugget of data—the address of this party. Our night could end up being a colossal waste of time. *Not for me. Not now.* Either way, I don't think Leon's slept properly in weeks.

Not like we're new to the waiting game. This has been our reality for the last twelve months. We get a tip from some scumbag loser, follow it, and hope it'll finally lead us to Bailey. One lead after another, and we've still got nothing except a few less losers populating the world and a new found penchant for bloody vengeance.

"Someone's gotta know something," Jasper whispers. "Lemme grab the next prick who goes to take a piss."

"Jasper," I growl in warning. "Don't do anything rash."

Of the three of us, he has the biggest reason to be losing his shit. Bailey's his younger sister. He won't stop until we find her and bring her home safely.

Movement from the window catches my eye. *Fuck. You're making me lose focus.* She lifts her black dress over her head slowly with her back to the glass. Tossing it aside, she shakes out her dark hair and pulls it into a ponytail at the nape of her neck. *You love that you're teasing me, don't you?*

I watch her every move, imagining my fist tugging that

ponytail, exposing her delicate throat to my waiting lips. Her pulse throbs as I skim my teeth along her neck, her soft moans, my favorite melody. Then her mouth quirks up in a seductive grin while she finally feels what her teasing does to me. *Smile now, Angel, because soon you'll be choking on my cock with tears running down your cheeks like my good little slut.*

Her body rocks side to side with the beat of her music as she slips a T-shirt over her head, giving me the slightest peek of a rib tattoo stretching across her side. I strain my eyes to make out the details of her ink, then snap a photo.

My skin tingles, tight and hot as my palm brushes my erection.

"No," I scold myself. *Not here and not yet.*

As I ready my camera to take another photo, she slips out of sight—likely into a bed—snuffing out my fantasy along with any remaining light.

Sighing at my misfortune, I slump lower and speak to the guys through my earpiece. "Anything?"

"Just the same handful of people. I think they're starting to suspect me. A few of them asked how I know the host. Not a trusting bunch."

"Nothing on my end." The sound of Leon's aggressive clicking muffles his voice.

"Dammit. I wish we had a picture of this guy." I rub my eyes, exhaustion catching up with me.

"They all look like a bunch of rich assholes. No one I'd peg as a kidnapper," Jasper says. Hushed voices filter through his earpiece along with faint classical music melodies.

"Well, *it is* a charity dinner," Leon says with an air of smugness.

"Oh, I forgot we were in the presence of a British aristocrat. Forgive me, sir, or should I say, Your Royal Dickness." Jasper attempts the worst British accent I've ever heard. So terrible, it's laughable.

"Cunt," Leon deadpans.

"Enough," I say. "I'm packing up my shit. I'll come back tomorrow."

"Meet you in—" Jasper's voice cuts out abruptly. I jump to my feet.

"Jas? You there?"

Leon pounds his keyboard, repeating my question. "He's offline."

It's probably nothing. A dumb tech error. Happens all the time. My tightening chest doesn't give a fuck about my excuses, though. I adjust the gun tucked into my waistband and draw in a quick breath.

"I'm going in."

I turn my earpiece off before Leon tries to tell me all the reasons not to. Jasper and Leon are my brothers. Not by blood, but in every way that matters. If there's even a slight chance that either of them are in trouble, nothing will keep me from them.

I'll check on you too, Angel. With one last look in the dim window, I step into the shadows, toward the back entrance.

CHAPTER TWO

DAMON

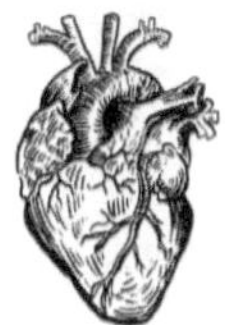

I watch my step, avoiding the uneven stone walkway and patches of dried leaves. As far as I know, the backyard is clear, but I can never be too certain. If I were thinking things through I would have had Leon double check the area from the neighbor's hacked security feed. He was probably biting his nails and cursing me out for my recklessness.

Murmured voices slip through the walls, mingled with the odd stray note from their music. With a house this old, I know I can get in easily. It's staying hidden that poses a problem.

Jasper hadn't mentioned exactly how many people are inside. Could be five or twenty-five. There's only one way to find out.

Weather-worn bricks scratch against my skin as I peer around the corner of the house to get a look at the backyard. Deciduous trees clutter the sprawling lawn like dusky giants. Maybe I did miss the Northeast? *So many hiding spots.* A cool breeze cuts at my skin just as clouds shift, allowing the half moon to bathe the space in silver light. I spot the back door, inconspicuous for such an elaborate home. Maybe they wanted it that way.

When I deem the area safe, I twist the handle on the shining knob and it turns smoothly, opening without a sound. It's either my lucky day or shit's about to get really bad. I'd bet on the latter...Lady Luck never liked me much.

The house smells like wood polish and cigarette smoke. I imagine a disgruntled housekeeper working diligently to keep the place tidy and cursing under her breath at the owner's refusal to smoke outside.

Who lives here with you, Angel?

A protective bubble expands in my gut at the thought of another man laying hands on her. *Find Jasper first, then get a better look at her.*

The sitting room lies dark and deserted. An unnatural quiet that has my hair standing on end. Parties shouldn't be this quiet. Keeping to the walls, I make my way past the sitting room and down a narrow hallway lined with expensive looking artwork, only stopping when I finally hear voices and the faint notes of music.

Around the corner, the hallway opens up to a large kitchen and open living area. Her bedroom must be down that hallway to the right. That's not where I need to focus at the moment.

My eyes adjust to the light as I roam them over the assortment of people in the room. All older, well dressed men and a few younger women. Jasper's nowhere to be seen.

I squeeze my palm tight enough that my short nails leave half-moon divots in my skin. Fucking loser from Palm Cove probably gave us bogus information. I told Jasper he reeked of desperation. That's how mistakes are made. How people are easily played a fool.

I watch the suits for a few minutes, listening for any bit of relevant information. Glasses clink, high-pitched laughter rings from a drunk woman's lips, jokes about so-and-so's golf handicap are thrown around. This has to be the wrong fucking house. These people are about as menacing as a senior sewing circle. But where the hell is Jasper?

During the next round of drunken laughter I use the noise buffer to creep around the corner in search of the staircase. The worn wooden floorboards creak beneath my feet as I grip the handle of my gun in anticipation. Just as I spot the stairs, one of the men says a name. *Brennan.* I whip around, holding my breath to listen in.

"Too bad Brennan's traveling. I haven't seen him since the last dinner party. When was that?"

"Must be at least a year ago," another man answers. "That was a night to remember." Laughter follows clinking glasses.

I fight the urge to turn my earpiece back on and let Leon know what I'd just heard, but a thump from upstairs draws my attention away. *Jasper.* With blood rushing in my ears and my gun still gripped in my palm, I make my way up the stairs as quietly as possible.

A second thud echoes down the hallway, followed by a groan. I pass a few closed doors, but I don't give a damn what's behind them. The only door I want is downstairs— *her's.*

"Fuuuck." There's no mistaking Jasper's voice.

Without another thought, I whip the door open, pointing my gun forward. Jasper locks eyes with me and all at once I take in the room. *Motherfucker.* Is he seriously getting blown right now? I'll kill him.

The woman starts to pull away, probably sensing me behind her, but Jasper grips her blonde hair tightly to keep her head in place. She moans around his cock, upping her pace as Jasper lets out a hissed groan.

Narrowing my eyes, I motion with my gun toward the door

and mouth, "Let's go." We need to get the fuck out of here. He widens his eyes and gestures for me to leave.

"Almost there," he groans, more to me than to the woman stuffed full of his cock. "I'm so close."

He's lucky I don't shoot him in the dick.

I slip out of the room before I do even worse than that and turn my earpiece back on. "Found him and I swear on my mother's grave that I'm going to kill that idiot."

"Do I want to know?" Leon answers in an irritated tone.

"Honestly, no. I'm getting out of here. Jasper's on his own. Meet you around the corner in ten."

"Good. I was just about to create a diversion and come looking for you."

"No need." I start back the way I came, letting my pulse slow down to a normal pace. I notice small details in the hallway that I hadn't before. A table with framed photos. A large vase filled with dried flowers. Heavy drapes hanging over the window down the hall. That smell of wood polish still lingers in the air.

Jasper sneaks out from the door down the hall as my foot hits the first step. I let out a quiet scoff, ignoring him, and make my way down the stairs against the noises of heated conversation.

"Bro, wait up," Jasper says through gritted teeth. I pretend he's not there, conjuring a picture of my angel's face in my mind so I don't lose my shit. "Come on, Damon, you're being a dick."

Jas may have three inches and a good thirty pounds on me, but that doesn't stop me from yanking him against the wall and getting in his face. "I'm being a dick? You compromised us for a blowjob from a drunken woman."

"She mauled me. Literally followed me when I went to take a piss. What the fuck was I supposed to do?"

I narrow my gaze and shake my head. "Let's get out of here. It's not important."

"She's still in there. Maybe you should take a turn…You're a little tense." Jasper steps aside and adjusts his shirt.

"I'm not tense and I don't want your whore. Christ, Jasper… Come on. If we're not out of here in the next five minutes Leon's going to go full *Leon*."

"Fuck."

"Exactly. So get some blood flowing up north and let's go." I grip my gun again, just in case, and follow the same path I took to get upstairs.

"I should say goodbye," Jasper whispers, craning his neck toward the party going on in the living room. "They might think it's weird if I don't."

"Who was the one bitching about getting out of here first?" I ask, growing more irritated by the second.

"My friend upstairs may have changed the tides for me. Plus, I want to find something about our guy. I'll just go schmooze a little, charm them, then duck out. Won't take more than a minute." He looks me over. "You sure you don't want to join me? Take a break from being creepy for once?"

I lift my middle finger, glancing at the Roman numeral tattooed between my knuckles before piercing him with my biggest fuck off look.

He raises his hands in surrender, fixes his hair, and walks in the opposite direction.

A few steps and I'll be outside, but I turn toward the dark, empty hallway instead. I know I shouldn't. I told Leon ten minutes and time's ticking. He's not a patient guy. A few minutes late and there's no telling what he'll do. I smooth my palms against the wood grain of her door, imagining her behind my closed lids.

Just one minute. One glance. Leon won't know a thing.

Cracking her door, I slip inside. The uncertainty of how I'll find her only adds to my giddy anticipation. My eyes dart straight to where she lies and I take in her still form. She's asleep on her side, facing away from me. One hand is tucked beneath her pillow, while a single leg peeks out from under her black blanket. I trail my eyes over her curves. The dip of her waist, her plump ass. My hands tremble with each step toward her. I can't get too close. Can't risk her seeing me here. Not before she gets to know me.

I breathe in her scent, filling my lungs enough to sustain myself until the next time. She smells so goddamn good—I knew she would. Like vanilla and spice...reminds me of a sugar cookie. Mouthwatering.

Time is ticking so I drink her in for another moment, memorizing the portrait tattoo on her thigh and the name of the band on the tour T-shirt she's wearing. All little details I'll store away in my mind.

There's so much to learn about you, Angel. Soon, there won't be any secrets between us. I'll know every single inch of your mind, body, and soul.

But first, what's your name?

I step around piles of clothes on her floor, resisting touching every item, and stop at her dresser. *You're a messy one, aren't you?* Paper notes, jewelry, tubes of lip gloss, and a half-empty energy drink are only a small part of what litters the furniture. I pick up one of the papers and read the name on the top. Blake Hyland. Letting her name roll around on my tongue, I sigh. Blake, the name of my future wife.

I pull out my phone, double checking that it's still on silent mode and take a picture of the document. It looks like medical paperwork. If she's sick, I need to know so I can take care of her.

Despite the mess, the room seems empty. No personal

touches. No photos or posters. As if it could belong to anyone. Like a blank canvas.

Are you just visiting?

If that's the case, I'll need to work fast. I can't lose her.

On the corner of the dresser, I spot her perfume bottle. An ornate glass sphere filled with amber liquid. I bring it to my nose, inhaling like one would a fine wine. I commit the scent to memory along with every detail I can see in the darkness.

Leon's counting down the seconds and I'm cutting it close. With a silent curse, I back away, grabbing a discarded pair of her panties from the floor and a necklace from the bedside table.

"Sleep tight, Blake," I whisper. "I'll see you tomorrow."

She rolls toward me as I reach the door. With one hand on the doorknob, I freeze, holding my breath. When she doesn't scream or jump up, I release my breath. Her eyes are still closed. Thick black lashes sweep the apples of her cheeks and smudged black eyeliner lines her upper lid.

It's not until I'm back in the cool night air, away from the incessant chatter of strangers, that I relax my grip on my gun. My hand grazes my pocket where I finger the thin chain of Blake's necklace and the soft silk of her panties. My chest loosens for the first time that night.

CHAPTER THREE

BLAKE

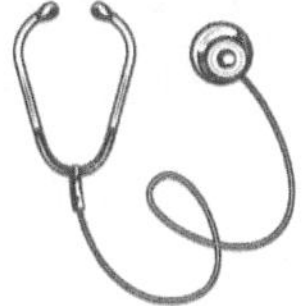

My eyes snap open and I push errant strands of hair out of my eyes. What time is it? From the excessive noise in the other room, Mischa and her pretentious friends are still partying. Not like that's a surprise. I'd love nothing more than to tell my brother how his *girlfriend* acts when he's out of town working for her father. The irony is, she calls it a charity dinner. The only charity going on tonight is funding her next shopping spree.

I roll over, forcing my eyes closed. 7 AM would be here too fast and I had to be on my A-game for pharmacology. It's already my toughest course and facing Ethan, with another one of his half-hearted apologies, only makes it worse.

I wasted three years with him. Three of my best years. And now every time I close my eyes, all I see is his scrunched up face as that undergrad bounces on top of him. *Freaking asshole.* I hope he fails out of med school.

Tossing and turning, I flip my pillow to the cool side and start to recite all the muscles in the body alphabetically. Usually that calms me. Clears my head. But for some reason, other than the obvious noise from the other room, I can't get my chest to loosen.

I can't shake an eerie feeling that someone was watching me. Call it intuition or paranoia but I swear a faint smell lingers in the air. Mint maybe. Smoke?

It's probably just Mom or Bryan coming for one of their ghostly visits again. It's been a few years. Not since college, when I swore to Falin that I'd see their outline in the shadows. If I tune out reality enough, I can almost imagine Mom sitting in the corner, smoking one of her menthol cigarettes.

"Guys, I know you're spirits and all but creeping on me when I'm asleep is still weird. At least if you're going to wake me up, do it in a cool way. Flash some lights or knock stuff over. This whole chill in the air, minty smell thing is so cliche."

Blake, you've seriously lost it.

I let out a nervous laugh until tears drip onto my pillow. If Ethan were here, he'd scoff and shove a pill down my throat. *"Talking to your dead brother again, Blake? You need to calm down. Take this."*

Blue, white, yellow. I've tried them all. Ethan's very own pharmacy provided by his doctor parents. Too bad the only thing they do is dull my feelings. Bryan is still gone. Mom too. Nothing can take that pain away.

Mischa's laughter echoes down the hallway. I'm seriously regretting choosing the downstairs bedroom. She's most definitely wasted by the sound of it—and not alone. A man's deep voice murmurs something and a high-pitched giggle follows. I catch the word "bedroom."

Maybe it's nothing.

I told myself when I moved in with my older brother, Brennan, that I wouldn't get involved in his love life. Mischa was already threatened by our close relationship before I moved in. She had to have hated me being here. From what little I know of her and her family, they aren't a warm bunch. She must not understand what a caring sibling relationship looks like.

I remember when I met her, she scrutinized me with her lips turned down and whispered in Brennan's ear. That night she barely said two words to me. Unfortunately, Brennan loves her, which means I have to accept her.

"Need more vodka," Mischa slurs loud enough for me to hear. She clomps down the hallway without any of her normal poised grace.

I reach for my AirPods on my bedside table, turn on noise canceling mode and start my sleep playlist. Instrumental versions of my favorite emo bands. My eyelids finally start to drift closed as the third song plays.

***

CLUTCHING my to-go cup of coffee between cold fingers, I navigate through campus. It's early September but already a chilly morning breeze drifts in from the river. My eyes are puffy and weighed down from the broken night's sleep, so the cool air is refreshing against them. Anything to help me wake up.

My pharmacology class meets in the historic section of campus. It's closest to the river and all the stone buildings are covered in climbing ivy. Our labs are held in one of the newer buildings, though. As much as I like working with top of the line equipment, there's such a disconnect between the north end of campus and the rest that it's almost jarring.

Funny how it worked out that the med school I got into happened to be fifteen minutes from Brennan's place. If it weren't for that, I probably would have transferred somewhere else, away from Ethan, this year.

My phone vibrates in my pocket. There's only one person who calls me this early.

"You realize it's only 8 AM here?" I say in lieu of a greeting.

"And I knew you'd be up for class," my brother answers. "I wanted to catch you. Pharmacology, right?"

"I have no idea how you remembered that. I can barely remember my own schedule."

I pause outside the building, smiling back at a girl I sat next to once, as she walks in ahead of me.

"It's my superpower, I guess," he says as he yawns. "Sorry, long day."

"Where are you this time? Lemme guess, London?"

"Nah, you know they won't let me back there after the teatime incident." He chuckles but I pick up on the exhaustion underneath. "Anyway, how's it going?"

"Do you want my honest response?" I ask, realizing he avoided answering my question.

"Always."

"I know I'm living with you for free and all, but is there any way you can tell Mischa to have her parties somewhere else?" *Or keep them upstairs if she has to have them.*

"I can try. But Blake, you realize we owe her a lot. You wouldn't have that free room to live in without Mischa."

"I guess, but Brennan, you're seriously undervaluing yourself. You've busted your ass for Mech Express. Yeah, Mischa might have helped you schmooze to her father, but you've put in the work. Alex keeps you busy nonstop." I soften my tone. "I don't know, I guess I just miss you. It's been too long. I haven't even seen you since I moved back and it's been way too many awkward meals with Mischa and her friends."

"I know, little bee. I miss you too. I'll be back soon, okay?"

Shouting cuts in from the background. "Gotta get going. Tell Mischa I'll call her tonight."

"Okay?" I start to ask why he can't just tell her himself, but I realize he already ended the call. "Weirder and weirder," I mumble.

Counting down the minutes before I need to go inside, I sip my coffee and lean against the wall of the building. The cool stone soothes the back of my head. I breathe deeply, pushing away the bubble of worry that creeps up every time I hear from my brother. It kills me that he's gone so much but I know he works this hard for me. To pay my tuition. Even though I argue with him every time I see him, he still insists.

I'll become a doctor but lose the most valuable thing of all: time. It's a trade off I question daily. The one resource we can never get back. But becoming a doctor—helping people like Mom and Bryan pull through. It's what I've been working toward for years.

My hand instinctively moves to fidget with my necklace, but I touch bare skin instead.

"Blake, you okay?" Julie calls, pulling me from my thoughts. "You look upset."

Plastering on a smile, I walk over to her. "I'm good, just realized I forgot to put my necklace on this morning. Didn't sleep well."

Julie shifts her bag and gives me a shoulder bump. "I hear you. I haven't slept since classes started." Her gaze lingers on my coffee cup, so I hand it to her without a word. She takes a long sip. "You're a lifesaver."

"No worries, it's my second cup." An engine rumbles and my attention shifts toward the parking lot, where a black muscle car is pulling in.

"Do you think Ethan is already inside?" she asks. I blink, breaking my stare away from the car.

"Oh...umm, no idea. I haven't seen him, so probably."

She squeezes me close and I have the overwhelming urge to shove her off. "I'm so sorry again. You guys were one of those dream couples. Everyone's been in shock over your breakup."

Yeah, no one was more shocked than me to find him screwing someone else. I give a quick nod and clear my throat.

"Sorry, I'm the worst. You probably don't want to talk about him. Come on, let's find seats in the back."

She pulls me forward into the lecture hall and my gaze lands on Ethan sitting in the seat closest to the door. He knew I'd have to pass him if he sat there. My shoulders tense automatically as his eyes rake me over.

I steal a final glance at that car one last time, wishing I could hop in the driver's seat and get out of here. Away from Ethan's watery-eyed stare.

"Bee, look at me," he whispers as I pass him.

Steeling myself, I let Julie pull me toward two empty seats in the back. Ethan's pained gaze follows my every move until the professor begins.

By the time class ends, I have a throbbing headache. I need more caffeine, food, and a nap, preferably in that order.

Julie puts her laptop away and turns to me, looking me over way longer than normal. "Want to grab some lunch?"

"I wish I could, but I have plans," I lie. I've had about as much of Julie as I can muster for the day.

She raises a brow. "A date?"

Why would her brain go there?

"No. Definitely not—"

"Baby, can we talk?" I jump at the sound of Ethan's voice, but quickly regain my composure. Ignoring the fact that he's standing behind me waiting for me to turn around, I answer Julie.

"Actually, I do have a date." I force confidence into my

voice, squaring my shoulders. "Yeah, it's just super new so I didn't want to tell you, but we're meeting for lunch."

Julie's face lights up. I know she's being nice but God, why are some people only happy if someone's in a relationship? What if I want to be single? Would she look at me with pity eyes everyday?

"I know what you're doing, Blake," Ethan says under his breath. He lays his palm on my shoulder. "We both know you don't have a date."

I stiffen and shrug his hand off. Every one of my instincts tells me to avoid his smug face but I can't stop myself from turning to confront him. "What's that supposed to mean?"

Julie lets out an awkward laugh and backs away. "I'll just give you guys some space."

"Nothing bad." He brushes his palm down his cheek. "Just, you know...I highly doubt you're already dating."

"Because I'm so heartbroken, right? Or is it because no one would want me?" Heat creeps up my neck, spreading to my face. "Is that it?"

"Baby... I—"

I put my hands up to silence him. "Stop. I'm not your baby, Ethan."

"I'm sorry. Can we please just talk? You deserve an explanation." His shoulders slump and he stares at me with his dumb blue eyes that have always been my Achilles heel. "Please?"

"Fine." I pretend to check a notification on my phone. He doesn't need to know my calendar is pathetically empty of anything other than reminders of assignments and tests. "I'll give you a few minutes."

He beams and slings his arm over my shoulder. The scent of his cologne is overpowering. I used to love how he smelled but now it only adds to my headache. "You're the best, baby."

"Ethan," I warn.

"Sorry, no more baby. It's a habit, I guess." He chuckles and squeezes my shoulder. "I'll drive."

I want to get him out of my personal space bubble. To take his hand off me and tell him where to shove it. I'm not sure why I don't. Maybe it's his familiarity hitting me? Or the fact that I feel empty inside and human touch is human touch?

With him holding me tight enough that I have a hard time walking, we reach his brand new Mercedes. A birthday gift from his parents. He opens the door and deposits me inside like he thinks I'll flee.

As he slides into the driver's seat, messing with the stereo and AC, I glance out the window at the glossy black muscle car still idling a few spaces away. Despite the tinted windows, I swear a pair of dark eyes track our every move as we pull away.

CHAPTER FOUR

DAMON

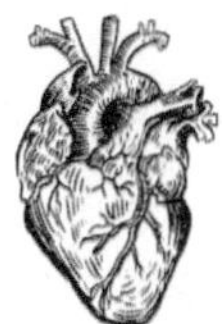

Everything about Blake's body language tells me she doesn't want to be near that prick. It takes everything in me to keep from ripping his arms from his body for touching her.

They drive a few miles from campus to a sushi place in town. Lucky for me, the hostess sits them in front of the window overlooking the street. My body aches and I need a smoke, so I hop out and lean against my car, being careful to stay out of her eyeline.

She noticed my car earlier. Stared at it with longing in her eyes. It's only a matter of time before she realizes my car is everywhere she goes. I know I'm fucked up, but I hope she does soon.

My heart races wondering how she'll react. Will she be afraid or intrigued? Will she confront me or avoid me?

People walk along the street, engrossed in conversation. Couples holding hands. Mothers tugging children along. Busy suits on their lunch breaks. I take a moment to admire the trees lining the street with their yellow and gold leaves while breathing in the crisp fall air.

It's been too long since Jas and I went hiking. It's always been our thing—get up before dawn and hike the toughest trails in town. We never talk much, just walk in companionable silence, taking in the sights and clearing our heads. Hiking is the only time Jasper doesn't talk nonstop. Leon and I joke that he's like a golden retriever on speed... We have to tire him out to get him to shut up.

We haven't hiked since Bailey was taken. Every minute has been filled with finding her. Well, almost.

I stub out my butt and walk it to the nearest trash can, getting a glimpse of Blake's profile. She's chewing her lower lip, focusing on the menu in front of her instead of the asshole who won't stop shooting his mouth off. The sunlight hits her dark hair, bringing out its indigo luster. My chest hurts from how perfect she is. So fucking beautiful. Even when she's clearly uncomfortable.

Fuck it. I guess I'm getting sushi for lunch.

I walk inside, never taking my eyes off Blake. Now that I'm within earshot of her, my pulse calms. The hostess directs me to a table across the room but still close enough to watch them.

I order an iced tea and take out my phone, pretending to idly scroll as I listen.

A different server stops at their table holding a large platter of sushi and a bowl of rice. She places it down and Blake looks it over, rolling her lip between her teeth.

"Dig in, baby," the douche she referred to as Ethan says. He grabs some chopsticks and rubs them together obnoxiously.

Blake reaches for the bowl. "I'll just have some rice."

I shield my face with my hand to get a better look.

"But I ordered all these rolls. Is this about that comment I made a while back? I was drunk, I didn't mean it. You're not fat."

My jaw clenches and I grip my phone hard enough to crack the screen. I'll kill him. Right here and now.

"Seriously?" Blake drops her fork and shifts in her seat. "I can't believe you'd bring that up. Especially now when I didn't even want to be here."

"Fuck, I'm sorry, baby. I know it's not an excuse, but my parents cut me off my addies and since you left I haven't been sleeping and classes are kicking my ass. Let's just eat and forget what I said."

Blake's expression softens and she picks up her fork again. "Fine, but I'm serious, Ethan. We're not getting back together. I don't care what you have to say."

He reaches across the table to take her hand. She visibly flinches from his touch.

"Ready to order?" The server steps directly in front of my view. Perfect fucking timing.

"I'll take a spicy tuna roll and a salad." I'm not particularly hungry, but I need something to keep my hands busy so I don't wrap them around Ethan's neck.

After thanking my server, she moves to Blake's table. "How is everything?" She glances at the rice in front of Blake. "Can I get you something else, Miss?"

"Oh, no, it's okay. I have food allergies. The rice is fine." Blake smiles politely as the server takes Ethan's glass to refill his drink.

This asshat takes her to a restaurant she can't even eat at. *I'd never do that to you, Angel.* He devours his rolls while Blake picks at her plain white rice. He never apologizes. Never mentions her allergies at all.

My jaw aches from how tightly I've been clenching it.

"Did I mention that my parents invited us to the gala at St. Luke's? They're going to introduce you to the president of the board and put in a good word for us. Last I heard they were only taking on a handful of interns next year, so we gotta make a good impression."

"Ethan... are we going to talk about what happened?"

He shoves another roll in his mouth and chews slowly. "It was one mistake, Blake. Jake's party and I was wasted. I didn't even realize she wasn't you until you walked in." He pulls a hand through his light hair.

Blake scoffs but keeps her eyes trained on his face while he spews even more obvious bullshit. He reaches for her hand again.

"I love you, baby, and I miss you. If you can't forgive me, at least come with me to the gala. My parents would love to see you and we can mingle with the board. You need those connections."

She offers a thin smile, while her gray eyes stay flat and lifeless.

Don't fall for his lies, Blake. He doesn't love you.

"You hurt me. It's going to take a lot for me to forgive you." Her gaze bounces between the nearly full bowl of rice and Ethan's hand before she pins him with her gaze. "But I'll go to the gala with you."

He leans across the table, invading her space and contaminating her perfect mouth with his lying lips. I wait with bated breath to see how she'll react. Surely, she'll slap him or at least curse him out.

My phone rings, dragging my attention away from Blake. I hit ignore and text Leon back.

Me: Hey, I'm grabbing lunch. What's up?

Leon: Found out more about our friends at the party. Jas just woke up. We're waiting on you.

I bring my attention back to Blake who's now standing and looking toward the restroom sign.

Me: Be there soon.

Ethan has his phone out, typing with a smug grin. He's probably texting his dude bro friends to tell them how Blake's taking him back.

Well, think again, Ethan.

I scrub a hand over my chin and pull out more than enough cash to cover my check and tip, along with one of my favorite little tracking devices.

Checking to see if Blake's still in the restroom, I walk past their table, accidentally knocking into it. Ethan drops his phone on the empty platter and raises his chin.

"My bad, man. I wasn't looking where I was walking." I shoot him a bright grin that he doesn't reciprocate. He examines me from head to toe, clearly adjusting whatever remark he was going to say.

"All good." Grabbing his phone, he wipes it with a napkin and continues texting someone named Aubrey.

"Have a good one." I force the words through a fake smile.

On the way to my car, I attach a magnet tracker to his rear bumper. When I take care of Ethan later, I want him to remember my face.

"DO you really need to take our one parking space for your bike?" I frown at Leon while I take off my boots in the entryway of our apartment, stubbing my toe on Jasper's amp. He keeps leaving it out here along with the tangled up pile of cords.

"Why are you asking stupid questions?" He leans back on the couch we recently picked up from a secondhand furniture store in town.

"What's a stupid question?" Jasper walks into the kitchen with a towel wrapped around his waist, drying his hair with another.

"Is that my towel?" I yank it out of his hands. "It is. Seriously? This better not have touched your dick."

"Chill, I just used it on my hair..." He grabs it back and slings it on a barstool. "*Today.*"

"I'll kill you." The wet towel becomes my ultimate weapon as I grab it and whip his retreating back.

"Ow, you asshole!"

"Are you two done?" Leon asks, shaking his head. "I've been waiting all morning to talk about this shit."

"I'll be done when Jasper says he'll stop flossing his ass crack with my towel." Jaw clenched, I level him with a defiant look.

"I lost my towels in the move and it's not like you haven't been all up in there before."

Leon pushes to stand and grabs a beer from the fridge, hiding his laughter behind his hand.

"One time in college! One fucking time and you'll never let me live it down. I was drunk and your ass and Sabrina's ass started to look the same, okay?" I angle my body toward Leon. "Tell him he's gotta let it go."

He swallows a long sip and raises his hands in surrender. "I'm not getting involved. This is why I won't partake in group activities... Lines and *bodies* get blurred."

Following Leon, I grab myself a beer and head over to the couch. "Okay, enough about Jasper's asshole. Let's focus on the assholes from the party last night."

"Nice segue," Jasper says. He pulls up a chair beside our makeshift dining table and workspace.

Leon sits next to me and immediately tosses a cushion at Jasper. "Christ! Put on some fucking clothes. The way you're sitting, I can see your balls."

Jasper snickers and throws the cushion back at his face. "Stop looking then."

While they argue back and forth until Jasper finally relents, I use the distraction to check my tracker app. The satellite map opens, showing Ethan's shiny new Mercedes as a blue blinking dot. It looks like he's parked at a building near the college.

Is Blake still with him? I need to get into her phone and email... find out when this gala will take place. I'm still berating myself for not bringing my cameras into her house yesterday while I broke into the party. There's so much I could be learning about Blake when I'm not able to be there.

"Alright, while you two arseholes were sleeping..." Leon points at Jasper. "Or out doing who knows what." He points at me. "I was working."

"Let me get you a medal," Jasper grumbles.

"Have you eaten yet?" I ask. "That tone usually means hanger."

Jasper cocks his head. "Not since last night. I'll order some pizzas." He grabs his phone from the coffee table, swiping through apps.

"For fuck's sake, shut up," Leon's irritated voice booms. He's the most patient out of the three of us but hell, when he gets pissed off, he gets *pissed off*.

We zip our lips and give him our full attention.

"Finally." He flips his laptop around to show us a photo of a young blonde woman on the screen. "Look familiar?"

"I'd know those lips anywhere," Jasper says, smirking.

"That's the woman who brought me upstairs. Wild one... The things she wanted to do to me."

"Her name is Mischa Orlova," Leon interrupts. "Daughter of Ivan Orlov... Russian millionaire shipping mogul."

"No shit?" Jasper says.

I take a good look at the screen, memorizing her features. "Makes sense that all the people at the party were rich suits. Do you know how this Orlov family is connected to Sweeper?"

And how is Blake connected to all of them?

"I'm still working on that. For a millionaire, Orlov has a squeaky clean record. Not even a speeding ticket since he moved here from Russia. I need to dig deeper. Sweeper could be working for Orlov, or it could be the other way around. I can't find much."

"From what I heard, the owner of the house travels a lot but a few people last night were talking about seeing him a year ago." While I think, I twist the stud in my ear.

"Jasper, what did you find out?" Leon asks. "Other than how good Orlova gives head."

"Like I said last night, nothing much. They were all tight-lipped." He smirks, and continues. "Talked about boring shit like golf and vacations. It'll take getting to know them better before anyone gives details. Or there's other ways..." He trails off, focusing his gaze on the wall.

"Whatever it is you're thinking, the answer is no," Leon says. "I know that piece of shit pedophile in Palm Cove wasn't the most reliable source by the time we finished with him, but his intel didn't come from nowhere. I think we should stick around, find out more."

"I volunteer to get more out of my new friend." Jasper grins. "From personal trainer to personal fuck toy... Who would have thought finding Bailey would take so much acting?"

"Because you'll really have to act to be blondie's fuckboy,

huh?" I tease him, but I'm more than happy he's willing to put himself out there. I'd done enough of that in Palm Cove, hanging around the diner to watch the prick across the street, and I'm burnt out. Sticking to the shadows works better for me.

I almost bring up Blake. From the look of her room, she's living there, at least temporarily, so she must know more about these people. As Leon fills Jasper in on details about Orlova, I decide I'll keep her to myself a little longer.

"I'll scope out the house, see what I can pick up," I say.

"Alright, so while you're doing that, Jasper, you'll get to know Orlova. See if she knows anything about someone named Sweeper. I'll keep searching for him and more about Ivan Orlov. I don't want any careless mistakes. We have no idea who we're dealing with."

I ignore the rest of their conversation and check my app again. Ethan hasn't moved from that spot. Brimming with restless energy, I get up and grab my shoes.

"I'm gonna go get started. I'll call you guys if I find anything."

"You don't want pizza?" Jasper asks.

"Nah, I already ate. Save me some for later." Without waiting for his reply, I walk out into the hallway, ready to see Blake again.

CHAPTER FIVE

BLAKE

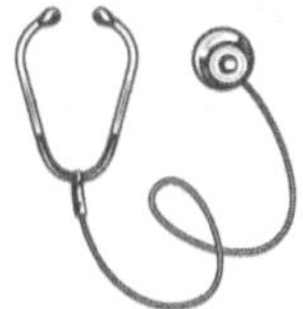

IT'S BEEN HOURS SINCE ETHAN DROPPED ME OFF AND I'M still pissed at myself. There must be something wrong with me for even considering forgiving him. Am I that lonely that I'd prefer Ethan to no one at all? That desperate to land the internship at St. Luke's?

I've read the same line three times on the screen in front of me and nothing's sinking in. Shutting my screen, I flop back against my pillows and close my eyes. I knew my second year of med school would be the toughest, but I guess I never took personal life issues into consideration.

I've already lost most of my undergrad friends from being "a bore." Their words. The only one still hanging on is Falin, but she's so far away.

Ethan is all I have left here, so it makes sense that I'm trying to hold on to our relationship. He gets my need to succeed. To get the coveted internships and graduate at the top of our class. Yeah, his reasons are to appease his parents whereas mine are entirely self-motivated, but at least they align.

A headache creeps in from the base of my neck, and my

stomach growls, reminding me again of my non-existent lunch. Mischa's downstairs with one of her equally snooty girlfriends. I could wait her out. Starvation is far superior to conversing with them.

I grab my phone to put on some background noise. Anything to distract me from my grumbling stomach. For some unknown reason, I open up my photo album and scroll through the photos from Jake's party. There's only a few, and one of them is of Jake's cat. I find the one I'm looking for, a selfie of me and Ethan sitting on a couch, holding glasses of wine. I was happy, right?

My smile wasn't exactly natural, but I looked comfortable. Ethan's eyes were already glassy and the night had just begun. Knowing him, he probably popped some benzos before the party. I can't believe I didn't realize at the time.

Flipping through my albums from the past year, I can't help but notice how few photos I have of other people. There's a couple of Brennan and me, some with Ethan, but they're all mostly screenshots of school stuff.

Maybe everyone's right about me? I'm a bore. A bookworm, studying obsessed, *bore*. What would Bryan think of me if he were here? He was always the life of the party, always the one to push me out of my shell. God, I miss him.

Out of instinct, I reach up to hold my necklace but then remember that I misplaced it. I've barely taken it off since he died, so it can't have gone far. This room is kind of a disaster too. If I clean then maybe I'll find it.

Turning my emo playlist up, I spend the next hour folding clothes and organizing paperwork. I put my dirty clothes in a hamper in the closet and straighten out my makeup and jewelry on my dresser.

I look everywhere and still don't find it. I'll have to check lost and found at school. Or maybe Ethan has it... although that's doubtful since today was the first time I've seen him in over a week.

Pausing my music, I crack my door and listen for Mischa. When all I hear is blissful silence, I head into the kitchen to make myself something to eat. It'll be another night of dinner, Netflix, and early bedtime so I'll be rested for classes tomorrow.

Our fridge is full of leftover appetizers from Mischa's party, food full of soy and wheat. The very ingredients that'll throw me into anaphylaxis with one bite. The only other edible thing is a bagged salad. After checking the sad status of my bank account and seeing that DoorDash isn't an option, I grab the salad and dump it into a bowl with some safe balsamic dressing.

Ethan's comment from earlier keeps playing in my head as I shove bites of lettuce into my mouth. The words swirl, looping around and coming back to the same two facts. *Fat and boring.* That's all I am to him. To everyone.

I can't take another bite or I'll barf.

Pushing the bowl aside, I cross the house and yank the front door open. I'm desperate for air… for anything that will ease the acid roiling in my gut.

Hunched over, I gulp a few deep breaths and let the cool air wash over my exposed skin until I'm covered in goose-bumps. An unexpected noise from across the yard startles me. I redirect my gaze in its direction but it's too dark to see anything beyond a few feet in front of me. The worn stone wall that surrounds the perimeter of the property should make me feel safe, yet I keep staring, wondering what lies behind it.

A chill seeps down to my bones. I shiver, unable to shake the feeling that someone or something is watching me. Wrapping my arms around my chest, I stare into the darkness taking in the stark tree limbs swaying in the breeze.

As I'm about to go inside, headlights turn the corner, illuminating the yard. "Nothing's there. You're seriously losing it."

Those headlights get brighter as the car turns into the driveway. Not just any car—Ethan's white Mercedes.

"What is he doing here?" Wrapping my arms around my chest to ward off the chill, I contemplate sprinting inside and hiding upstairs. He'd leave after a few minutes... I think.

While my feet and brain take their time waging war against each other, Ethan gets out of the car and makes it halfway down the walkway.

"Bee?" He clutches his chest in surprise. "What are you doing out here?"

I give him a quick assessment. He doesn't look drunk, but I was never any good at realizing when he was high.

"Getting some air. Why are you here?" I force my face into a neutral expression and shift my hands to my hips.

He opens his mouth to start talking but I'm distracted again by a rustling sound in the yard.

"Wait... Quiet for a second," I say, bringing my finger to his lips.

"What?" he asks, his voice muffled.

"Shh. I think something's out there."

We pause for a few breaths, listening. Nothing breaks the silence—no nightbird's calls. No branches rattling in the breeze. No distant car engines. Only eerie silence.

Ethan grabs my finger and sucks it between his lips. I hate myself when my stomach flips and tingles spread along my skin.

"Nothing's there, Bee. Let's go inside." He grabs my palm and kisses the outside, holding it to his lips for an extra beat. Drawn to his warmth, I move in closer, grateful for his familiar comfort.

I'm disappointed in myself for allowing him to squeeze through the crack of the wall I've carefully constructed. But I shove that thought away and nod, letting him pull me inside.

Forgetting that he's never been to my room here, I lead him down the hall, both of us quiet. I'm sure he realizes that one wrong word would get him a swift kick out into the cold.

His lips are on mine before I can close the door, kissing me hard and fast, pushing his tongue between my teeth. I open for him, trying with all my might to clear my mind of the intense resentment I feel in his presence and instead focus on my senses. The feeling of his palms as he grips my ass. The sounds of my moans into his parted lips. The smell of his body wash, so familiar to me. The taste of his tongue as he glides it against mine.

"You missed me, didn't you, baby?" He speaks low against my ear. "I knew it."

I grip his shirt, unsure if I want to shove him away or pull him closer. Before I decide, he yanks my sweats down with one hand and palms my tit with the other. I'm only wearing a tank top with no bra and the scratch of the fabric against my tight nipple is unfortunately exquisite.

He plunges two fingers inside me, rougher than normal, and I yelp against his lips. "So wet for me. Get on the bed so I can show you what you've been missing."

I push my laptop to the side and climb onto the comforter, pulling my pants and underwear down the rest of the way. He's not wrong, I am wet for him. *I hate myself.*

He doesn't hesitate, just shoves his jeans down to his ankles and kneels in front of me. I reach for him, craving connection. Warm body against warm body. That's all this is. No feelings, only need.

Slowly, I slide my hands under his shirt and run my fingernails over his sensitive skin until he hisses in a breath. I'm desperate for him to reciprocate. Touch me, anywhere, in any way.

But he doesn't.

He lunges forward, hovering over my body, and glides the head of his cock over my wet slit. I gasp and buck my hips, attempting to give myself the pressure I crave. When I reach to touch myself, Ethan grabs my hand and holds it above my head while he jerks his cock inside me.

I close my eyes and retreat into the safe space in my mind. If I try hard enough, maybe I can feel good with Ethan. At least sex is easy with him. Comfortable, if dull. But dull can be a positive thing sometimes.

While he pumps his hips, realization hits me and I tense my muscles. "Wait, did you bring a condom?"

Mid-thrust, he stops and curses. "No. Why would I?"

He starts to press into me again but I lurch backwards, knocking him off-balance. "We can't do this. Not without protection."

"Fuck." He kneels and takes a few deep breaths before moving toward me. "You can't leave me like this, Bee. Come on, baby. Look at what you do to me." He strokes his cock and gazes at me with hooded, expectant eyes.

I know what he wants from just that look. Even as he climbs off the bed and lines his swollen cock up with my mouth. "Suck it, baby. You're so good with that mouth."

Every bit of romantic feeling that was bubbling in my chest falls flat the second he pushes his cock past my lips. I want to shove him away. To bite it. To make him hurt.

But of course, I don't.

I open wide and he rams his cock to the back of my throat, pumping himself in and out like I'm nothing more than a hole to be filled. "Yes, fuuuck, Bee. Suck it, baby. Hollow your cheeks."

Tears leak down my face as his cock hits the back of my throat again and again. I pump the base of his dick with my fist, wanting to finish him quicker. To be done with him tonight.

"Goddamn, baby." He pulls himself out to the tip and pushes back in, making me gag. Images of him with that undergrad fill my mind. The way her head was thrown back as she rode him. The look in his eyes before he realized I'd come into the room. The sounds they made. His grunts reminded me of a feral pig. The same grunts he let loose now.

Screw *him*.

I yank my head back and shove him off me at the same time, grinning as he stumbles on his ass.

"What the fuck?" he spits. "Bee, I was about to come."

"You have a hand. Finish yourself off." I smile in triumph as I wipe my mouth and grab my clothes.

"You're a real bitch lately, you know that?" He fists his cock, jerking it hard and fast, filling my bedroom with his groans. "This what you want, Bee? To make me suffer?"

With one last thrust his body trembles and he comes, shooting onto my comforter. I watch him hold his dick and catch his breath, pissed that as much as I hate him, seeing him finish himself turned me on.

"You should go," I say. I need time to dissect what the hell tonight was and if I was being honest, I needed to make myself come after being left high and dry.

He pulls his pants up and tucks his softening cock away. "Yeah, I'll go." Hesitating for a moment, he adds, "Are we still going to the gala next week?"

My eyes roll of their own accord. "Yes, I said I would go so I'll go."

He inclines his chin and leaves without another word.

While I lie in my bed, equally frustrated and angry, my phone pings.

Ethan: I'm sorry, Bee. I want us to go back to how we were but I get that you're not ready. I'll make it up to you tomorrow.

I reread the message a few times, sitting with his words. I have no idea what to feel anymore. Do I want what he wants? To go back to how things were when I'm not sure they were working to begin with.

I pull off my sweats and get ready for bed. Ethan's cum spot is half dry on my black bedding by the time I wipe it down with a damp cloth. Nothing about seeing it there is sexy. Not anymore.

Clouds shift in the dark sky, to reveal the shining half-moon. Its light casts a pearly glow into my window. I close my eyes and rub my clit until I come. It's quick and efficient. As my eyes flutter open, I swear I see a shadow shift outside my window. My pulse quickens as I dart to a sitting position and grab my phone.

Is Ethan that desperate that he'd creep outside my window? I call him, forcing my breathing to slow with each ring.

"Hey, I'm glad you called. I was starting to think you were still mad."

"Where are you?" I ask.

"Home. You don't have to check up on me, Bee. I told you it was one time." He continues rambling about trust and how he loves me but I barely hear him.

I'm too focused on the shadowy form outside my window. "Ethan, someone's outside."

There's a tremor in my voice as I stumble away from the window. "It's probably a deer or something," Ethan says. "Did you lock up when I left?"

Shit. I didn't.

"Stay on the phone with me." My legs shake but I push

myself to jog down the hall and to the front door. I have no idea where Mischa is or if she's even coming home, but if she does, she has a key.

I lock the door and run back to my room, shutting the door and locking it. I'm panting when I register Ethan's voice again. "All good now?"

"I think so," I say.

He laughs and tells me he'll see me tomorrow before ending the call.

I glance at the window, feeling equally curious and terrified. Was I seeing things? It's been a long, emotional day. Maybe I'm just jumpy. I'm still not used to living this far outside of town in a house this old and creaky. It's like something out of a horror movie being this deep in the woods.

I stare at the space in the yard for a full minute, finding nothing amiss. It's another hour before I fall asleep, imagining a pair of dark watching eyes beneath my closed lids.

CHAPTER SIX

BLAKE

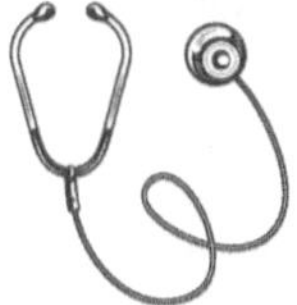

AFTER AN ENTIRE DAY AT THE LIBRARY, THE LAST THING I want to do is get into a fancy dress and go to some gala. Especially as Ethan's date. After the last week, I'm still not sure how I feel about him. My body reacts to his touch, which I'm chalking up to nothing more than familiarity. I wish my damn vagina would get the *Ethan sucks* memo.

I peek out my window, still shaken from the past few nights. Understanding that my mind can deceive me doesn't explain the prickly feelings I've been having each night. Like hundreds of eyes are watching me in the dark.

Instead of getting changed in my room, I grab my strapless bra and dress and head into the bathroom. I swear all the windows in the house have drapes except my room. As soon as my schedule allows... shopping here I come.

Mischa opens the front door as I'm crossing the hallway. *Great.* Just who I want to see. I'll be the bigger person, as always. "Hey. How's it going?"

She looks up from her phone and peruses me like I'm on display. "Is that a dress?"

With the navy blue dress slung along my arm, I nod. "I have this gala to go to tonight. It's for the h—"

She cuts me off. "A gala?"

"Yes. That's what I was—"

She takes a few steps toward me and pulls the dress off my arm. I'm taken aback by her sudden movement. It's rare that she spends more than thirty seconds talking to me, let alone shows care about what I'm wearing.

"This dress is garbage."

Oh. There's the Mischa I know.

"It's not," I rebuke. "It was expensive when I bought it." *Five years ago.*

She walks into the kitchen still holding my dress. "It's hideous. This color doesn't suit you at all. Come."

I don't have a choice but to follow her upstairs and into the bedroom she shares with Brennan. "Mischa, what the—"

"Hush. You'll wear something of mine." She tosses my dress across the room and opens her closet. She must be on something if she thinks I can fit into her clothes.

I'm a size sixteen on a non-bloated day and Mischa must be an eight if I had to guess. Plus, our proportions are different. I have an hourglass figure and DDD tits. Mischa is built less curvy. She does have a nice ass though, I'll give her that.

She's flipping through dress after dress until she stops and pulls out a black gown. "Here it is. You'll wear this."

"It looks beautiful but I don't know. I wouldn't want to ruin it by accident. I can be so clumsy." I rattle off a few more excuses that don't seem to reach her ears. "What about the size? I'm sure it won't fit."

Again, her clear blue eyes rake over my body. Heat spreads to my cheeks.

"It was a gift from Milan. They sent the wrong size but I kept it anyway. Take it."

I realize she's serious so I take the gown from her outstretched hand. It feels like creamy velvet or spun silk. One touch and I know it's expensive. Expensive and fragile. I'll be on edge wearing it all night, but now that I'm looking at it, I don't think I can give it up.

"Thank you," I say. "I'll have it dry cleaned and give it—"

"No." She waves me off. "Keep it. I have no need for it." She closes her closet and turns to stride out the door.

"Okay," I say, still confused by this entire encounter. "I'll just go get ready then."

She's already on her way downstairs.

My phone rings as I get back to my room. I'm about to side button whoever it is when I see Falin's name lit up across my screen.

"Oh my God, you're actually calling me," I say in a shocked tone. I clutch my chest for added flair.

"You're clutching your chest, aren't you?"

I double check the phone to see that it's not on video call. "No. Definitely not. I just miss you! I haven't heard your voice in a million years."

Like my brother, my best friend travels for months at a time for her big tech company job. Her latest trip was to China for over a month. I love that for her but it makes keeping up with our friendship tough. I haven't even told her about Ethan or moving in with Brennan.

"I know, it sucks. I promise you've been on my mind though. How's life? Classes? My oh-so-favorite mommy's boy, Ethan?"

Cringe.

I know I should tell her the truth. It's sitting on the tip of my tongue but I don't want to worry her. Not when she's likely on the other side of the world. Knowing Falin, if I were to tell her about Ethan's mistake, she'd fly here and kick his ass. And she could totally take him down.

"Everything's fine. How are you? *Where* are you?" I prop my phone up on the bathroom counter and grab my makeup bag. Might as well get ready while we catch up.

"Back in the states for now. But don't change the subject, I can read you like a book. What's going on?"

I finish applying shadow to my eyelid and take a breath. "I'm getting ready for this gala thing. Ethan's parents are introducing us to the board at the teaching hospital and I need to make a good impression."

There. It's enough information to keep her satisfied.

"So things are okay with Ethan?"

"Yup. Things are great," I lie.

"You remember my dad's a cop right? He taught me a lot of things. Like how to tell when someone's bullshitting me." She uses that *I mean business* tone and I shiver.

With my foundation puff halfway to my face, I huff. I'll have to give her something. "Okay, fine. I moved in with Brennan about a week ago. But before you ask, it's only because I need a calm environment to focus on studying. This year is already kicking my ass and it's just started."

She's quiet for a second and my heart rate kicks up. Having a police officer for a father makes her slightly terrifying. I'm about to ask her to say something, but she beats me to it.

"I'm all for that plan. You'll get more time with Brennan and some much needed space from Ethan. How did he take it?"

"Oh, you know... he's fine." I finish blending my foundation and grab my mascara.

"Right," she says, drawing out the word. "Before I have to hang up, I can take some PTO between projects. I was thinking about coming out for your birthday."

"Really? That would be amazing."

"I'll check flights and let you know dates. We both seriously need a night out. I miss my Blakey." I feel myself start to tear up when she says her nickname for me. "Go get ready for your party. Kick that board's ass... in a good way. They're going to love you."

I laugh and dab at my eyes. "I hope so. If I don't get into St. Luke's, the next option is over an hour away."

"You got this. I'll try and text you tomorrow." I hear her doorbell ring in the background.

"Who's that?" I ask in a playful tone. "Tonight's hookup?"

She laughs but evades my question. *"Gottagobye."*

Definitely a hookup.

ETHAN PICKS me up in an Uber and I know within the first minute that he's not sober. He's stumbling over his words and being extra handsy, pawing at me with slowed movements.

"Someone fucked up my car last night. Smashed my windshield and keyed the doors. I'll find the motherfucker. My parents are going to kill me if they think I did it." His eyes dart around wildly, watching out the window like the culprit will jump out at us.

"I'm sure they'll understand." I know better than to ask questions or engage further. It won't get me anywhere when he's like this.

"I'm fucking shaky." He reaches into his jacket pocket and pulls out a pill bottle.

"Ethan..." I start but decide better of it. If he wants to take something, then so be it. I honestly don't care anymore. All the more reason for me to end things with him after the gala. I watch him pop two pills into his mouth and dry swallow them.

He seems to calm almost immediately. Gotta love the placebo effect.

"I need you to make us look good tonight, Bee. Everything is riding on this." He wraps his clammy hand in mine.

"I know."

"Good." For the first time since I got into the car, he meets my eyes. "You're wearing a lot of makeup. Do you think that's a good idea?"

"I'm not. What are you trying to say?" He trails his eyes down the rest of my body and I cringe.

"The red lipstick and that dress. Your tits are hanging out. You realize these are respectable people, Bee. My parent's colleagues. This gala is $500 a plate. You think they want to hire someone who looks like a whore?"

He may as well have slapped me across the face. I don't respond. It wouldn't accomplish anything, not with him like this. He's mumbling under his breath and texting God knows who, so I pull my jacket closed and turn my head to focus on the passing cars out the window.

We pull up to a building in the historic district of town. A looming Victorian turned banquet hall. As soon as the Uber stops, I fumble for the handle, anxious for air. When Ethan tries to take my hand, I step away, walking as quickly as my heels allow on the unsteady cobblestone path. If he thinks I'm going to act all lovey dovey after what he said, he's sorely mistaken.

I admire the ornate staircase and grand windows as we walk across the entryway. This area is filled with historic homes, but none quite as impressive as this one. If this were another time with another date, I could imagine having a great night here. Romantic even. But I look at Ethan, whose pills must be starting to kick in by the slump of his shoulders, and sigh.

For the next hour we're introduced to at least twenty different people. Doctors, administrators, volunteers. Ethan's mother gushes about her son every chance she gets.

Did they know he's studying to be a surgeon? Lie.

Or that he's at the top of his class? Also not true.

Not once has she mentioned me, other than introducing me as her son's date. And as for Ethan, he's barely coherent enough to make conversation, let alone jump in on my behalf. My cheeks sting and hands shake by the time dinner is served.

A dinner of fish atop a plate of pasta. I try to flag the server down to ask for an allergy menu, but in the bustle of demands from other, more important-looking people, I'm ignored.

"Excuse me," I say to Ethan and the six others at our table. I grab my purse and head toward the restroom.

The halls are narrow and dim and I have no idea where I'm going. I'm too frazzled to stop and find someone to ask for directions in the maze that is this huge building.

Tears prick at the corner of my eyes and I finally stop to lean against a wall, reveling in the quiet. If I leave now, Ethan wouldn't even notice. But that would give him exactly what he wants and I refuse to give up this easily.

The sound of nearby footsteps startles me but as I turn my head toward the noise, no one is there. I'm left with that prickly feeling again. Like spiders crawling on my exposed skin. Goosebumps pop up along my arms and all at once an overwhelming need to be anywhere else takes root.

I rub my arms and come face to face with Ethan as I turn the corner. His eyes are glassy and he's stumbling his steps.

"Bee, there you are. They're asking about our next exam dates and I dunno. Lessgo." He grabs my arm with more force than necessary but I stand firm. Whatever I was thinking about not giving up flies out the window.

"No, I'm going to call myself an Uber. Tell your parents

thanks for the invitation." I pull away and start to dig my phone out of my purse.

He's inches from my face before I can find it. "Bee, don't be like that." He plants a wet kiss on my lips before I have a chance to move my face away. "Come on, baby. I'll be good out there. Promise. I need you, baby."

"Ethan, come on," I plead.

His hands snake along my arms as he buries his face in my neck. He's murmuring nonsense, begging me to stay.

"What do I have to do, Bee?" His hot breath fans across my cheek. "Do I have to fuck you right here? You'd like that, wouldn't you? All dressed up like a cheap whore."

I'm immobile. Frozen, while he paws at my waist. He crowds me against the wall with his frame and presses his erection against my stomach. "No," I manage to whisper.

He lets loose a manic laugh under his breath. I'm trembling, unable to do or say anything to get me out of this situation. And I hate myself even more. Whatever he took in the car had him acting like a different person. Like a monster.

"Everything alright over here?" Ethan steps back at the intrusion, giving me a chance to regain feeling in my limbs. I turn toward the resonant voice as a man steps out of the shadow.

His golden brown eyes lock onto mine. They're sharp and full of fire. As I take him in, I realize everything about him looks angry. His tense square jaw, his inked flexing fists, his strained posture. Even his outfit is intimidating—all black with the exception of a dull silver buckle on his belt.

I should be afraid, but I'm not. If anything, I'm relieved.

Ethan looks the man up and down. "Yeah, I'm talking to my girl."

The man's lips pull down and his brows furrow. A deep crease forms between them. His gaze bounces between me and

Ethan and I realize I'm holding my breath. When he locks eyes with me again, I try to convey gratitude in my expression. As much as my frozen body will allow me.

"I was actually looking for the restroom," I say. "Do you know where it is?" Seconds go by with his gaze pinning me to the wall. I lick my dry lips and look away.

"Yeah, it's around the corner. Want me to show you?"

"No, it's fine." I don't bother looking at Ethan as I force my legs to carry me away from them and whatever this weird encounter is. I don't know this man but the tension in the hallway is a powder keg ready to blow.

CHAPTER SEVEN

DAMON

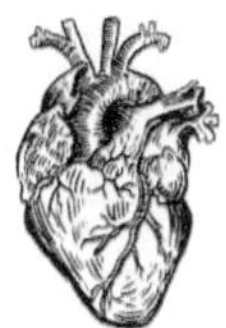

I'll kill him. *No. Death is too simple. A piece of* shit like him doesn't deserve the easy way out.

Blake picks up speed with each step and as much as it kills me to put distance between us, I'm glad she's not here to witness this.

The waste of space in front of me stumbles toward the wall and mutters a curse under his breath. "Whaddya want, man?"

I smile wide, showing off my dimples. The docile lamb hiding the sharp-toothed wolf beneath. "Just making sure you're alright. Weren't you saying you needed to take a piss?"

"Did I?" he asks. He takes stock of his body and nods. "Yeah, I guess I do."

"I'll lead the way."

He plods behind me, holding onto the wall for balance.

Those hands were all over Blake. That body flush with hers. Those sloppy lips kissing her precious skin.

My blood boils with each racing thought. I don't know how I manage to make it to the men's room with the red film over my field of vision.

We stop at the door and I push it open, letting him enter first so I can lock it behind us. If he thinks it's odd that I'm following him inside, he doesn't say.

They've kept much of the original structure of the building with some obvious upgrades like urinals and multiple sinks. My eyes go directly to the vintage cast iron radiator against the wall.

I can smell the heat in the room. Hear the popping sounds from the steaming contraption. I'm already flushed from how warm the space is.

We stand side by side in the urinal and I continue with my friendly small talk.

"So you and your girl looked like you were having some fun." My eyes stray back to the radiator as my hands twitch.

It takes him a second to respond. Pissing and talking at the same time are apparently too much for him to handle. "Nah, she's a prude. It wasn't going anywhere. Was trying to get her back on my good side."

My nostrils flare as I try to hold it together.

"Yeah? Why's that?" I ask, tucking my dick away.

"Who knows this time. Bitch is always on me about something." He grabs the wall for balance while he continues pissing.

I don't allow him another second. Grabbing him by the throat, I squeeze until he's gasping for breath. The piece of shit dribbles piss onto my black boots. *That won't do.*

He's too uncoordinated to put up any kind of fight. It's almost too easy. I hate when it's too easy. "You don't deserve to breathe the same air as her," I seethe. "You're a waste of fucking space."

I let go, step back, and punch him in the gut until he doubles over. "What the fuck?" he rasps and coughs, sinking to the tile floor.

"No, no, Ethan. We're not done here." He tries to crawl away, but I grab him by his suit jacket and pull him up, wiping my boot against his slacks. His flaccid dick flops out of his unzipped pants. "You must be a real smart guy, medical school and all."

"Please," he groans.

"Oh, now you have manners? Too bad you didn't have any when Blake was telling you no. Now back to what I was saying. You must be a genius to get into medical school... Wouldn't have anything to do with mommy and daddy? Or how about that brilliant girlfriend who you've been leeching off for years? No... that's all the brainpower of Ethan Porter, future surgeon."

I drag him over to the radiator and soak in the fear on his face. Much like how Blake looked when I found her in the hallway.

"Tell me, doctor, what happens when skin is held against a balmy 150 degree slab of cast iron?" He tries to pull away but I grip the back of his neck. "I'm no genius, not like you, but I'd guess it's not a fun time. Shall we experiment?"

"No... no, please," he begs, as I pull out my gun and press it to the back of his head.

"Try anything and I pull this trigger." With my free hand I hold his torso against the heated metal, pressing down to ensure his useless dick gets the brunt of the heat. "Let me hear you count. You're smart enough to do that, right? It's all in the name of experimentation." He's whimpering and pleading so I push harder. "Count, or I shoot."

"One," he cries. "Two..." He's struggling to free himself but I hold tight. I want him to feel the hurt that Blake felt when she found him fucking someone else. His pathetic dick will never hurt someone again.

"Listen to me closely, Ethan." I lean over his hunched body.

"You'll never go near Blake again. Don't talk to her. Don't touch her." He nods between sobs. "Did I say to stop counting?"

"Ten, eleven..." His body shakes with each heaving word.

"If I find out you've disobeyed me... and I will find out, I'll come for you. Do we have an understanding?"

I wait a few more seconds until he's nodding vigorously before I toss him to the floor. He curls up in a ball, clutching his dick. My balls shrivel up when I take a peek at the scalded flesh. Ouch.

"Well, it's been fun. There's just one more thing," I say before whacking him across the temple with the barrel of my gun. His head falls to the side as he goes unconscious. "Can't have you ruining the rest of Blake's evening."

I drag him into a stall and flop him onto the toilet. He'll take a nice rest and when he wakes up, I'll be long gone. And now Blake will have her chance to shine with those pretentious assholes. All night long she's been hidden in Ethan's shadow, but not anymore. She'll get that internship, if she still wants it. Whatever Blake wants, I support her.

Ethan's phone vibrates in his pocket so I grab it and hold it in front of his face to unlock it.

Aubrey: Still coming over later?

Shaking my head, I swipe away and open his photo app. There's one of Blake laying in bed with a book propped against her folded knees. A coy look lines her lips as her smokey gaze meets the camera. I swipe again and find a selfie of the two of them. My free hand clenches. Blake's eyes look lifeless. She's not happy here. He's never made her happy. But I will.

I open an album labeled "private." "Oh, Ethan," I tsk. "I did the world a favor today, didn't I." Photo after photo taken from the internet, teenage girls in varying states of undress fill the album, mixed with nudes of himself and other women he's slept with. None of them are Blake. Not that I wanted to see those in his phone. Blake's body is for my eyes only. Seeing these bolsters the choices I made for him. My instincts are rarely wrong.

I drop his phone into the toilet, shut the stall door, and head out into the hallway. The burst of adrenaline that fueled my actions begins to leave as quickly as it came on. My legs shake and my head spins. I need to see that Blake is alright before I leave here. Fuck. I wish I could take her home with me. Tell her how I feel. But it's not the right time, not yet. I make my way back to the edge of the banquet hall, careful to avoid being seen.

There she is.

My beautiful angel in her silky black dress. Her hair falls over her collarbones and onto her chest in waves. I'd give anything to wrap it around my fists. She's at the table, biting her plump lower lip, and chatting quietly with the couple beside her. I see that she hasn't touched her meal and instantly know why.

I pull a young waiter to the side as I step farther into the banquet room. "Hey, you see that woman over there? Black dress, dark hair." I point discreetly and he nods. "She has food allergies and can't eat whatever they served." I pull some bills out of my wallet and hand them to him, clapping him on the shoulder. "Make sure she eats something."

"Alright, no problem, sir." He pockets the cash with a grin and walks directly over to Blake.

Leaning against the wall, I watch her face light up as he takes away her untouched plate. Warmth fills my chest. I'm entranced by her. Plain and simple. I could stand here and watch her for hours. But I don't, not when Ethan could wake up at any moment. *I'll see you later, Blake.*

LEON'S BIKE is once again in our parking space when I pull up to our duplex apartment. I'd be shocked if it wasn't. Before I climb the stairs, I take a peek through the open blinds of Mrs. Langston's place and see the TV on but no one watching it.

I'm about to head upstairs when she comes around the corner with a bag of trash. "Mrs. Langston, let me grab that for you," I say, heading back to the driveway.

Her face lights up when she sees me. "Thank you, handsome."

She's in her frayed terrycloth robe and a pair of worn Crocs and her graying hair is twisted up in a bun. "No problem. I'll just walk this to the can."

"You're home early for a Saturday night," she says with a lilt in her voice. "I saw my favorite cutie leaving earlier. I bet he's on a hot date."

I chuckle. She really likes Jasper. "Don't worry, Mrs. Langston, he's saving himself for you."

"Call me Dolores, sweetie. You boys are just the cutest. If Herb and I were blessed with a son, I'd want him to be just like you." She pinches my cheek right where my dimple pops. "Make sure you remember to make time to clean the gutters soon. Snow will be here before we know it."

"I'll make sure. Do you need anything else tonight?"

"No, don't worry about me. You have a fun night. Blow off some steam."

Oh, Dolores, if you only knew.

"Okay, I will," I say, smiling.

She heads back to her apartment downstairs while I take her trash to the can. We struck gold finding a landlady like her. She's a widow. Quiet and mostly keeps to herself, except for when Jasper comes and goes. Clearly, she's picked a favorite.

She owns the building and was ecstatic when we told her we'd be happy to clean the gutters and mow the lawn for her. So ecstatic in fact, she didn't even ask for identification. She handed us the keys and we handed over three months worth of rent in cash.

Leon's at the kitchen counter, staring at his phone. He doesn't look up when I greet him. "Everything okay?" I ask. I toss my jacket on the couch and sit down with a groan. Adrenaline crashes fucking suck.

He types something and ignores my question.

Okay then.

I'm starting to think Leon is struggling worse with Bailey's disappearance than Jasper. He's barely sleeping, only eating when we force feed him. Every time I'm here, his face is buried in a screen.

Makes sense when I think about it. Leon's been in love with Bailey for as long as we've known him. They'd finally just started hooking up a few weeks before she was taken. A fact that Jasper knows nothing about. There's no way I'm saying shit either. That's between the two of them.

"Hey." I try to get his attention again. "You eat today?"

Nothing.

I get up and grab the phone from his hand.

"What the fuck?" he responds, finally acknowledging me. "When did you get back?"

I widen my eyes. "Like two minutes ago. Man, I say this as your best friend, you need to take care of yourself. Come on, let's have a beer, eat some food."

His shoulders slump. "I'm not hungry. I ate..." He grabs his phone back and checks the time. "Well, fuck me. I ate this morning. I didn't realize it was after eight."

"This is what I mean," I emphasize. "Give me the phone

and get your ass on the couch. I'm making dinner." He drops his phone in my outstretched palm and rubs his temples.

"Fine, but I was just messaging with someone who might know something. I'm working on narrowing down our list of locations to stake out."

I open the fridge and find nothing but beer and a box of leftover pizza. That'll have to do. I throw a few slices on a paper plate and nuke them for a minute. While I wait, I open some beers and bring one to Leon.

"That's good. Hear anything else about the house from the other night?" *Blake's house.* My ears perk up as I wait for his response.

"Jasper's out with that woman tonight, fishing for more info. Otherwise, nothing. Orlov is squeaky clean. I can't find anything about someone named Sweeper anywhere. Even the cameras Jasper planted the other night have been pretty dull. Just Orlova and some other woman seem to be there most of the time. No sign of a man yet."

Cameras?

My throat goes dry so I gulp down some beer. I should have realized Jasper would have planted some. He better not have put anything in Blake's room.

"Damn. When I was in there briefly I was getting tax evasion vibes, not kidnapping. But I guess it doesn't hurt to keep an eye. Where did he put cameras?" I feign nonchalance and get up to grab the plate of pizza.

Leon takes the plate with a muttered thanks and bites into the slice like a starved animal. "I guess I was hungry." He chews, takes a sip of beer, then answers. "Kitchen, living room, entrances. Why? You see something?"

"No, like I said, nothing out of the ordinary. Was just wondering." I fold my pizza and take a bite.

"I think he put one in the bathroom too, pointed at the shower." He shakes his head. "Fucking Jasper."

My hand pauses halfway to my mouth. He can't be serious? I know Jasper's an idiot but he's not a perv. No one gets to see Blake's body but me. "You're serious?"

"Wish I wasn't. Don't worry, as soon as I saw the feed, I shut it down. I gotta say though, man, that brunette... Fucking hot."

"Delete it," I seethe.

He raises his brow. "What?"

"Delete the fucking footage." I drop my half-eaten pizza and clench my fist.

"I didn't save it, brother. Calm down." He narrows his eyes. "What's with the meltdown?"

"Nothing. It's just fucking creepy. We're not those guys. I'm gonna kick Jasper's ass when I see him."

Leon sighs. "That makes two of us." I sit forward with my hands on my thighs. "He told his parents where we are. I heard him on the phone with them earlier. I swear he got hit in the head one too many times playing ball."

I groan. We've decided to keep certain things to ourselves. Mainly, where we're living. We don't need Mr. and Mrs. Shea knocking on the door for Sunday dinner and seeing guns and surveillance equipment laying around the apartment. They think we've started a consulting business and are helping out with the search for Bailey during our downtime. Yeah, we take on odd jobs here and there. Mainly Leon with his tech shit. But the majority of the time we're chasing leads. Plus, Leon's rich British daddy left him a nice, fat bank account when he turned eighteen. Leon hates using the money, but he knows we have no choice, not while we're focusing so much time on shit that doesn't pay.

"You think they'll show up?" I ask. As much as I love the Shea's, it's not a great time.

"Nah, or at least I hope not. We're far enough away that they won't want to drive to see us." Leon reaches for his phone again and checks the screen.

"I'm gonna head out for a bit. Check out a couple potential leads," I say. I'm restless and exhausted at the same time. If I were to try to sleep right now, I know I'd be tossing and turning, thinking of Blake. I get up, throw my plate away, and set my empty beer bottle on the counter. "You want to come? Get some air?"

"Nah, I'm good. I'll see you later though." He's back to typing on his phone so I leave him to it. I'm halfway out the door when he interrupts. "Wait, come back. I just got something."

Looks like you'll have to wait, Blake.

CHAPTER EIGHT

DAMON

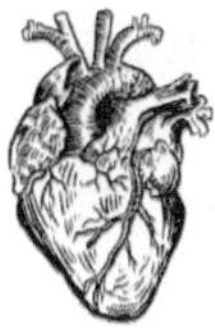

We're driving through the dark streets, heading toward the highway. Leon seems like he's alive again for the first time since we left Palm Cove. His leg vibrates in the passenger seat while he types the address into his GPS.

"I'll call Jasper to meet us there," he says.

"Back up a sec. Where are we going and what the fuck is going on?"

He takes a breath and looks up from his phone. "I've been working this lead since we got here. Telling this guy named King that we're looking for work. That we've been recruiters down in Florida and just moved up here. I dropped the loser from Palm Cove's name and said he told us to meet up with someone named Sweeper. Long story short, we got a meeting with him."

I let his words sink in. He's been working nonstop like an animal and we finally got something tangible. "Fuck, yeah," I say. "So where are we headed?"

AFTER PICKING up Jasper at a bar in town, we pull up to a club called Velvet. My mind's whirling with the new information Leon was able to find. This day has had so many fucking ups and downs, it's a wonder I haven't crashed yet.

"A strip club?" Jasper says as he rounds the corner. "So cliche."

I chuckle and shake my head. He's not wrong. We take a few minutes to get our shit together and stories straight—fake names, history of how we met, and a few other random facts. When we're somewhat sure of ourselves, Leon gets out and leaves his gun on the floor of the car.

"No weapon?" I ask, adjusting my own. He paces for a moment then reaches for it. "Good choice," I say.

"I don't know. I'm sure they'll pat us down. Feels useless to bring them." He's probably right, but I'd rather err on the side of caution. Plus, if they do take our guns, I still have a few tricks up my sleeve.

Weaving through parked cars, we approach the venue. Two huge dudes with scowling expressions flank the entrance. They wave us through without question. Leon seems to know where to go, so we follow him, but I stay on guard.

It's a small club, not that I've been to many, but the ones I have been to were larger than this. There's one main low stage in the center of the room surrounded by high-backed red armchairs large enough for two. The lights are dim with the exception of a few well placed spotlights directed at the two attractive women currently dancing to a remixed R&B song.

I don't linger on them for long. There's only one woman I want to look at. We head toward the bar and order drinks. Leon leans in and speaks low to the bartender.

"I don't know about this," Jasper says, eyeing the area. "I feel like he's getting desperate and jumped on this too fast."

Jasper's never the anxious one. Our role reversal puts me on edge, but I trust Leon.

"He's been on this lead for a while. It'll be fine." I take another look around at the men and few women occupying chairs and bar stools. Not one looks intimidating.

Leon hands us our drinks. "Okay, the bartender is going to lead us to the back. King owns the place... He's back there with a few of his guys."

"We have a meeting set up right? You told him we were coming?" I ask to be sure.

"Yeah, of course." Leon's eyes dart nervously; Jasper clocks it too. "What? Drink up."

Jasper and I share a silent look before I narrow my gaze at Leon. "What's with the face? Shifty eyes, clenched jaw, and do I see a bead of sweat?"

"You had the same look that time you stole my favorite shirt and stained it," Jasper says. "We both know you suck at lying."

He scratches the stubble on his chin and schools his face into the most fake neutral expression I've ever seen. "I'm not lying."

"You look like the picture of guilt," I say. "It's actually freaky. Blink, man."

He blinks dramatically. If we weren't in a situation where we were possibly about to meet a brutal criminal, I'd laugh.

"Follow me," the bartender says, coming around the side of the bar and laying a hand on Leon's shoulder. Jasper and I follow close behind.

I whisper, "You better fess up right now. What are we walking into?"

"Fine. This may not be a scheduled meeting. And when I say may not be, I mean it definitely isn't."

I clench my fist. "What the fu—"

"Come on, I didn't want to bum around while these fuckers could know something. It'll be fine."

"Why does it sound like you're trying to convince yourself of that more than me?" I reply.

"Told you," Jasper says low enough for only me to hear. "My gut never lies."

"Your gut is usually telling you that you ate too much Taco Bell. But I'll give you this one."

I suck in a breath and prepare for the worst as the bartender knocks on a door at the end of a long hallway. We step inside an office that's roughly the size of our entire apartment. The space is a stark contrast to the rest of the club. Bright overhead lights, metal shelving filled with boxes and bins, one large wooden desk in the back of the room. It looks more like a storage closet than an office.

We follow the bartender over to the group of men around the desk. A few older guys sit in chairs holding glass tumblers, while two younger and bigger guys stand beside the desk. Sitting in a leather chair, eyeing us as we head his way, is who Leon's been talking to.

He's a middle aged white guy in a polo shirt. The type you'd expect to see playing a round of golf or shopping with his wife and kids at Costco. The one difference is his shrewd light eyes. He scratches his blond thinning hair and sets his hands on top of his desk.

The bartender introduces Leon, takes our empty glasses, and hurries back the way she came. "Gentlemen, as you can see I'm currently entertaining guests." His words carry a hint of a Russian accent as he gestures to the men. Their posture visibly stiffens in response. "Unless the reason you're here can't wait until tomorrow, I'll have to ask you to leave." He subtly nods his chin at one of the men standing beside him.

Leon jumps in. "I'm sorry to come by unannounced. I'm

Randy, we've been talking." King's sharp eyes narrow. "From Florida," Leon adds.

The man standing to his left bends to speak into his ear and realization blooms on King's face. "Randy, that's right." He drums his fingers on his desk. "Why are you here and who are your... friends?"

"We can leave," one of the seated men says. "It's no problem."

King laughs and my skin crawls. So much for Costco dad. This guy's creepy. "I'm not done with you two. Stay awhile. Finish your drinks." He focuses back on us. "Go on."

I stay locked in on the three men around the desk while Leon stumbles over his words. "I have a lead... some girls. The pick up's tomorrow. I wanted to bring you in... Call it a good faith gesture."

King clasps his hands together and laughs again. This time my hand inches toward my gun. "And what makes you think I'd be interested in that, Randy?"

Leon's quiet for a moment as the tension in the room rises. "Based on our conversations. You mentioned girls and I—"

Both men shift, drawing their weapons before I can react, but Jasper's quicker than I am. He faces them, gun drawn. Leon and I follow suit, aiming our weapons at the three men behind the desk.

"Do you think I'm stupid, Randy? You come here, to my place of business unannounced, and expect me to what? Agree to work with you?" The two men in front of the desk try to abandon their seats but he fixes his gaze on them. "Did I tell you to move?"

"No—no, but—"

King nods to the man on his left and he shoots one of them in the leg. "Try to move again... I dare you," he says.

They curse and bite back screams. My focus isn't on them, not while guns are still pointed at us.

"Greg, remind me to can those two idiot bouncers for not patting these ones down," King says. "Where was I?"

"Listen," I say. "We'll leave right now and forget this ever happened."

They laugh and look behind me where two more guys have appeared from nowhere. They're blocking the door, their weapons drawn.

Jasper and I exchange glances, while Leon seems to be deep in thought.

"I don't think so," King says. "What's going to happen is you three idiots will drop your weapons and walk slowly over there." He points to the back side of the wall near the metal shelves. "Then my boys will pat you down."

I blink at Jasper, trying to relay my thoughts. Leon catches my eye and jerks his chin slightly. "And what if we refuse?" I ask.

"Then you die, genius," the stocky guy to the right says. "Lower your weapons."

With my hand shaking, I begin to squat, but at the last second, I aim and shoot out the overhead light above us. The distraction causes all out chaos to ensue. Leon and Jasper drop low, firing their weapons. I manage to hit the stocky one and he goes down.

Sparks drop from the ceiling as I duck behind a box and fire off a few more rounds. "Let's go," I shout, hoping the guys can hear.

King cowers behind his desk. Figures, a guy like him is all talk. I'm dangerously low on ammo. I assume Jas and Leon are too.

Gun pointed at the remaining two, I crouch and head toward the door, hugging walls and boxes. I'm so close. Right there. *Bam!* A bullet smashes into the wall beside my head. Fuck. I aim and fire, hitting one of them in the shoulder.

"D," Leon calls. "Come on." He's made it to the door with a hunched over Jasper by his side. Steeling myself, I dart forward and follow them out the door. I grab a nearby chair and jam it under the doorknob. It should buy us a few minutes.

"Fuck!" I yell. "We can't go through the club. There's gotta be a back entrance." Jasper groans and Leon hangs back, sinking to the floor. Jasper's shirt is soaked through with blood. "Shit, Jasper. Hang in there." I face a frozen Leon, shock catching up with him. "Hey, stay with me. We gotta get the fuck outta here. Hold him up, I'll grab the other side. They're gonna come for us. We didn't kill them all."

Leon nods and speaks low to Jasper. He's the biggest of the three of us so carrying him isn't easy. I spot an exit sign glowing in the dim hallway and say a silent thanks that one thing's working in our favor. We stumble to my car and drape Jasper's groaning form into the passenger seat.

"He needs a hospital," Leon says. "But fuck, they're going to ask what happened to him. What do we say? We can't tell the truth."

"Let's just get the hell out of here and we can figure something out on the way," I say.

"Y-yeah, alright," Leon stutters. He climbs in the back and takes off his shirt. "Jas, here, hold pressure."

Jasper groans and presses the shirt against his shoulder. "Fucking hell."

"Keep pressure on it," I order, gunning the engine as we peel away. My gaze darts between the road ahead and the rearview, scanning for potential followers the entire drive home. I can't let anything happen to him. I fucking refuse.

"Let's get him upstairs," I say, pulling as close to the steps as I can. "I have a plan."

Jasper moans at my side. His face is so fucking pale. "I'll be okay. I can walk."

"The fuck you can," I tell him. "Sit your ass down. Leon, go make sure Mrs. Langston isn't out."

"It's 2 AM, I think we're okay," Leon says. How the hell did it get that late?

It's a struggle, but we manage to get him upstairs and into his room. Jasper lies on his bed, bleeding onto his sheets while Leon grabs our one clean towel to staunch the wound. He pulls me to the side. "What now?"

"Stay here and keep him comfortable. I'll be back soon."

CHAPTER NINE

BLAKE

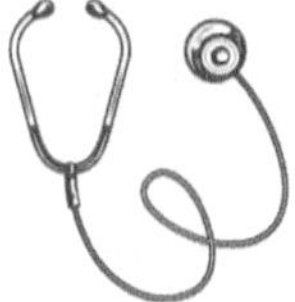

I FINALLY FELL ASLEEP AFTER A FEW HOURS OF TOSSING and turning. Every time I closed my eyes, I'd picture Ethan's face as the ambulance took him away. He wouldn't look at me, wouldn't say a word to me.

Something happened after he found me in the hallway, but I still have no idea what that was.

My eyes jerk open from the sound of a car engine outside. Is it Ethan? Possible, but unlikely. He's probably still at the hospital, unless something's changed. I check my phone and it's just as blank as when I went to sleep. My ears perk up for the sound of someone coming to the door but when I hear nothing for a few minutes, I roll back over to face the wall.

I'm in that magical place between sleep and dreamland when I feel something cold and hard press against my head. I freeze, unable to say a word. Everything inside me is screaming to move... to do something. But my muscles lock and my throat constricts.

"Blake," a voice—clear and deep—speaks, breaking the stillness in the room. "Listen closely. I'm not going to hurt you. I'd never hurt you, but I need you to come with me. It's important."

My heart pounds so hard I can feel it in my throat. I'm still frozen, disconnected from my body, but somehow I find my voice. It's like speaking through a tightened windpipe. "Who are you? What do you want?"

"I'll explain on the way. There's no time." He pulls the gun away from my skin and I finally gather enough courage to turn and face him. He's wearing a black fabric mask. It covers everything but his eyes. I can't make out much in the dark other than his large frame and black clothing. Even so, I memorize whatever features I can. It'll be important for later... if he lets me live through this.

Channeling the same energy I use with Ethan when he's not himself, I speak slowly, but my voice comes out shaky. "N-no. I'm not going with you."

"I'm not asking you, I'm telling you. We need to go."

My pulse pounds like a drum in my ears. "If you're not going to hurt me, then why do you have a gun aimed at my head?"

"If I put the gun away, will you come with me willingly?" He's so calm, like holding a gun to a sleeping woman's head is an everyday occurrence.

I have a choice to make. A choice that could cost my life. God, I wish I'd let Brennan give me those self-defense lessons. *Brennan*. He'll flip out if something happens to me. I can't leave him, not after losing mom and Bryan. Hesitating, I nod and clear my throat.

He fixes his amber eyes on me as he puts his gun behind his jacket. There's something familiar about those eyes, but I can't place them. "You have five minutes to get ready. Do you have a medical bag?"

Wait, what?

"No—I'm only a student. What is this about? Who are you?" His phone vibrates from his pocket and he finally breaks his gaze away from me. It might be the only opportunity I have to run.

"Leon," he says into his phone.

With him distracted, I dart up and kick him as hard as I can in the balls. Brennan may not have taught me much, but I know you can't beat a ball beating when it comes to these situations. He groans and drops into a hunched crouch while I run like I've never run before.

I'm out my door, and instead of heading through the front, I stop in the kitchen and grab the first knife out of the wooden block on the counter. Clutching it to my chest, I sprint through the rest of the house and out the back door.

Cold air hits my bare legs but I ignore the discomfort. I know my feet will be ice soon, but I'd rather risk frostbite than death. I'd take any number of injuries over death. My pulse screams in my ears and my chest heaves as I run across the backyard.

"Blake," he calls. From the sound of it, he's just left the back door. "Come on, I'm not going to hurt you."

Says every serial killer, everywhere.

I duck behind the closest tree to catch my breath. Where can I go? We're so far out in the middle of nowhere, the closest house has to be a half mile away. Dead leaves crunch with every step. He's getting closer.

Think, Blake. You're smart.

"You know Blake, I live for this. *Hide and seek.* It's my favorite game. And guess what? I always win."

My legs tremble, fear-struck and cold. It's either I sit here and freeze until he finds and takes me, or I make a run for it. I don't hear any heavy steps or branches snapping. He's waiting for me to move like a hunter stalking his prey. This prey won't go willingly.

I take off, sprinting toward the woods. My feet throb from stepping on sharp sticks and rocks. I push past the pain. The shelter of the woods is close. There's more places to hide, less light. When I lose him I can walk alongside the road until I reach a neighbor's house.

Another few paces and I'll be safe. Or at least *safer*. Panting, I reach a copse of trees and lean back to catch my breath. It's quiet again and I'm filled with as much relief as panic. He could be anywhere.

With another breath, I'm ready. The knife close to my chest, I turn to sprint again, but he appears out of thin air.

"Found you." He grabs me around the waist and pulls me against his hard chest. I thrash and swing my arms, attempting to graze him with the knife to no avail. He plucks it easily from my outstretched hand and tosses it aside.

"No!" I scream as he lifts my feet off the ground. "Put me down!"

His low tone in my ear quiets me. "Keep thrashing and screaming, Blake. I fucking love it."

Whimpering, I twist again, trying to break free of his hold but he's too big. Too damn strong. "Please," I whisper. "What do you want?"

"There's my sweet girl. I love this side of you almost as much as I love your feisty side. You submitting to me is music to my ears." There's a hint of pride in his voice, like he's in awe of me.

"You're crazy. I'm not submitting to anything." I flail, kicking out and back to hit him where it hurts again.

He hoists me and tosses me over his shoulder like I weigh nothing. "No way, Angel. I need those and so do you. Can't make a baby without them."

My stomach drops. He's more than crazy, he's flat out psycho. As he jogs toward the house, all my blood rushes to my head. "Put me down. I won't run."

"Even if I did believe you, I'm still going to carry you. Your feet are destroyed."

He cares about my feet, but chases me through the woods. Again, psycho.

"I'm too heavy to carry. Let me walk."

He scoffs and continues. His hand on the back of my bare thigh scorches my chilled skin. "Too heavy? Absolutely not. I can and will hold you for hours. Against the wall, in the shower." He glances at the side of the house. "Right here in this yard."

My stomach flips at the thought of being pressed against the side of the house. There's something obviously wrong with my brain if I'm having those kinds of feelings. It's from the blood rushing to my head... that's all. "I thought you said you wouldn't hurt me."

"I think you misunderstand me, Blake. When I say I'll hold you against this house, I mean, you'll be climbing me like a tree, nightshirt hiked up to your hips, pussy soaking wet, begging for me to fill you with my cum."

I'm stunned silent. No one's ever spoken to me like that. He's vulgar and blunt... and I have no idea what he wants with me.

By the asphalt below us, I can tell we've reached the driveway. I try to crane my neck to see where he's taking me but between my position and the darkness, I can't make out much. He opens a car door and finally loosens his palm from my thigh, dropping me into a passenger seat.

His chest brushes against my own as he leans across to buckle my seatbelt. I catch a hint of mint as his face gets closer. "Safety first." My breath catches in my throat as his masked face brushes the crook of my neck. "Don't even think of trying to run again while I walk to the other side of the car. I will catch you and next time, I won't be so nice."

Alarm bells blare. Run, hide. Do not let him take you without a fight. My body's gone into full blown shivers as he closes my door. I reach for the handle with my trembling hand. It's right there, I could open it and run. But the moment passes as quickly as the thought. He gets into the driver's seat and starts the engine.

A blast of warm air hits my skin and I shiver involuntarily. I'm colder than I realized. The heat permeates the car with his scent. Mint and earthiness. It's overwhelming. With the glow of the dash lights, I can see more of his profile. His chest hugs his black shirt, lean but strong. He's tall, unable to fully stretch his long thick legs even with the seat pushed back much farther than mine.

He reaches into the back seat and drops a hoodie in my lap. "Here, I know you're cold."

The kind gesture shocks and confuses me. He's just ripped me from my bed but is worried about me being cold and hurting my feet. At first I think about tossing it back in his face, but another bout of shivers rattles me and I think better of it, pulling it over my head instead.

He backs out of the driveway and for a short while there's only the purr of his engine and the sound of Chino's melodic voice coming from the speakers at a low volume.

"You can take off the mask," I say. "I'm picturing you looking like some kind of Freddy Krueger under there." He scoffs. "Seriously. Why wear a mask and then say all that stuff about me begging you for... uh, you know what, nevermind."

Smooth, Blake.

My cheeks flame and I shut my mouth.

"Begging for my cock," he says casually.

I swallow and focus on the blurring trees out the window. "Yeah. That."

"Maybe I do look like Freddy. What then?" he says, challenging me.

"Nothing... It wouldn't matter because what you said won't ever happen. I'll never beg you for sex. You're a psycho kidnapper. Plus, I have a boyfriend." He's quiet and it unnerves me. I'd much rather spar with him than sit here wondering what's going through his head. I'm stuck reading body language.

His hand rests on the shifter and I can't help but watch the way his knuckles flex as he squeezes it. I try to figure out what his tattoos are. Any details will help me later when I go to the cops. It looks like Roman numerals on his fingers and an anatomical heart on his fist.

"Just wait," he says. His tone is so arrogant it does nothing but irritate me further. We're on a main road now, not far from campus. The streets are pretty much deserted at this time of night but I notice a few landmarks. He speaks up. "We need supplies." I'm about to ask what type of supplies when he stops me. "Don't ask questions, I know you were about to. My face is covered but my eyes work just fine. All you need to know is someone was hurt and I need you to patch him up."

"You can't be serious." My mouth drops open. "I told you before, I'm a second year student. I've never worked on an actual person before."

"You'll do fine." He stops my argument by putting his hand on my thigh and squeezing gently. "Now, where can we get supplies?"

I must be as crazy as he is. That's the only reason I have for giving him the address to Ethan's father's office. "You'll have to break in," I say. "It's my boyfriend's father's practice, but I've only been there a few times. I don't know if there's an alarm."

He grabs his phone and presses the screen. "That's no problem. You worry about what you'll need." With the phone to his ear, he speaks to whoever picks up on the other end. "Hey, I'll be there with help soon. I need you to put on your masks."

What the hell am I walking into?

CHAPTER TEN

DAMON

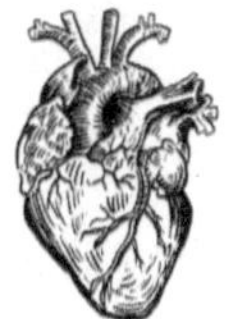

Breaking into that doctor's office was too easy. It was keeping a grasp on Blake that was the difficult part. We managed to get in and out in about ten minutes. Would have been faster if I trusted her to gather everything on her own without trying anything. I hate that she doesn't trust me. That the start of our relationship has to be this way. She'll come around soon enough. She has no choice.

I park on the street in front of the apartment with a bag full of medical supplies and a bottle of antibiotics. Blake's absently biting her lip in the seat beside me while she studies the exterior of our place. I know what she's doing. Stashing all this information away for later so she can tell the cops. That won't happen.

"Ready?" I ask, although her answer won't matter. She shakes her head.

"I can't do this. What if I make things worse?"

That's what she's worried about. She's an actual angel, I knew it all along. I reach for her hand. She flinches at first but then lets me cover her hand with mine. I smile beneath my mask from how perfect our joined hands look. One day there will be a ring on her finger, a big fucking diamond that tells the world she belongs to me.

"I believe in you. You're brilliant and caring and anyone would be lucky to be your patient." She shivers from the feel of my thumb rubbing circles on her palm. The unease on her face changes as I speak. My eyes linger on her chest as she takes a few calming breaths. "Ready now?"

"I guess I don't have a choice." With another squeeze, I release her hand. "Freddy?"

I can't help but laugh. "Yes, Blake?"

She swallows hard. "If I can't save him—whoever it is up there—promise you won't hold it against me?"

The fear in her voice kills me. "Come on, Doc. They're waiting."

LEON PULLS me into his bedroom and yanks his mask off. "What the bloody hell, D? Please tell me this isn't what it looks like!"

Blake's in Jasper's room, doing her thing. I was able to hear her initial thoughts before Leon interrupted. He's lost a lot of blood but thankfully is still conscious. The bullet went straight through the muscle, missing his brachial artery by less than an inch. I want to be in there with them to help. Blake needs me.

"And what would that be?" I lean against the doorframe and pull my mask off as well, scrubbing my hand over my face. It feels like I've been awake for days and my body is screaming at me over it. I don't feel like dealing with a Leon talk, nor do I care what he has to say.

"Oh, I don't know. Maybe that you kidnapped a woman

and forced her to come here. Is she even a doctor? We can't fuck around with this, Jasper could—"

"Could what? Fucking *die*? You think I haven't thought about that. You can't say shit to me. It's your fault we're in this mess." I force air into my lungs and silently count down from five before I fucking lose it.

Leon slumps on the edge of his bed, resignation in his tone. "I'm sorry, okay? We'll deal with the repercussions of tonight later. Let's just make sure Jas pulls through. You sure about this girl? Where'd you find her?"

"Of course I'm sure about her. She's in med school, we started talking recently, that's all you need to know." I drum my fingers against the wall and avoid his scrutinizing gaze. "What?"

"I know who she is. It took a minute but I knew I recognized her. She's the brunette from that house. The one I saw in the—"

"Don't finish that sentence," I seethe. "I don't want to go in there and shoot Jasper all over again for putting a camera in my girl's bathroom."

He plays with his lip ring, a habit he always does when he's thinking. And the guy's always fucking thinking. "You're dating her? How'd that happen? We've been working nonstop since we got here."

"What's with the cross-examination? I wasn't aware my personal life was on trial." I walk into his ensuite and take a quick piss with the door open. I know Leon, and he's not done grilling me.

"She got a mask kink or something?" he asks as I shake my dick. *Fuck.* I'm so damn exhausted I didn't think of a reason for the masks.

I flush and face him as I wash my hands. "Fine, Leon. Since

you have to know my business, we're not dating. Or she doesn't know we are yet. Happy?"

He grabs me by the shoulders and spins me to face him. I don't put up a fight. It's not worth it. If I know Leon, and I do, he'll go through what Jasper and I have coined *The Stages of Colter*. Colter being Leon's last name.

Step one: he'll stress the fuck out over whatever I tell him—red face, lip ring twisting.

Step two: he'll berate me like I'm a child in his pretentious British accent. I'll ignore him even though I'll want to punch his stupid, handsome face.

Step three: satisfied that he's said and done all he can, he'll stoop to making passive aggressive comments any chance he gets. Step three is usually where I get way too close to smothering him in his sleep.

And finally, step four: acceptance. We'll hug it out and he'll say he's washing his hands of me, which really just means he's given up on whatever the issue is and we can go back to living with normal, pleasant Leon. By pleasant, I mean insufferable. But fuck, I love the guy like a brother, so what can I do?

"You're obsessed with her, aren't you? Tell me you haven't gone full Olivia." He's referring to the woman I had a thing for in Florida, which we've already gotten past stage four on, so there's no reason to bring her up.

"It's not like that. Blake's different. And we already cleared everything up with Olivia. Left it in Palm Cove. I don't know why you're bringing her up. Come on, we need to be there for Jas." I shrug away from him and cross the room, ready to be done with this conversation.

"Right then, but we're not finished discussing this," he says, his voice full of defeat.

"Yeah, whatever," I mumble, pulling my mask back over my face. We both have more important things to worry about.

Soft light filters in through Jasper's bedroom window, casting Blake in an ethereal glow. I stand outside the door for a moment, listening to her gentle encouragement and watching her careful fingers stitch Jasper's wound. She's holding her chin high, exuding confidence, but I know the Blake beneath that facade. She's terrified that she'll fail Jasper, somehow lose him while trying her best. She wants to please him... to please me. If it takes me a lifetime, I'll show her that she's perfect. That she's more than enough. I'll stoke her flames and happily get burned in the process.

"How's it going, big guy?" I move to the side of the bed, eyeing Jasper's half-masked face. His eyes are hooded but open and his breaths come in shallow pants. I try to keep my tone upbeat even though seeing him this way twists my insides.

"Never been better," he says through gritted teeth.

"Grab me that gauze from the bag," Blake says. "And I could use more light."

"You got it, Doc." I grab what she needs and stand next to her, holding my phone flashlight against Jasper's stitched wound. "Looks good, nice and clean."

She shrugs. "Yeah, well, I'm doing what I can. He got lucky, although I'm worried about nerve damage and there's always the chance of sepsis. Any number of things can go wrong. Like I said, I've never done this before, only read about it."

"What?" Jasper rasps, meeting my eyes.

"Don't worry about it," I reply and turn back to Blake. "What else can I do? Are you hungry? Thirsty?"

"Don't think I can eat pancakes while I'm cleaning a bloody wound, Freddy." She's playing with me and I fucking love it.

"Freddy?" Jasper asks.

"Yup," she says. "Freddy Krueger, my new kidnapper." Jas manages a strained laugh.

I press against her back and lean in to speak low in her ear.

"Should I buy some special gloves just for you? I do like to play with knives." She sucks in a breath and the apples of her cheeks color. "You're so pretty when you blush for me."

"Nothing I do is for you," she says after regaining her composure. Too bad for her, I can read her body like a book. "Grab me the wound wash."

I help her finish up, passing her supplies and holding the light when she needs it. We make a fantastic team, if I do say so, but I already knew that we would. Leon pops in to check on things, barely meeting my eye. He thanks Blake and apologizes before letting me know he's going to get some sleep.

Blake bandages Jasper and I have him swallow some antibiotics and a couple of leftover pain pills I found in his stash. They're old as fuck, probably from one of his many football injuries in college, but I figure anything helps. He's asleep before I turn the lights off.

"He'll need to be monitored closely for infection in the upcoming days. His bandages need to be changed daily and the wound needs to stay clean." She bites her lip and gazes at a spot on the wall. "Oh, and his antibiotics and some anti-inflammatories. He'll be in pain when he wakes up."

"Got it," I say on a yawn. With Jasper patched up and asleep I feel my body starting to crash. I give Blake a once over and see that her nightshirt is stained in blood. "Come with me. Let's get you cleaned up."

She meets my gaze with wide, blinking eyes. "Then you'll take me home?"

"I'll be honest with you, Blake. I'm about to pass out where I stand. It's been a long fucking night for both of us. Let's get cleaned up, sleep some, and after you check on my friend, I'll bring you home." I don't wait for her response before I start walking toward the bathroom that Jasper and I share. Blake hesitates but then follows me.

"You promise you'll bring me home later?"

She's twisting the edge of her nightshirt, waiting for my response. "I'm too exhausted to bullshit you."

Hoping I've made her feel comfortable enough to believe me, I step in front of the bathroom sink and pull my shirt over my head. I want to rip this fucking mask off my face but I still can't trust that Blake won't go to the cops. Not yet.

I feel her eyes on me from the doorway as I wipe myself down with a damp washcloth. Showering takes more energy than I have at the moment, so this will have to do. I pull my mask up to brush my teeth quickly and swipe on some fresh deodorant.

"You can join me, I won't bite."

Her tongue darts out to moisten her lips. I can't break my gaze away from her perfect mouth. "I'm okay. I can clean up when I get home."

I grab a fresh washcloth and dampen it with warm water. She watches me with wide eyes as I step closer. I expect her to back away or flinch but she freezes. Gently, I skim the cloth against her cheek, testing her. When she sucks in a breath, I inch closer, our bodies almost flush against each other.

As I reach her other cheek, she shakes her head slightly, snapping back to the present. "No. Don't touch me." She pushes my chest, and I stumble against the edge of the counter.

"Blake," I scold. "That wasn't very nice." Her fight is the spark that ignites my blood. I close the distance between us, crowding her against the doorframe. Her throat bobs as she gulps audibly. "Let me."

With my free hand, I cup her chin, hard enough that she knows I mean business without hurting her. She wraps her hand around my wrist and squeezes. "What's your problem, Freddy? I'm not a child. I can wash my own face."

"Trust me, Blake, I know you're not a child." I draw the

cloth over her cheeks and down the slope of her neck. The loose neckline of her shirt slides off her shoulder, revealing a small bumblebee tattoo. I skim it with the cloth as her chest heaves and her dark lashes flutter. She digs her fingernails into my skin, but I continue cleaning her, loving the fact that she's leaving her mark on me.

I bring the cloth lower, washing the dip of her collarbones, right above the swell of her perfect, full breasts, then back up the column of her neck. Time is suspended as her gray eyes lock onto mine. I imagine dropping the cloth and wrapping my palm around her graceful neck. I'd push her against the tile wall and bite that plump bottom lip between my teeth.

Her eyes seem to darken as her lips part. "I-I think I'm clean now." Shoving me away again, she twists out of my grasp. It takes me a moment to reconnect with my surroundings.

"Come on, let's get some sleep." I brush against her in the doorway and head across the hall to my bedroom. She's frozen where she stands.

"I'll sleep on the couch," she says with her chin raised.

"No. You're sleeping in here, in my bed." Her mouth opens to argue but I add, "I can carry you again, or you can walk. Your choice."

"But you said—"

"If I was going to fuck you tonight, Blake, I would have done it already. Get your sweet ass in here before I throw you over my shoulder again."

She closes her mouth and listens like a good fucking girl. Crossing my bedroom, I pull out a clean T-shirt and a pair of gym shorts for her to change into. "Sit on the edge of the bed."

"Why?" I'm too exhausted for her questions. She squeals as I pick her up and plop her on the edge of my bed. Kneeling before her, I hold one leg at a time against my knee and wash her dirty, cut up feet with the washcloth. "You don't have to," she argues.

"I know," I say, meeting her gaze. Once I finish cleaning her off, I grab a pair of thick socks from the bin in my closet and pull them on her feet. "That's better. I'll turn around so you can change."

Her gaze bounces between me and my folded up clothes beside her on the bed, like she's at war with herself. "I don't need your clothes. I'm fine."

Huffing, I crouch down and hook my fingers into the hem of her nightshirt. She scrambles back, so I let go and hold my hands in front of me. "Either change, or I dress you. Your choice. I don't want blood on my clean sheets."

She blinks and nods to study the filthy nightshirt. Resignation spreads across her face as she silently grabs the clean clothes beside her. I can't help but smirk while I turn to face the wall. Knowing that my clothes are against her bare skin has my heart thumping in my chest.

A few minutes go by, and the rustle of fabric quiets. "Safe to turn around?"

"I guess," she whispers under her breath. I face her and momentarily lose my train of thought when I see her full tits in my black T-shirt.

I stand and pull the corner of the blanket down for her, gesturing for her to climb in. She looks utterly confused but lets out a tired sigh before relenting. All tucked in with my blanket up to her chin, she asks, "Where are you going to sleep?"

"I'm gonna go check on my friend again. Close your eyes, Angel. Get some rest." I turn out the light and leave her exactly where she belongs.

Jasper's still fast asleep and breathing normally. Thank fuck he's alright. Blake saved his life tonight and I'll be eternally grateful.

I linger for a few minutes, letting myself calm down from the image of Blake between my sheets. Her beautiful body curled up against mine while we rest our weary heads. She's everything I've ever wanted and more.

Back in my room, Blake breathes in a steady rhythm. She's fast asleep on her side, cuddling one of my pillows to her chest. I pull off my mask and watch her from the shadows. All the tension she carries in her face disappears when she's asleep.

If I could carry all her burdens, I would, but I know one thing: I'll sure as shit make sure she has a lighter load from now on.

I slide my jeans off and grab a pair of sweats. I'd normally sleep naked but I'm taking it slow with Blake. I need her to trust me, to know I'll always protect and care for her, even if that means pushing her out of her shell. Or punishing her when she needs it.

I lay beside her, keeping a few inches between our skin. I'm drawn to her in every way and being this close only makes me crave more. *Fuck it.* I draw her against me, my arm around her waist, as sleep begins to claim me.

CHAPTER ELEVEN

BLAKE

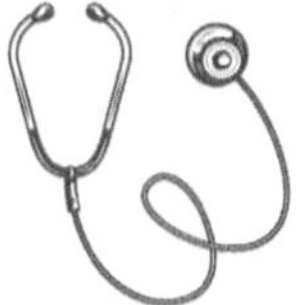

I WAKE AS THE LATE AFTERNOON SUN STREAMS THROUGH the blinds. I'm in a stranger's bed and should be panicking, but instead I'm experiencing an odd mix of disorientation and restfulness. I can't remember the last time I slept that hard.

The other side of the bed is empty but there's still an indent from where *he* slept. I reach out and brush my hand over the spot but pull back quickly. What's wrong with me? Am I wishing for him to still be in bed with me? That would be insane.

"Morning, Angel, or I guess afternoon." I jump back at the sound of his deep voice. "Didn't mean to scare you. I was letting you sleep a little longer."

He's leaning against the far wall, holding his phone in one hand at his side. Sadly his chest is covered by a clean shirt and he's wearing a pair of low slung gray sweats. Can't forget about his trusty mask. Seeing him there, by the light of day, is nothing short of surreal.

"Last night felt like a dream, a nightmarish fever dream," I say, stretching my arms over my head. I realize how badly I need a shower, a toothbrush, and some deodorant. "How's your friend?"

He sits on the edge of the bed beside me, overwhelming me with his masculine smell—like he's fresh out of the shower. It's subtle and natural, nothing like Ethan's cologne. "He's doing alright. Still in pain, but he was up and about this morning. All because of you."

I can't help the small grin that lifts the corners of my lips. "I'm glad he's okay. Still not happy about you breaking into my house and kidnapping me. Not cool at all." I poke his chest to punctuate each word but he grabs my hand.

"I think you liked it," he says, rubbing circles on my palm. God, that feels good. I'm ashamed at how my body reacts to him. I pull my hand away before whatever this is goes too far.

"No... I can assure you I didn't." I inch away from his thick thighs. Those sweats that leave little to the imagination.

"You can't tell me our little game of hide and seek didn't soak your panties, Blake. That you weren't hoping I'd find you and punish you for running." My mouth goes dry and I stop my eyes from fluttering closed. No. I hadn't thought about him punishing me. Not at all. "That's what I thought."

"I didn't say anything," I argue.

"You didn't have to. I can read you like a book." He pulls his mask up a few inches, showing off his chiseled jawline and perfectly shaped lips. My breath catches as he leans closer. "I can tell when your pulse is fluttering, right here." His lips hover over my racing pulse point. "Or when you're holding your breath, here." He moves lower, grazing the swell of my chest with his teeth. I let a breathy exhale slip out and feel his lips turn up against my heated skin. My head lolls back to accommodate his size as he lifts onto his knees in front of me. I'm staring at his perfect lips with all the right words spilling from them and I feel myself coming undone. "Or when you're silently pleading for me to suck this bottom lip between my teeth."

I whimper as he inches closer, knowing that I'd let him do it. This completely unhinged man... this stranger. I'd let him kiss me here and now in his bed. His warm breath fans across my parted lips and I close my eyes. "I know you, Blake, and with every passing day you'll know me too."

My eyes snap open to find him climbing off the bed. I'm mortified. I almost let him kiss me and I don't even know his name. He pulls his mask back down and watches me from the doorframe. "I'll bring you home after you check on him."

I can't meet his gaze, not after whatever that was. "You can just call me an Uber."

"Look at me, Blake." I hate the way his voice drips dominance. How every time he opens his mouth, I feel like I'm his to control. Well, he can't control me. Not now, not ever. I turn my head to face the other side of the room. "Blake," he repeats, coming closer.

"What?" I finally reply. I don't need him climbing back on the bed again with that whole, *I can read you* thing.

He guides my chin, turning and lifting it to meet his gaze. I've never seen eyes like his. They remind me of warm honey. The black ring encircling his iris creates the most hypnotic contrast of color. I hate that he draws me in.

"The only car you'll ever get in again will be mine. No one else carries my precious cargo."

His fists ball at his side as he backs away to leave the room. I'm left stunned on his bed, wondering who the hell this man thinks he is to talk to me that way.

AFTER MY NAMELESS masked lunatic drops me off, I spend at least thirty minutes soaking in the shower. His scent is all over me and it's messing with my head. Once I've scrubbed him away, I can start to put yesterday out of my mind.

Mischa's still not home. Come to think of it, I haven't seen her since before I left for the gala. It isn't unlike her to leave town on a whim though. At least according to Brennan.

The house feels cold and empty without my brother. I miss his laugh, and the way he always teases me. He's the only one who makes me feel safe and loved. Except for Falin, but it's different with her. I have no idea where in the world Brennan is but I grab my phone and text him anyway.

> Me: Hey, it's been a bit. Just wanted to check in and see how you're doing? Love and miss you!

I don't expect a fast reply. Even when Brennan's home, he's never the best at answering messages. He's more of a "randomly call you at 8 AM" type person. While I have my phone in hand, I scan through all the messages and emails I missed while sleeping the day away. I should have been studying for my tests at the end of the week, but now it's late and I'm mentally drained. I send off a text to Ethan to see how he's doing. I still have no idea what happened or why he was taken by ambulance. My guess is it had something to do with the pills. Thank God that worker interrupted him in the hallway when he did. He was acting super off.

After throwing on some comfy pajamas, I check the fridge for anything edible but shockingly it's bare. Instead, I grab a box of the gluten free crackers I bought the other day and go back to my room. Let's just hope none of my future patients ask me for nutritional advice. Crackers and water... The ultimate struggle meal.

I flop on my bed, scrolling social media. Ethan's mom posted a few photos from the gala. Of course, I'm not in any of them. I never expected to be. There's a staged photo of a few of the board members with Ethan and his parents. Where was I when this was taken? Thinking of the gala brings me back to everything that happened afterwards.

I Google the number for the Willowbrook non-emergency police line and stare at it. There's no reason for me to be hesitating, yet I am. Their names and faces may be a mystery, but I know the color of his car and maybe I could lead them to the apartment?

Swiping the Google search away, I open Maps and attempt to figure out a possible address for the place. It was dark both times and I was conveniently distracted. Let's say I don't call. The worst thing that can happen is I walk away slightly traumatized but weirdly exhilarated. I wouldn't be implicated in a breaking and entering for Dr. Porter's office and I'll have successfully worked on my first gunshot wound.

Groaning, I close the apps. Who am I kidding? I knew all along that I wouldn't call. Whatever trouble those guys are in, I don't want to add to it. Despite the whole kidnapping and criminal behavior situation, they seemed like nice enough guys. Kind of goofy if I'm being honest. Which is probably why one of them ended up shot.

And Freddy, or whatever his name is, thinking he's all tough and domineering. Like he knows me so well. He doesn't. There's no way someone I've never met can claim to know me.

My phone vibrates and I pick it up. There's a text from an unknown number.

845-555-0912: Check your front door.

A wave of panic twists my gut. After last night, there's no way I'm going to unlock the door for anyone.

Me: Who is this?

I force myself to head down the hall and peek out the window. It's too dark to see anything, but it doesn't look like anyone's there. My pulse is erratic as I wait for a response.

845-555-0912: Don't tell me you've forgotten me already?

I read over the message as a gif of a Ghostface mask is sent.

845-555-0912: If you're going to call me a horror movie character, I'd much rather Ghostface than Freddy. Wink emoji.

What the hell? This man is unhinged, but for some reason I'm grinning like a fool. I go to the front door and crack it open. There's no sign of him or his car, but there's a paper bag, closed with a piece of string. I grab it quickly, then shut and lock the door.

I'm afraid to look inside the bag. Flashes from the movie *Seven* creep into my mind. Brad Pitt hysterically yelling, "What's in the box?" It could be body parts for all I know.

Taking a deep breath, I pull the string and peek inside. No body parts. There's a few different takeout containers, a hard seltzer, an organic juice blend, and a card. Whatever's in the containers smells amazing, but I'm sure I won't be able to eat it. I'm almost convinced Freddy wouldn't poison me the old fashioned way, but he wouldn't know about my allergies.

I open the card first. There's a watercolor night sky on the front. He's written a note on the inside.

I wish I could be with you enjoying this meal, but I have some work to do tonight. Before you ask, everything is from an allergy friendly restaurant. Leaf and Ladle. It's a few towns over. Wheat, soy, nut, and dairy-free.
Sweet dreams, Angel. I'll be seeing you soon.

I'm absolutely floored. No one, not even my own family has ever taken this much care about my food. How did he know? My stomach growls as I open each container. There's a grilled chicken over quinoa dish with veggies. It smells garlicky and delicious. The next container has some sort of hummus with pita and sliced veggies. I pull off a piece of the pita and dip it before stuffing it into my mouth. It's freaking amazing. I never get to eat bread products because of my wheat allergy. The last one has an incredible looking chocolate brownie in it.

I'm so touched I could actually cry. I carry each container over to the barely used dining room table and crack open the seltzer. Before I dig in, I text him back.

> Me: I don't even know what to say except thank you. This looks so good.

I start to cut into the chicken when he responds.

> 845-555-0912: I'm glad. Can't have you eating crackers for dinner.

I stop chewing and reread his message. Crackers... How did he know that?

> Me: Umm... ok, stalker.

845-555-0912: What? It was an educated guess.

Yeah, okay. I glance around the empty room. "Are you here?" When he doesn't answer I yell. "Hello?"

Maybe it was a guess. Still, it's pretty damn creepy. I take a few more bites of my meal and start to feel full. There's no way I'm not leaving a bit of room for that brownie. Picking up my phone, I click on his number and change the contact name to Freddy. Then I take a screenshot and send it to him.

Freddy: I thought I've upgraded to Ghostface. Freddy's a creepy child predator.

I snort in the most unattractive way. A few pieces of quinoa fly across the table.

Me: Until I see what's under that mask, I'm afraid you're stuck with Freddy.

Warmth spreads in my belly from the seltzer. I rarely drink, so when I do it doesn't take much to get a buzz. I know I'm here all alone and the guy I'm talking to is the definition of a red flag, but this feels good. It's been so long since I've smiled and laughed and enjoyed good food. I can't remember the last time.

Freddy: Is that a proposition, Blake? Should I come show you?

I almost choke on a sip of seltzer. Do I want that? I keep telling myself I don't but the way I'm flirting says otherwise. Heat spreads across my cheeks and down my neck as I imagine what he looks like under that mask. If his jawline and mouth are any inclination, the rest of his face will be just as hot.

Me: Noo, I'm all good. Aren't you working, anyway?

Freddy: Liar.

He doesn't answer my question and that's fine. I don't need to know what he's doing.

Me: Not a liar.

I smile.

Me: If you don't want me to call you Freddy, give me your name.

He doesn't respond right away so I start cleaning up the containers. I'll have food for the next day or two with all of this.

With everything put away, I grab the card and head back to my room, checking over my shoulder the entire time just in case.

CHAPTER TWELVE

DAMON

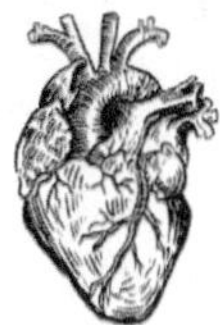

Leon and I are the definition of laying low for the next few days. We didn't want that, especially Leon who can't sit still for the life of him, but waking up to messages from the criminal you shot will really slow a guy down.

Another burner phone casualty. At this rate we should buy them in bulk.

On the plus side, laying low has given me some extra free time to keep an eye on Blake. She's been busy with her classes but I've been there, watching from the parking lot and making sure that piece of shit Ethan hasn't been hanging around. Leon's on my ass about my relationship with Blake, saying we can't involve anyone else in our lives. Classic step two behavior. He doesn't understand that she could never be a burden.

I'm pacing around, so sick of being limited to this apartment and my car, when Jasper hollers from his bedroom. I know he's hurt and all but he's really been milking it for all its worth.

"You called, Your Highness," I say, taking in his crumbled

bed strewn with wrappers and the anime playing at full volume from his laptop.

He pauses the show and holds up an empty pill bottle. "I just took my last pain pill. Can that girlfriend of yours get me some more?"

I don't bother to correct him. "Doubtful. Can't you just take some ibuprofen?" He narrows his eyes in his most menacing expression. "Fine, I'll see what I can do."

"Snacks too." He waves an empty chip bag. "Brand name, not that generic shit."

I grind my teeth but keep quiet. Leon's in the living room working on his computer, doing who knows what. There's code of some sort on the screen, but nothing I can read.

"The king is out of meds and snacks. Feel like getting out of the house?"

He leans back and scrubs his hand over his face. "I should. I'm going crazy in here with him. But one of us should stay in case he needs us."

Or a certain someone finds out where we live and comes to end us.

"Got any connections for painkillers?" I ask.

"Maybe... but I don't want to poke around too much right now. Is it the worst idea to take him to a hospital? He's stable now. We could go a few towns over. Say it was a hunting accident."

It's not a terrible idea. "Still risky," I say. "I'll see what I can do first."

He doesn't have to say anything, I already know what he's thinking. "Meaning, you're going to involve her?"

Ignoring him, I peek my head in Jasper's room. "I'll be back. If you need anything yell at the grumpy bastard in the living room."

I hop in my car as the last of the sun's light dissipates. Dusk always has a way of hiding things in plain sight, so I pay extra attention to my surroundings.

> Me: You up for a little breaking and entering again?

> Blake: I haven't heard from you in days and that's what you text me…

I grin and head toward her house.

> Me: Missed me, Angel?

I make it halfway there when she responds.

> Blake: What do you need now?

> Me: Be there in a minute, meet me outside.

As I reach her driveway, I pull my mask over my head. It would be nice to know that I can fully trust Blake. She hasn't called the cops yet, but I haven't shown her how unhinged I can be. She's seen a taste of my dark side but will she stay when I show her exactly who I am?

I go to the passenger side and open the door for her. When she sees me, she rolls her lip between her teeth, hesitating at the entrance. Can't blame her. Any sane person wouldn't willingly offer herself to a masked man who held her at gunpoint. I wait a moment, watching resignation bloom on her face, and smile beneath my mask. She's starting to trust me.

I drink her in as she walks to my car. The way her full hips sway in her tight high-waisted leggings. How her tits barely fit in her crop top, making it ride up as she walks. My palms itch to wrap around that sliver of exposed skin. To mark every inch of her as mine.

She slows her steps as if she can read my mind. That won't do. I meet her halfway and wrap my hands around her waist, drawing her closer, eliminating the space between us. She fits so perfectly against my chest, her head just reaching the bottom of my chin. The hitch in her breath makes me instantly hard. I know it's fucked up but I love that I make her nervous.

"Did you wear this tiny shirt just for me?" I slide my hand up her back until I reach the edge of her shirt and slip the tips of my fingers under the fabric. She's so soft against my calloused fingers.

"N-no," she stammers as my fingers glide higher, reaching the clips of her bra. I stop and relish the way her body responds.

I wrap my fist into her wild hair and tug, tilting her head until she's looking into my eyes. Her gasp is music to my ears. "Yes you did. Everything you wear, everything you do, is for me, Blake. Because you're mine. This body is mine. Every inch of your soft, perfect skin belongs to me."

Her tongue darts out to wet her lips and her eyes burn with smoky heat. She blinks and gives me a shove. "Get fucked, Freddy. I'm going back inside."

"The hell you are," I say, circling her wrist and tugging her back to me. "Get in the car."

She scoffs and shakes her head. "You know for someone as crazy and possessive as you seem to be, you're really giving me nothing in return. You want me? My body? But won't even tell me your name. Even Ethan—"

"Don't say it." I grind my teeth. I can't stand hearing that fucker's name from her lips. "Don't say his name."

She cocks her hip and smirks. "Ethan wouldn't be such a coward." I feel my blood boil.

"Oh yeah, Blake? You want me to be like Ethan?" I brace a

hand on either side of the car, caging her in until there's not an inch between us. "You like this? Should I pull on your clothes? Stick my tongue in your mouth? Fuck you when you're telling me no?"

Her chest heaves but she doesn't back down. "It wasn't like that."

"Wasn't it? Or how about I go fuck someone else then come crawling back to you?"

"Fuck off." A tear leaks from the corner of her eye and I back away a step. "Leave me alone."

I smooth my finger down her face, capturing her tear. "I'll never leave you alone, Blake. That's the difference. I'll never do what he did. When I say you're mine, that means you're the only one I see, the only one I want, the only one I need."

Without thinking it through, I pull off my mask. Blake's breath catches in her throat and she leans closer. "You. At the gala."

"That's right, sweetheart." Wrapping my hands around her waist I pull her in and ghost my lips over hers, capturing her breath. "I'm everywhere you are. Remember that."

Stepping to the side, I open the car door and usher her in. She's rendered speechless, a rare feat. I lean in and buckle her, before whispering against her ear. "Say his name again and I'll stuff your mouth so full of my cock that you'll be tasting me for weeks."

Grinning, I shut her door and walk around the car.

***

"WHEN YOU SAY BREAKING and entering, what exactly do you mean?" We're a few minutes from her house and she's finally speaking to me again. She's avoiding looking at me though. I'll have to change that later.

"My friend ran out of painkillers," I tell her. "He's miserable and we're trying to avoid taking him to a hospital."

"Because you're criminals," she states matter-of-factly.

I raise a brow and laugh. "No, we're not the criminals. But we need to avoid any complications, like the cops."

"Which is exactly what a criminal would say." She folds her hands over her chest, squeezing her tits together. Fucking hell, they're perfect.

"Criminal, vigilante, call me whatever you want. Just tell me where I can get meds." I pull up to a red light and glance over at her. She's biting that lip again, thinking.

"There might be some at Eth—" She stops, taking in the way my body instantly stiffens. Will she test me? I'd love to teach her that my threats are never empty. "You're ridiculous." She huffs but continues. "*His* parent's house. *He* always got his meds directly from their stash at home."

Sounds like a sure thing. "What's their address?"

It takes us about thirty minutes to get there. Darkness swallows the car as I turn off my headlights and park down the road from the address. While Blake unbuckles, I open my app and check to see where Ethan's car is, finding it still parked at his apartment near campus. Was he still in the hospital? Or nursing his wounded dick at mommy and daddy's house? I'd love to pop in on him and say hello.

"What should we do if they're home?" Blake says, pulling her hair up.

"I'll worry about that." She has no idea how well I keep to the shadows. We start our ten minute walk to their house, Blake carrying her black backpack purse.

There must be an acre or more of property between the giant new builds in this neighborhood. All perfectly manicured lawns and gleaming aluminum siding. I prefer older homes, built with character. Not these cookie cutter wastes of space.

The studio apartments I grew up in would fit inside these homes ten times over and still have enough room for a family of four.

"You want a house like this one day? A big mansion for Doctor Blake?"

She's thoughtful as we walk. I wait for her to answer, listening to the sound of a screech owl in the distance. "At one time I did. I guess I thought if I had a big house, a fancy car, enough money in the bank to blow cash on a whim, that I'd finally have made it. Been someone my family could be proud of."

"Makes sense," I say. "It's what most people want out of life."

She shrugs. "I guess. I just don't know if that's the life for me anymore. Living in that big house, alone most of the time, has been pretty eye opening. That and seeing how Eth—*he* lives. Money can change people, but I won't let it change me."

"So no mansion?" I ask, taking her hand. She glances down at it before pulling away.

"Nope, I'd much prefer a smaller house. Older too, something with character." I know my dimples are out as I grin.

"We'll need enough bedrooms for our kids though," I say. She slows her steps and glares at me, crossing her chest.

"Once again, you're insane. I don't even know your name."

I contemplate blurting it out right then and there but edging her is so much more fun. "I'll tell you my name when you're ready to scream it, Angel. Until then, you'll just have to use your imagination."

"I can't with you." She rolls her eyes and looks away. I still catch the way her cheeks darken for me.

We're close enough to the house that I can see light pouring through some of the windows. She points to smoke coming from the chimney. "Look."

"Looks like the good doctors are in." I pull a hand through my hair. So much for this being a straightforward in and out job. "Let me make a call."

"I guess I can tell them I stopped by to check on Eth—"

"No," I say, looking up from my phone. "You don't need to do that."

"Bossy, much?" she mumbles under her breath.

You have no idea.

CHAPTER THIRTEEN

BLAKE

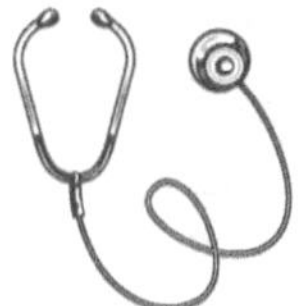

I stand to the side while he makes a phone call, breathing in the comforting smell of chimney smoke while listening to crickets chirp. Normally, I'd be creeped out being on such a dark street late at night, but for once I'm enjoying it. I guess being near Freddy is weirdly comforting. Man, I need therapy.

"Okay, the docs are about to get a call about an emergency break-in at their office. They'll have to go down to the station and fill out some paperwork." I shake my head. Not a bad idea, but I won't tell him that. The last thing this man needs is a bigger ego.

"What about Ethan?" I ask, realizing my mistake as his eyes darken. "What if—"

His large body looms over me as he holds my chin in his grip, tilting my face up so I have nowhere else to look but directly into his eyes. "This is your last warning, Blake. Say his name again and you know what happens. I don't care where we are, or what we're doing. I'll choke his name from your throat."

I'm panting from a mix of fear and arousal. It was one thing when he wore the mask, but now, hearing the dirty things he says... while looking like that... my body can't help but react.

Swallowing down the lump in my throat, I rephrase. "What if he's home?"

"Leave everything to me."

Like clockwork, five minutes later the Porter's luxury SUV pulls down their driveway and speeds away in the opposite direction. Freddy grins and wraps his hand in mine, something I don't totally hate, although I won't admit that to him. We stay in the shadows of the property, skirting around any traces of light.

"You're almost too good at this," I whisper. "It's creepy."

He lets a low chuckle permeate the air but doesn't respond. I have no choice but to be pulled along by him, watching him scout the home like a pro. Not a criminal, my butt. I'd bet he robs houses for a living.

Once we've done a few passes, he asks, "Do you know where they keep the meds?"

I nod. "Upstairs, but I don't know if they're locked up. Sometimes they'd do that to keep *him* from cleaning them out."

He tips his chin in approval, whether it's from not slipping and saying Ethan's name or from knowing where to find the pills, I have no idea.

"I found our best way in through the back door. Once we're in, you lead the way." A thrill runs through my veins. I've never done anything even remotely bad, never even thought about it. "You're grinning."

I force my face into a neutral expression. "Am not."

"Okay, Blake." He uses his sarcastic tone. The same one he used when he called me a liar.

We get inside exactly as planned. It took him no more than thirty seconds to pop the lock. If criminal acts impressed me—

which they don't, but if they *did*—I'd be impressed. Maybe even a little turned on.

He motions for me to go first, so I move ahead and guide us through the house I've visited often, yet always felt like an outsider in.

We cross their family room and go through the open plan kitchen. I listen for any noises but the house is completely silent apart from the click of the heat here and there. Where they had the fire going earlier was now just a pile of ash around a half burned artificial log. Two wine glasses sit on their coffee table, half full, with the bottle beside it. Looks like we interrupted a romantic evening. Oh well.

Freddy's close enough that I can feel the heat of his body radiating onto my exposed waist. It's helping my pulse slow to a normal rate as we slowly step up the stairs. We pass an empty guest bedroom and bathroom but I slow as we get to Ethan's bedroom. There's bouncing light coming from the crack at the bottom of the door. His TV's on, I'd guess. I gesture with my finger and mouth, "*His room.*" Freddy pulls me along.

He's right, of course. What if Ethan decides at that moment to go get a snack? It's weird that he's here to begin with. Whatever happened at the gala must have been serious enough to warrant him sleeping back at home.

We head into the Porter's dark bedroom and I shut the door behind us. "Okay, let's check their bathroom."

I've only ever been in here once or twice, for the same reason that we're here now. I remember the first time Ethan came in here searching for pills. He got so excited from finding a mother lode that he tried to fuck me on his parent's bed. I wouldn't let him get too far, instead distracting him and pulling him into his bedroom.

"Nice furniture," Freddy says. "You ever fuck on that bed?"

Was he a mind reader? "No. Why the hell would you ask that?" Heat spreads from my neck up.

"If you were in my house, I'd fuck you on every surface I could." He shrugs like he's casually discussing the weather and heads into the bathroom while I ignore the growing ache between my legs.

We open every cabinet and pull out every drawer but the most interesting meds we find are a bottle of Xanax and a stash of THC gummies. Oh, and can't forget about the year-long supply of Viagra.

"Shit," he says, pocketing the pills. "Anywhere else they could be?"

"I don't know. Like I said, they've recently kept things locked up because of Ethan's problems." I bite my tongue as soon as I let his name slip, waiting for him to scold me or worse, but his eyes light up instead.

"Ethan," he says. "Come on."

Confused, I follow him from the bedroom and down the hall. He stops in front of Ethan's door. I whisper, "What are you doing?"

"Getting our meds." He slowly turns the door handle and peeks inside while I stand there in shock. He's not seriously going in there with Ethan? He's not that crazy? I step away from the door, wrapping my arms around my chest while I wait for a fight to break out. A few seconds go by and it's quiet. He pokes his head out. "Come on, he's asleep."

"This is too risky," I whisper-shout. "Let's go, we can try the office."

He grabs my hand and pulls me inside. Ethan's in bed, flat on his back and snoring lightly. The light we saw creeping through the door is from *The Office* playing across his mounted flat screen. Ethan looks like he's lost weight in the short time since I've seen him. Even in sleep his face looks scrunched in pain. On his bedside table, I spot a few prescription bottles. Freddy seems to eye them too and heads right for them.

"Bingo," he whispers. "Here, put these in your bag."

I feel guilty stealing meds from someone who obviously needs them. If he didn't have the means to get them replaced right away, I'd be fighting Freddy on this.

Ethan startles in his sleep and I jump. My nerve endings are shot. This is so wrong. "Let's get out of here," I say as quietly as I can, and pull Freddy toward the door. He stays put, even when I pull again. I look at him and raise a brow in question. "What are you doing?"

"On your knees, Blake." My thoughts freeze as I take in the serious expression on his face. God, he's devastatingly hot... Looking at him like this, in the dim light, makes my knees weak.

"Let's go," I whisper again.

"What did I say would happen if you said his name again?" His jaw tenses as he drops my hand.

"I didn't," I argue, fighting the dizziness that overcomes me.

He unbuckles his belt, making no effort to stay quiet. Ethan stirs again, murmuring in his sleep. He can't be serious. There's no way.

When he unzips his jeans, my stomach clenches. "One thing you need to know about me is I always keep my word."

Did a part of me want this? Every time I said Ethan's name, a little voice in the back of my head wondered if he was serious. I test him again, anticipating his reaction. "But what if Ethan wakes up?"

"I hope he does," he growls, pushing me to sit on the edge of the bed. Anxiety courses through me and I hold my breath, waiting for Ethan to jump up and freak out. A second goes by, then two, and Ethan still sleeps soundly. He must be doped up on a buttload of meds for him to not hear us or feel the weight of another body.

I'm flushed and panting as he pulls his cock out of his jeans and brings himself to my eye level. He's rock hard and so thick I don't think I can wrap my whole hand around him. "Are you ready for your punishment, Blake?" I whimper, unable to form words. "Swallow my cock. I want you to choke on it, so you never say another man's name again."

"Oh, God." He fists my hair and brings my face to his dripping tip. I grip his thighs and pull back, but he's got me in a tight hold. This is wrong on so many levels, but I'm soaked and aching, mouth watering for him. I'm not going to give in easily, though. I clench my mouth shut, gnashing my teeth together.

"Open up or I'll make you." He grips his cock in his fist and slaps my cheek with it. I gasp, stunned. He does it again and a small whimper escapes my lips, the perfect opportunity for him to thrust into me. With one hand tangled in my hair, he moves the other to my jaw, pulling down to open me wider as he shoves himself into the back of my throat. "That's my good little slut. You're nice and wet for me."

Holy shit.

He draws himself out and pumps back in, hissing a breath that sounds so erotic I clench my thighs together. Every ounce of restraint I have snaps and I close my eyes, hollow my cheeks, and suck hard. "Fuck, Blake," he groans, loud enough that any sober person would wake.

His groans drive me to open wider, take him deeper. He pulls out and I swirl my tongue over his tip, swallowing his salty pre-cum. I open my eyes and look up at him from under my tear-stained lashes. He's looking at me like I'm the best thing he's ever seen. Like I'm perfect in his eyes.

I stroke as much of his base as I can without yanking his pants down while licking and sucking his tip. His thighs flex. "Fuuuck... so good."

His hold on my hair tightens as he fucks into me, pumping

deep into the back of my throat before pulling out and slamming back in again until I gag. Saliva drips down my chin as his thrusts become jerkier. I'm rocking the bed, right up against Ethan's leg, but my focus is on him and only him. He's close to coming so I suck harder, matching his pace.

He groans and holds my head still as his cock jerks inside me. "Fuck, baby. Drink up."

His cum drips out over my open lips. While he's still hard against my tongue, I swallow him down along with every drop that he gives me.

Finally, he releases his hold on my hair and my shoulders sag. My body's trembling so much I don't know if I can walk. Before I can wipe my face with the back of my hand, he grabs a pillow from Ethan's bed, pulls the case off of it, and uses it to clean me up. I don't expect the nice gesture. Something about it has me feeling warm and fuzzy. Maybe it's the fact that Ethan's never once cared for me after any kind of fooling around. He's never even offered me a washcloth after sex.

The more I think about it the angrier I get, until I'm stopping Freddy from putting his cock away. "Wait, let's clean you up." He tilts his head, watching as I go to Ethan's dresser and grab his favorite T-shirt. He bought it on his first day of freshman year at the college store. I spread it out and use it to clean every last drop of cum and spit from his cock. Then, with a smile, I fold it and put it back where it was. "Now you can put it away."

"I don't know, I think I'm ready for round two," he says with a smirk. "Watching you use his shirt like that... fucking hot."

Licking my lips, I contemplate all the things I'd like to do with this man but quickly come back to my senses. "Let's get out of here."

He runs his palm over my hair, fixing the wild strands.

"Damon," he says. I look at him with wide, questioning eyes. "My name is Damon."

"Hmm, I think I like Freddy more. It's grown on me." He scowls as I tease him. "Oh Freddy, right there," I moan in a fake sexual tone and then laugh.

He picks me up and throws me over his shoulder, spanking my ass with his large palm. "I think you need to be punished again. You liked that last punishment too much."

He carries me that way down the stairs and through the house. Once we're outside and my feet are back on the earth, I look up at him. His deep brown hair is tousled from running his hands through it. The spider and webbing tattoo on his neck stands out against his fair skin. All of his facial features look shadowed out here with the only light coming from Ethan's house. More menacing. But I realize I'm not afraid of him, not anymore. I can't tell if I'm disappointed or relieved.

"Race you to the car," I say, sprinting ahead of him. I know how much he loves to chase but I'm just now learning how much I love to *be* chased.

CHAPTER FOURTEEN

BLAKE

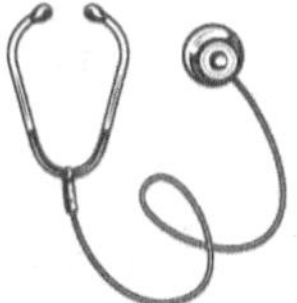

I'VE WOKEN UP EACH MORNING TO A LITTLE GIFT FROM Damon on my bedside table and today is no different. He's left an iced latte—my favorite—and a single white rose. It's unnerving how he's able to get in and out while I'm asleep, but I haven't questioned it. If I'm being honest, his creepiness makes me feel special and cared for, in my own weird way.

Since we broke into Ethan's parent's house a few weeks ago, I haven't seen Damon in person. He's seen me, apparently. I've been trying not to read into it too much. We're both busy. School and studying for me and whatever criminal shit him and the guys do. I refuse to be desperate and chase after him. He knows where I am, obviously. And he has my number... He can learn how to use it more. It's just funny how he was all, *you're mine, Blake... growly possessive crap.* Well, where's the follow through, huh? He can show up when I'm asleep but then ghosts me all day. Not cool.

I scoot up in bed and take a sip of my latte. Perfectly made, damn him. Since I'm feeling kinda feisty this morning, I grab my phone and send him a text.

> Me: At least you're a creeper who brings gifts... thank you.

While I wait for a reply, I scroll up to our last few messages. Not that I know him well, but I've gotten a feel of how he texts, and something was different. I know he's safe or there'd be no bedside table gifts, but something has to be going on.

> Me: I hope everything's ok...

He's fine, I'm sure of it. I just wish I didn't care so much. Pushing him out of my mind, I scramble around to get ready for another long day of classes. Microbiology and pharmacology will be the death of me.

THREE HOURS and one massive headache later, I'm finally free. My stomach growls from skipping breakfast and I've had to avoid Julie and her questions about Ethan for the last hour. If I knew what happened to him, I'd tell her, but I'm in the dark as much as she is. Thinking of Ethan had me thinking of Damon and what we did on Ethan's bed. My cheeks reddened while we chatted, so much so that I cut the conversation short.

Walking through campus, I take in the gorgeous reds and golds of autumn and breathe in the faint scent of wood smoke in the air. They've decorated the outside of the old buildings with potted mums and pumpkins. I love everything about this time of year.

Opting for the cafe on campus instead of going into town, I order another iced latte and one of their chicken quinoa bowls. All the bread and baked goods smell incredible, but because of my allergies, unfortunately, I can only smell them. There's a free table by the window so I snag it and check my phone while I wait. My stomach flutters when I see a reply from Damon, still listed as Freddy. At this point I don't know if I'll ever change that.

> Freddy: You're welcome, Angel. Don't worry about me, make sure you take care of yourself today… drink water, eat lunch, don't work too hard.

There's the overbearing guy I know.

I bite my lip and think of a reply. Something that says, I want to see you again but doesn't sound too clingy. Oh God, it's been way too long since I've done this awkward "getting to know a new guy" thing. I hate how unsure I feel.

> Me: Sitting at the cafe right now.

I glance over at the few full tables where couples are chatting, or friends are meeting up between classes. If I don't want to be alone all the time I guess I should put myself out there. I know just how to get to him.

> Me: I'll talk to you later, this guy from class just sat down with me.

I click my phone off and grin. I know I'm being a brat and playing right into his possessive, jealous nature when instead, I could easily admit that I miss him and want to see him. It's immature and irresponsible, yet I can't help but picture his face when he reads the message. Maybe that makes me just as nuts as he is.

The server brings my lunch and I scarf it down, feeling my headache subside with each bite. In the spare half hour I have left, I grab my laptop and work on some of my ethics assignments. They're pretty straightforward but I try to write well thought out responses. I had the same professor last year and he loved to have us do impromptu presentations, so this year I'll be padding my answers just in case.

Clouds roll in, blocking the gorgeous fall sunshine by the time I pack up and leave the cafe for my last class of the day. In case I get lucky enough to get rained on, I zip my computer into my bag and shrug on the sweater I brought with me.

It's a ten minute walk to the building and I'm speed walking. My phone beeps from my bag but I ignore it as the wind picks up. The building is within my line of sight when the first few drops of rain sprinkle on me.

"Shoot," I say, picking up my pace. "Come on, I'm almost there." No amount of pleading with the elements helps. The sky opens up and the soft sprinkles become a steady downpour. The few students around me race to get indoors, stomping through quick forming puddles in their pursuit.

I tug my bag higher on my shoulder and start to jog, when someone grabs me from behind. Disoriented, I swing my bag and struggle to break free until I hear his voice. "Where's your lunch date? Not very chivalrous of him to let you walk to class alone in the rain."

His smooth voice sends a tingle along my skin. "He had to go," I lie. Damon chuckles, his warm breath skating along the curve of my neck. He spins me around and I'm struck silent by the heat in his amber eyes.

Rain is coming down in sideways sheets, muffling our voices and the sounds around us, but I hear him clear as day as he says, "If you think I'd let another man enjoy your company, you're mistaken. There was no lunch date... if there were, he'd be dead."

"How would you know? You haven't been around," I yell as rain pelts my face.

He swipes his hand through his hair and pins me with his gaze. "I know. Trust me on that." This man is the most frustrating, egotistical, annoying... I stew over a response but I'm cut off by him leaning in. "If you were trying to make me jealous, it worked. That was a very bad thing to do, Blake."

I scoff and turn my face away but he grabs my chin like he always does and draws me back to him. My skin is electric where he touches me. "What are you going to do about it?" I challenge him.

He claims my lips, rough and punishing. My heart pounds against my chest as he fists my hair and pulls me closer. Everything disappears. The rain. The students dashing to class. The entire world around us. There's only him and his demanding kiss. My nipples harden to sensitive peaks against my soaked shirt and I moan into his mouth.

He pulls back, leaving a fire in his wake. Our breaths come in uneven pants and I'm reluctant to let him go. I've never been kissed like that. Not once in my twenty-four years.

He swipes his thumb across my bottom lip. "Smeared your lipstick."

"Oh," I say dreamily. I blink and come back to reality. "Shoot, I need to get to class."

That dark laugh escapes his lips again. I hate how much it affects me. "I should drag you to my car and spank that sweet ass for being bad, but I won't. Not yet, at least. I'll think of something much better."

He'd spank me? The thought doesn't totally freak me out. If anything, I feel an ache growing in my core. "I'm not a child. You can't punish me."

"Get to class, Blake." He responds with a grin and walks leisurely back to his car, not caring that he's completely drenched too. Huffing, I turn and book it to class. I only look over my shoulder once, but when I do he's still there, standing outside his car, watching me.

A shiver runs down my spine imagining what he has in store for me.

I DECIDE to take advantage of the empty house and sit cozy by the fireplace. Normally when it's just Mischa and me here, I keep to my bedroom. I should ask Brennan if he knows where she's been lately. She hasn't been home all week.

After sitting through ethics class in drenched clothes, even the sparse fire I managed to get going and my warmest pajamas aren't cutting it. My body is chilled down to my bones.

I add another log from the stack I found in the garage and go put some water on for tea. While I'm in the kitchen, I imagine all the changes I'd make to this house if it were mine. It's too big, but at least it has some of the home's original features. Intricate crown molding, heavy wooden doors, and I'm pretty sure the windows are original too. I grab a mug and a peppermint tea bag and imagine how the space would look with black cabinets and white marble countertops.

I grab my phone to look up ideas when I notice a text from Falin.

Falin: Hey, call me when you get this!

I hit call right away and she answers on the first ring. "Tell me you love me," she says instead of a greeting.

"Um, hi. I love you?" I say. I'm only mildly confused; this is Falin I'm talking to after all.

"That sounded more like a question, but I'll take it. Guess what?" She sounds frenzied compared to my relaxed, quiet tone. The tea kettle whistles so I busy myself pouring the hot water into my mug.

"A spot finally opened up for you in the country's best grippy sock jail?" I tease, stirring some honey into the mug.

"I wish," she says. "This is even better. I just booked a flight to visit for your birthday!"

I grin ear to ear. My birthday is in a week and with Brennan still overseas, I had a feeling I'd be spending it alone. "Oh my God, I'm gonna cry."

"Not allowed because wait until you hear what else I did." I make my way back into the living room, clutching my steaming mug. My insides twist with anxiety.

I love Falin like a sister but usually our ideas of fun are wildly different. There was the trip we took to Vegas in college when I lost her for two days. Turns out she was having the time of her life with this couple she met at the casino. Or the time she booked us a dinner reservation and it ended up being at a "clothing optional" restaurant. I had no idea those existed but apparently they do. I'm all about a natural dining experience but something about knowing another person's wrinkly balls or sweaty butt shared the same chair as me really killed my appetite.

"I'm afraid to ask," I say, then correct myself so I don't hurt her feelings. "Because I know how hard it will be to top my twenty-second birthday."

She's quiet for a moment before laughing. "Shit, I totally forgot about the clowns."

"Lucky you," I say. "Anyway, spill. What did you plan?"

"I got us tickets to this spooky burlesque show! I've heard amazing things about it so when I saw them coming to your area I knew we had to go. It's on your birthday too. I may have DM'ed them and let that info slip."

I release a breath. A show doesn't sound too bad. If I can

fake a phone call and go blend into the back of the crowd, I may be able to get through it relatively unscathed.

"That sounds so fun. I'm just happy to see you, I can't wait to squeeze you!"

"Me too," she says. "I miss you too much, babe. It gets lonely traveling all the time, new cities every month. We need to have a cozy day too. Horror movies, tons of junk food, all the gossip. I miss that the most. But for your big day, we're going all out."

"All out?" I ask. "The show is perfect. That's all I need. And a cozy day sounds amazing, I can't wait."

"Well, prepare for some shopping too. There's a dress code for the venue. I'm thinking slutty vampire brides." I laugh as she rambles different costume choices. "Fake blood but tastefully applied. Oh, and fangs... Fangs are so hot."

"What am I going to do with you?" I say as I shake my head.

"Love me forever, of course."

"You know it." We chat for a few more minutes about her itinerary and by the time we end the call I'm more joyful than I've been in a long time. Falin has a way of blowing into my life like a storm, right when I need her most.

CHAPTER FIFTEEN

DAMON

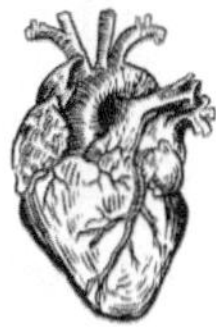

LEON'S ON THE PHONE ASKING FOR AN UPDATE. "I JUST left and the place is still vacant," I tell him.

We got tired of laying low recently so we have adjusted our efforts. Now instead of being trapped in the apartment, he has me watching that club night and day. Whoever that King guy is, he's not dumb. By the time we decided to venture out to get more intel, they'd completely vacated the space. It's like every lead we had vanished into thin air.

"Fuck, I almost wish they'd make a move." I could tell that Leon's pacing from the other side of the phone. "I hate to say it, but maybe we should get out of here. Florida's a bust but I might have someone in DC worth looking into."

My stomach plummets five stories. "Calm down, you're reading too much into this. I'll keep an eye on everything as much as I can and maybe we call in some help until Jasper's healed up. I think Jas still has the number for that investigator his parents hired. Maybe he's available."

There's no way I'm leaving. Not unless Blake's coming with me.

"That bloke? He was a waste of space, mate. Plus he's proper by the book from what I remember, completely opposite from how we operate."

"But anything helps, right? I'm not saying we gotta move him into the apartment and become best friends." Christ, Leon was going to lose his hair from stress if he didn't calm the hell down.

"I suppose." He sighs and I hear the slight change in his tone. "I have to track down his details."

"Don't worry about it, I'll take care of it. You just keep doing your thing." I pull onto Blake's street and park around the corner. "I'll be home late, don't wait up."

"Where are you?" I'm about to answer but he sighs. "Nevermind, I already know." He ends the call without saying goodbye.

"I'm genuinely hurt," I say into the phone before swiping out of the screen. That guy needs a hobby or a girlfriend... or both. He's become a massive asshole. I click my app that leads to the camera feed I have of Blake's bedroom. It's dark and empty. Tilting my head, I double check her location from the GPS tag I put on her old Honda and the other one I slipped into her backpack. Both have her pinned at home. She must be somewhere else in the house. I'm happy to see my efforts while she's been busy with classes have become useful.

I zip my black sweatshirt and pull the hood up. It's not raining as hard as it was earlier, but it's coming down enough that I'm not thrilled to have to walk in it.

Making my way down the dark street, I imagine what Blake's doing inside. What she's wearing. For a second, I almost text her and tell her to strip bare and get on her bed, but that would ruin my plan. Instead, I spend the walk imagining her bent over for me. Slapping her round ass until she has a permanent handprint. Until she's soaking wet, begging to be fucked. I'm so hard that I need to adjust myself.

Her car is in the driveway and the house is dark. It won't be difficult to find her, though. I start by doing my normal rounds around the property, checking that she's safe. When I'm satisfied that no one has tried to harm her, I peek into each window, one by one. The thing I love most about these old houses... the ease of opening windows.

Blake's in the living room, curled on the couch with her feet under her while a fire burns in the fireplace. She's on the phone, laughing. I curl my fists, wondering who she's talking to. It's nice to see her smile though. She's been down lately, too much work and too little play.

Once I hire that PI, it's me and you all the time, baby. You won't remember what it's like to be alone.

She finishes her conversation and spends a few minutes sipping from a mug and scrolling on her phone. I wonder if she's reading our messages? My curiosity gets the best of me so I pull out my phone and text her.

> Me: It's the perfect night for a fire.

She adjusts her feet and sits up, looking around the room. Her expression isn't one of fear, it's more anticipation.

> Blake: Where are you, stalker?

Her and her nicknames. The list keeps growing.

> Me: I'm working. Just wanted to check in and see if you're still wet from earlier.

I watch her shake her head and pull her hair into a messy bun. I hope she keeps it like that, I'd love to give it a hard tug.

Not for long.

I can't wait to hear her gasp my name. My real name this time.

She lets the fire burn down to a few embers then heads toward her room. Once I'm certain she's not coming back, I pull the window open and climb inside. Warmth surrounds me and fuck, it feels good. I've been soaked for the better half of the day and the cool air didn't make it any better.

Shrugging out of my hoodie, I lay it beside the fire to dry, then do my nightly ritual of checking the house. Leon may be focused on the empty club but my focus is right here. If there's people after us, it's only a matter of time before they find Blake. I won't let that happen.

Satisfied that all is well, I linger outside Blake's door and listen. The only sounds I hear are the occasional ticks of the heating system and steady barrage of rain against the roof. The long day of classes and being stuck in the rain wore my angel out. I almost feel bad disturbing her. But she wanted this when she provoked my jealous nature. She'll learn that I mean every word that I say. Without making a sound, I sneak into her bedroom.

I'll never get over how perfect Blake looks asleep. She's on her back, clutching a pillow to her chest, her hair above her head like a halo. Her face is serene, those pert lips slightly parted and releasing slow, steady breaths. One leg is stretched out on top of the blanket and her oversized T-shirt rides up her thighs.

She's in the perfect position.

CHAPTER SIXTEEN

BLAKE

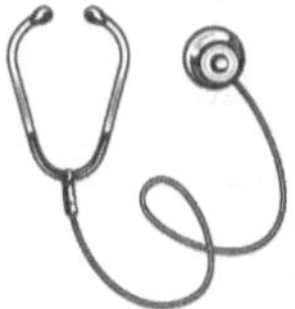

Gasping, my eyes dart open but all I see is inky blackness. I take stock of my limbs, attempting to move them, but I'm restrained.

"What the hell?" I yell. "Damon? Are you in here?"

My arms are tied above my head, I assume attached to the headboard or some other anchor, and my legs... They're spread wide enough that my muscles are pulled taut. I thrash from side to side, whimpering. This is not my idea of fun sexy time, not at all.

I feel movement from the end of the bed and my heart pounds frantically. "Damon? Answer me." Cool air reaches my exposed flesh causing me to shiver. I'm overcome with emotion. Fear, anger, lust. So much that tears leak onto whatever blindfold covers my eyes.

"Shh," he finally says. He drags a finger along my inner thigh and I shudder. "Don't cry, Angel."

"Damon, what the hell? Take this shit off me." I sniff and try to gain control of myself. This isn't the first time I've been in a situation like this. I was in high school. He was older, he didn't like that I fought back, so he made it impossible for me to move. By the time he was done with me, I didn't care to move anyway... I stayed curled in a ball for hours. "Please," I cry.

He's silent but I feel his solid weight as he positions himself over me. I breathe in and bring my mind to a different place. A happy place where Damon is just a normal boyfriend. I'm not fourteen anymore, and this is different. Damon is different. My body relaxes slightly, but I'm still on edge.

"I wish you could see how perfect you look spread for me like this. This cunt is all mine, Blake. You're going to learn that when you're good, you get rewarded." He drags his finger up my thigh and between my legs. The rush of fear I felt minutes ago turns into something else entirely. A throbbing ache that grows with each filthy word from his lips. I try to arch toward him, though the smart part of my brain tells me to do the opposite, but the restraints are too tight.

"Please," I beg. This time for an entirely different reason. The heat of his hand hovers over my sex, so close to where I want him.

"You want me to rub your clit? Make you come?" His voice is as strained as my body.

"Yes, please." It's been so long since I've been touched like this. With Ethan it was always about his pleasure. Maybe I'd get off every so often, but mostly because I did the work.

His warm breath tickles my skin as he shifts his weight. "Or how about I feast on this delicious pussy? Do you want that, Blake?"

My entire body is on fire. I need something. Anything.

Just touch me.

I nod, and whimper as his finger slides up my slit. It takes me by surprise how quickly I shift from anxiety to desire.

He brings his finger to my lips and shoves it in my mouth. "You're so wet, baby. So desperate to come."

I'm literally panting with need but the bastard doesn't care. He's slow and methodical as he hovers right over where I want him. I manage to buck against him, and moan from the quick second of pressure on my aching clit. I try again, but he holds my stomach down.

"Uh, uh. I'm in control." He ghosts his lips over my pussy again and again, each time just barely touching me. I let out a frustrated groan as he licks so delicately along my lips.

"Please, Damon. I can't..." I'm two seconds away from crying. He scrapes his teeth over my clit and I hiss. "God, yes."

He does it again, this time clamping down and sucking hard enough that I thrash. I'm climbing higher and higher, as long as he keeps going... just like that. With the perfect amount of pressure, he buries his face and devours my pussy. I wish I could watch the way he's moving against me but being deprived of sight adds to my pleasure somehow. Helps turn my brain off.

"I'm so close. Please," I murmur, along with a string of other incoherent words. His teeth scrape again and my pussy starts to spasm. "Oh, my God."

As I'm about to fall over the edge into bliss he pushes off me and I'm left with nothing but cool air against my hot flesh.

"Damon? Why'd you stop? I was right there!" I'm nearly sobbing. I wish I could see his face, reach out to touch him. Anything but his silence. "Freddy?"

"Do you think you deserve to come?" he finally whispers. Realization blooms across my covered face. This is about the lunch date comment. His *punishment.*

"I-I'm sorry. I know I was bad to egg you on. Take off my blindfold. I want to see you." Tears prickle my eyes again, seconds away from a full on outburst. He moves, and finally I'm able to see his outline in the darkened room. He climbs off my bed and stands at the edge, like he didn't just have a face full of my pussy. "You can come sit with me, you know. I won't bite."

It's hard to see his expression but I imagine his smirk. "What if I want you to?"

"Well, that's a different story. Come sit, I promise I'll bite." I make a show of struggling against my restraints in hopes that I won't have to beg him to untie them.

He pins me with his intense gaze and swipes his hand over his wet lips. "I was promised a bite."

Playfully, I lean as close to him as my ties allow and nibble his arm. "Hmm, needs a little salt and pepper, but not half bad."

"You know I'm planning on making you stay like that all night," he says, tilting his chin toward my hands.

"Can I ask you a question?"

He sighs, and relaxes against the headboard beside me. "Anything."

"Do you get off on this kind of thing? Punishment and all that?" I'm genuinely curious. I've only ever seen bad men say and do stuff like he does, but I know deep down he's not that way. At least not fundamentally.

"Yes," he answers candidly. "I was hard as a rock the whole time I tied you up. Couldn't wait to see you wake up afraid. To hear you whimper and gasp."

I roll my lip between my teeth. "You know, I think I kinda like to be afraid. That burst of adrenaline when something scares me. But..." I hesitate, thinking over my words. "Only with you. Only because I know you won't actually hurt me like I've been hurt before."

I've let too much slip. Damon's not one of those emotional, lovey dovey guys and here I am telling him exactly how I feel, like a complete idiot. He's going to ghost me for sure.

"Who hurt you? Was it Ethan?" His body goes rigid beside me. "Tell me, Blake."

That's the part of my admission he's focusing on. Wow.

"Untie me and I'll tell you," I say, flashing him the biggest grin I can muster for a woman who's just been woken up and denied an orgasm. He shakes his head and heaves a breath.

"I can't deny you anything when you smile." I'm glowing a little inside knowing that I hold sway over him, until he leans over and says, "But know this: you try any of that date shit again, and tonight will be nothing compared to what I'll do."

My lips turn down and eyes widen. I don't want to know.

He takes his time with the restraints, gliding his palms over my skin until I'm aching all over again. Particularly when he traces the path to my ankles with his tongue.

Breathe, Blake. Do not jump this man.

Stretching out until my muscles pull in painful pleasure, I turn to him and say, "Thank you."

"You're really playing it up for me," he says.

"What do you mean?"

"The whole sweet angel bit. Thank you, the cheese grin, the *only with you.*" He chuckles dark and low. "I know there's a devil lying in wait. So go ahead sweetheart, make me fall even harder for you."

I can tell I'm blushing. I only hope he can't see. "I don't know what you're talking about."

"Back to what you said before. Who do I have to kill?" The way he can go from flirty to lethal in the span of seconds is all sorts of terrifying.

I sigh, not wanting to get into the story. What will it accomplish to dredge up shit that happened ten years ago? Damon's clenching his jaw so hard it could crack steel, so I know I need to give him something. "It was a long time ago."

"And? I don't care if it was twenty years ago. Tell me. Was it Ethan?"

I clutch my pillow to my chest and flip to my side. "No, Ethan's an ass but he's never actually hurt me."

"Then who?"

I close my eyes and imagine the last time I saw him. The long strands of black hair that hung over his narrow face, gaunt from drugs. His stupid chest tattoo—a heart with barbed wire. Bryan and him got their first ones together and thought they were so cool.

He always smelled like a Spencer's store mixed with menthol cigarettes. I stopped shopping there after everything happened. If I focus hard enough, I can feel the pain of him sinking into me... The bite of his fingernails against my flesh. The way the restraints clinked against my old metal bed frame, like warning bells.

"He was my brother's friend, five years older than me. They were in a band together and I looked at him like he was a god. He had this laugh that you could recognize across a crowded room. Everyone loved him. I thought I did too."

Damon pulls my head into his lap and I shiver when I feel how damp his jeans are. It doesn't matter. I'll take the comfort, wet pants or not. He pulls my hair tie out and strokes the loose strands. His fingers are magic.

"What's his name?" he asks.

I'm hesitant to utter it. It wouldn't be that difficult to find him. Falin and I did a few years ago, one drunken night in college when I told her everything. I know Damon won't relent though, so I take a breath and release it. "Trevor."

"Trevor, what? I need a last name, baby."

I shake my head. If I give that out, I know he'll find him. As much as I hate Trevor for what he did and how he ruined me, he was Bryan's best friend. Bryan wouldn't want anything to happen to him.

"I can't," I say. "You don't understand." He quietly strokes my hair; the only sound is the rain against the window. If this is a tactic to get me to talk, it won't work. He doesn't ask anymore questions but scoots lower against the bed. "You're not going to ask what happened?"

"No, I don't need the details unless you want to tell me. I know enough to assume."

I think about his words and appreciate him more and more. Most people want every detail, relish in any drama they can get their hands on. "What if I say he stole my box of crayons in school? Or took my lunch money?"

Damon chuckles. "I'd still kill him."

"You're unhinged, Freddy."

His body sags as his breathing slows. "Still Freddy, huh? I guess I should stop by the Halloween store and grab a glove and a striped sweater."

"Yup. With you in my life, I'll never sleep again."

"For all the best reasons... I can promise that. Not tonight though, you're still in trouble. No getting yourself off either. I'll know."

I can't see how he'd know if I masturbate in the privacy of my room, but somehow I believe him. "Power trip," I say under my breath. My heavy eyelids fall and the last thing I remember is his breathy chuckle before I pass out.

CHAPTER SEVENTEEN

DAMON

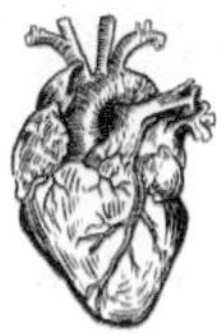

I watch Blake sleep peacefully for about an hour before I tuck her in and leave. It's not that I don't want to curl up with her and get some shut eye. I do, so fucking badly, but I can't stop the racing thoughts.

Blake didn't have to spell out what happened to her. What she told me was more than enough. I laid there, seeing Blake's tear-streaked face behind my closed lids, and knew I wouldn't rest until I made it right.

My headlights reflect on the rain-soaked street when I pull up to the apartment. The rain's lightened up, thankfully. Leaving Blake's warmth was tough enough, but going out into the rain again made it that much harder. I inhale the comforting smell of wet leaves and damp earth. It takes me back to playing in the woods as a kid. My mom would hand me a cup of Kool-Aid and lock the door behind me, telling me not to come back until the sun went down.

I never had many friends back then; we moved around too much. Different towns and different junkie boyfriends. They'd doctor hop, using a bullshit injury to get their fix of oxys, until those sources ran dry. My friends became the salamanders I'd catch underneath soggy logs or the stray cats I'd steal cans of tuna to feed.

Most kids would hate getting locked out of the house the way I did. But not me. I preferred to be out there instead of trapped inside while they were high. I still prefer the outdoors to any four walls.

My life changed the moment I met Jasper, one hot summer day catching crawdads in a murky stream. We were fourteen, both awkward ass kids. Jasper hadn't gotten contacts yet, or discovered the power of weightlifting. I was even scrawnier than him, but I'd gone through a growth spurt that year and none of my clothes fit. The first thing he said to me was, "Hey, did you raid my sister's closet for those shorts?"

After that, we spent the whole summer together. I ate meals at his house. Slept over most nights too. The Shea's took me in, and by the time my mom was ready to leave town, I begged her to let me stay. I couldn't move again, not after I finally had somewhere to belong.

I'd put up too much of a fight while she was coming down from a week-long bender. With shaking hands, she patted me on the shoulder, got into her waiting cab, and left me. I only found out that she died a few years later, from the cops going through her stuff and finding an old report card. I'd gotten straight A's. They tracked me down and left the information with my high school guidance counselor.

None of that matters now. I didn't need to go inside all fucking sad and nostalgic while Leon was keeping a keen eye on me. Pulling myself together, I peek into Dolores's window and see her TV on—some soap opera looking show. Smiling to myself, I get ready to deal with the guys.

I have accomplishments to focus on.

Getting Leon to help me find this Trevor guy.

Hiring the private investigator to take over some of my responsibilities.

And sneaking off to make Trevor pay.

Nothing to it.

I REALIZE it's long after midnight when I walk inside and find Leon asleep on the couch, laptop open on the coffee table. Jasper's in a similar state, except his computer is showing the "Are you still watching this?" screen and his hand is in a bag of chips.

Quietly, I shut his screen and pull the open chip bag away from his bed. I guess I'm a mama bear tonight, tucking everyone in nice and cozy. I hope Blake's still sound asleep.

There's slim pickings in the fridge, but I luck out in the freezer and find a microwavable burrito. It'll have to do. Once it's ready, I take it into my room along with Leon's laptop and settle in on my bed.

"Alright, motherfucker. Let's see if I can find you." Between bites of burrito, I scroll different social media profiles and Google listings. Using the information I know about Blake's past, I'm able to somewhat narrow it down, but I'll admit that I'm kind of shit at this sort of thing.

I try different combinations on the search bar. *Trevor, band, Oak Falls, NY.* That brings up a bunch of useless shit. Next, I try the name of her high school and the year I assume he graduated, according to the age difference Blake mentioned. *Trevor, Oak Falls High School, Class of 2013.* A few different articles about the school pop up but nothing that mentions a Trevor, unless she was talking about a janitor named Trevor who won employee of the year for the district. He's not a complete rule-out, but he wouldn't be my first suspect.

Fuck, I feel like damn Sherlock Holmes. How the hell does Leon do this all day? About to give up, I hop on Facebook and search for anyone who graduated that year from Blake's school. Thoughts of her face keep popping in my head, how broken she must have felt. I want to throw the computer against a wall.

Time for a smoke break.

Leaning against the front steps, I take a drag and blow the smoke out slowly. It does little to calm me. At this point I know there's only one thing that will.

A dark colored car with tinted windows drives by and maybe it's my imagination but it seems like it slows as it passes. I shake off the prickly sensation that crawls up my skin. I'm just cold. The temperature's dropped since I got home and I'm out here in a T-shirt. *Real smart.* Still, I keep my eyes pinned on the vehicle until it's completely out of sight.

I wake up to Jasper standing over me. Hell, I don't even remember falling asleep. "Late night?" he asks. "Hope you didn't download any more sus porn onto Leon's computer again. He'll fucking beat your ass." He grabs the laptop and clicks a few buttons. "Damn, I was secretly hoping you did so I could see him kick your ass. I'm bored as hell."

I grab my extra pillow and toss it at him. "Get out."

It would be a miracle if he actually listened. "What do you got going on today? I just finished *Death Note* again. I think this was my third rewatch. No, wait, maybe the fourth. Anyway, I had this dream, I found a Death Note and had a hot anime girl-friend and I was—"

"If I buy you food, will you shut up?" I groan against my pillow. I love Jasper but holy hell, he's annoying sometimes.

I can tell I've caught his interest. I push up onto my elbows and he's already out of the room.

"I take it that's a yes?" I yell.

"I'll never deny my body the sweet thrill of breakfast foods.

Ohh, bacon. It's been so long since I've crunched into a nice thick piece. Or do I want sausages, spicy with maple syrup drizzled over them. Help, I can't choose!"

He can't be serious? One peek from my doorway and I see that yes, he is serious. He's standing there idling about bacon or sausages.

"Throw on some clean clothes and I'll get you both," I say. "And run a brush through that hair, you look like you're building a nest up there." I guess getting shot and being laid up in bed did a number on a guy's hygiene routine.

"It's not that bad," he says, making me scoff.

"I guess your mirror was injured too?" I love fucking with Jasper's fragile ego. Almost as much as I love picking on Leon for being a boring British bastard.

Cleaned up and smelling fresh, thanks to me reminding Jasper that deodorant exists, we pull up to the local diner. I've only ever had takeout from here, but the guys love the place. It's got the retro feel with the jukebox, red and white booths, and neon signs. Reminds me of the places we'd stop in our travels from town to town when I was a kid.

We grab a booth in the back and settle in. I watch Jasper shift around with a grimace on his face. "How are you feeling? You're up and around a lot more. Still on pain meds?"

He scans the menu and answers without looking up. "It's not as bad as it was. Honestly, I feel like I'm more sore from not working out than from the healing. Oh, stuffed French toast!"

"Get whatever you want, it's my treat," I say. Am I kissing ass so he'll back me up with Leon later? Maybe. Even so, it's nice to get some time out of the apartment together.

"You're not getting in my pants later, even if I order the most expensive shit on the menu." He cracks a Jasper, megawatt grin while I toss a piece of ice from my water glass at his head.

"I draw the line at lobster," I say. "While we're on the subject of your pants, no sane woman will wanna get in those pants again unless you start showering more. We share a bathroom. I know that it hasn't been used as much."

Our waitress comes to take our order. Black coffee and a breakfast sandwich for me, and half the menu for Jas. Jasper calls the older woman sweetheart and flashes another grin. I'm pretty sure she floated back to the kitchen.

"Lining up more cougars for the back burner?" I tease, tapping my fingers on the table. "Dolores not enough woman for you?"

"Blasphemy," he says. "Dolores is enough woman for the three of us. I don't know how her old man handled her."

Shaking my head, I picture a younger Dolores. "She was probably hot back in the day."

Jasper leans in conspiratorially. "Don't tell Leon this or I swear I'll key your car." I choke on a sip of water—he'd never. "Dolores posed for Playboy back in the 70s. She pulled it out to show me when we first moved in."

"I bet that wasn't all she pulled out." He kicks me under the table. "So... how was it?"

"Tasteful yet erotic. Chub inducing. Mr. Langston was a lucky man." We laugh as the waitress returns to fill my mug with steaming hot coffee. I take a sip and feel it scald my throat on the way down, adding to the warmth in my chest. I didn't realize how much I needed this. No stress, just me and Jas being dumb like we always have. The solid six hours of sleep might have helped too.

Jasper stretches his neck from side to side, rubbing his injured shoulder. "You take your meds this morning?"

"No, I gotta take them with food or I'll barf. I'm worried it's not healing right. You think you can get Blake to come back over and take a look soon?"

I've purposely kept Blake away from the guys since that night. I've told myself it was to keep her safe from retaliation but a part of me wanted her to myself. It's always been dog eat dog with the three of us when it came to girls. Jasper would be drowning in more pussy than he could ever need. He's a 6'4" jock with blue eyes and sandy blond hair. The prick went through puberty and turned into Charlie Hunnam. Next to him, I never stood a chance.

Then there was Leon, with his tan skin, dark hair, hazel eyes, and British accent. He might have played the quiet one, but the second he opened his mouth he had them. The hot, smart girls with their secret Dom kinks were his thing in college.

And for me, I did alright. I've always been a one woman guy though which never worked well for me in those days.

Our plates come, distracting Jasper from his question. I can't hide Blake from them for long. Not with how serious I intend our relationship to be. "I'll see if she can stop by after class this week."

He cuts into his French toast like he's never seen food before, shoveling monster bites into his mouth. With a mouthful he says, "Thanks, man."

Speaking of Blake, I haven't checked in on her yet this morning. I grab my phone and pull up my GPS app. Blake's in class, exactly where I knew she'd be. My shoulders relax as I drink more of my coffee. I wish she was here in the booth beside me. I'd love to rest my palm on her thigh, drag my fingers up along the length until she squirms.

> Me: Sleep okay, Angel?

Jasper finishes chewing and looks up from his plate. "So you really like this girl, huh?"

I glance at my phone screen on the table and wait for a response like a lovesick puppy. "Yeah, she's incredible. So fucking smart and gorgeous. She makes me laugh."

"You guys fuck yet?" He waggles his brows and it's my turn to kick him under the table.

"That's my future wife you're talking about," I say.

He holds his fork up in surrender. "Sorry, you know me... I can't help but ask. From your response I'm assuming the answer is no, though. I wonder how her friend is doing, the blonde I met at the party."

"She hasn't been around. Blake mentioned that she'll sometimes take off to join her brother for work trips though."

He shrugs and finishes chewing a piece of bacon. "I know Leon wanted me to keep an eye on her, which I don't mind doing in the slightest. You know I have a thing for blondes."

"Your dick has a thing for anyone with a pulse," I deadpan.

"You're an ass."

My phone vibrates with a text from Blake.

> Blake: I would have slept better if someone didn't leave me all hot and bothered.

Fuck, this isn't the time or place to be having a daydream about last night. Blake was so wet and ready for me. The sounds she made. Her startled face when she woke up restrained. I drop my fork and gulp more coffee.

"Is that her texting you?" Jasper asks, polishing off the last bite of food on his plate.

I nod and text her back.

> Me: If you're good and don't touch yourself, maybe I'll reward you later.

"Dude, you're so down bad. The dimples are out." Jasper

watches me like a hawk. It's quite creepy if I'm being honest. I hope I don't look at Blake that way.

"Shut up, or I'm gonna send you in the back to wash dishes." My phone goes off again.

Blake: What if I already did? ;)

This fucking woman will be the death of me. My leg vibrates under the table while I think of a clever response.

Blake: Just kidding… Did you spin out for a second there?

Me: I'm going to spank that ass raw tonight.

Our waitress drops off the check and the to-go box I got for Leon. She gives Jasper a wink before walking over to her next table. I pull out my wallet and notice she left her number on the check.

"See what happens when you clean up and use deodorant?" I pass the check to him and he smirks.

"I'm back on my game."

We're getting in the car as my phone vibrates again.

Blake: Looking forward to it.

CHAPTER EIGHTEEN

DAMON

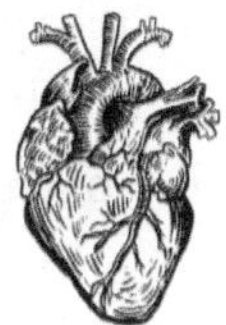

Leon's outside smoking a cigarette when we get back. He spots the takeout bag and tips his chin in our direction. "Was wondering why it was so quiet inside."

"Brought you home an egg sandwich." I lift the bag up like an offering. "I had to get Jas out of the house. You're next."

He takes the bag and we head inside. While Jasper and I sit on the couch, Leon grabs an energy drink from the fridge. "I let the club fuck up get to my head. Now that I see Jasper's up and moving, I'll feel better about doing the same."

"Aww, you were worried about me?" Jas teases. Leon rolls his eyes and sits on the couch with us.

"Of course, you bloody idiot. It's my fault you almost died." He unwraps his sandwich and takes a bite, keeping his eyes low. "I wouldn't be able to live with myself."

"Fuck ups happen," I say, squeezing his shoulder. "Next time we plan better, that's all."

"At least we have Blake now," Jasper says. "She patched me up nice."

That's my woman.

"She did do a good job," Leon says. "Everything going okay with her?" They both stare me down. It's not like I fuck up that much. Some women haven't *loved* some of my tendencies. But that just meant they weren't the one.

"Everything's great. She'll be by this week to check up on Jas. I actually have a favor to ask though." He chews a bite of his sandwich slowly while a smug grin starts to form.

"What is it? You need help setting up cameras in her house? Didn't Jasper do that already?"

Jasper's distracted on his phone and doesn't hear his name mentioned. "It's not that. I need help finding someone. I tried last night with the information that I have but came up short."

He crosses his arms over his chest and leans back. "So what you're saying is... you need help from the master?"

"I refuse to call you that," I huff.

He chuckles, all arrogant and obnoxious. This is why Jasper's my favorite. For today. Until he pisses me off too.

"I'm just messing with you. Grab my computer. I'll find whoever it is."

It takes Leon less than ten minutes to find our guy. I hate to admit it, but he is the master. He won't hear it from my lips, though.

"Why did you need to find this guy?" he asks while I take down all the information on my phone. Jasper's ears perk up too.

"He hurt Blake and I'm gonna make him regret it." There's no beating around the bush. That's what it is, plain and simple. You hurt what's mine and you face the consequences.

"I don't like the sound of that," Leon says. "Shouldn't you be watching the club today?"

"I forgot to tell you, I got in touch with that PI, Ray. He's in. I gave him a brief update on the phone but told him you'd get in touch from a more secure device."

"That's good," Jasper says. "I know he didn't find much at first but maybe he's gotten better."

"I suppose it can't hurt. Just try not to get too distracted. We need you." Leon's smug expression turns serious and I nod.

"Don't worry, finding Bailey is still my top priority. She's my little sister too, in every way that matters." Saying it out loud makes a nice, fat pang of guilt grow heavy in my gut. It's selfish to want time with Blake when I should keep my focus on Bailey. I know that. But she came out of left field and I can't let her go. I refuse to. She's under my skin, running through my veins, squeezing my heart until I'm weak. When I'm not near her, I physically ache. It's not a choice anymore. I have to be with Blake. If we need to make accommodations to our plans then so be it.

Jasper stands and slowly stretches his shoulders with a groan. "So, who are we killing today?"

LUCKY FOR ME, Trevor lives a few towns north in the next county. If I had to travel far that wouldn't be ideal, not when I had plans with Blake tonight.

"So this Trevor guy was friends with Blake's brother when they were teenagers and he..." Jasper gestures with his hands rather than saying his thoughts out loud.

"Groomed her and assaulted her. You can say it, Jas. Letting it out will help you when we see his greasy face." I grip the wheel like I'm pulling a trigger. "I'm gonna need you to keep me calm. You know I can get carried away."

"Bro, you should have brought Leon. You know I've never been the 'calm down' friend. I met Blake once and that's enough for me to want to end this piece of shit. Hell, even if Blake was a complete stranger, I'd still take pleasure in watching the light seep out of his eyes." Jasper cracks his neck, then his knuckles one by one. He's right, I should have made Leon come. The two of us unchecked will result in major fuckery.

"Simmer down, killer. I know you've been cooped up but we need to be smart. We're going into a high school, can't just fucking murder a guy there."

"What if Leon jams the security cameras? Then can we?" He sounds like a little kid asking for a cookie.

I massage my aching temple and groan. "Christ, I don't know... maybe? Call him and see if he's free to help."

How did I suddenly become the responsible one in this situation?

We pull up to Blake's old high school. Turns out the Trevor I found during my own search—Mr. Janitor Of The Year—*is* the guy I was looking for. Interesting that he's still sticking around fourteen year old girls.

"We should wait until dark," I say. It looks like there's still some students and faculty lingering for after school activities. "Can't take unnecessary risks."

Jasper nods and takes out his phone to scroll videos. While we wait, I picture a young, impressionable Blake getting off the school bus everyday, walking those front steps, and going through the motions after her innocence was shattered. Did anyone know? The fact that she lost her mother and brother was common knowledge I got from a quick search on the inter-net, but she was older than fourteen when they passed. Were they there to comfort her?

With each passing minute I grow more and more enraged. I assume Jasper feels the same, as he's gone quiet since we parked. On one hand, sitting here for all this time let me work on a plan.

Leon: I did what I could with the cameras. I wouldn't do anything stupid though.

Me: Thanks, man.

Jasper closes out his YouTube video and puts his phone in his pocket. "Do we have a game plan?"

"I think so, just one second. I want to text Blake." Jasper grins and grabs his mask from the backseat.

Me: If you could say one thing to Trevor, what would it be?

She's going to know I'm up to something, but it's too late for her to try and stop me. I heard the vulnerability in her voice last night, saw her tears. What happened to her affected her in every aspect of her life since then. I only wish she were here with me to get revenge herself.

Blake: What are you doing? Where are you?

My phone rings immediately and Blake's name flashes on my screen. I hit the red button. "Let's go."

I nod to Jasper and we get out of the car and start walking toward the maintenance entrance. "What's Blake saying?"

Me: Answer the question, baby.

Blake: Fine... I'd tell him that he ruined me. That I still see his stupid chest tattoo sometimes when I close my eyes. That he never deserved Bryan's love.

That right there is exactly what I need to hear. I can't wait to hold Blake in my arms tonight and bring her the gift of closure. Or better yet, I'll save it as a special birthday gift.

AFTER DROPPING Jasper back at the apartment, I drive straight to Blake's house. I'm exhausted and oddly emotional about getting this closure for her. Normally this kind of thing would get me fired up, but tonight all I want is to comfort Blake. Maybe spank her gorgeous ass too, but in a caring way. Hell, she's making me soft.

I don't bother to park around the corner or case the property this time. I'm laser focused on being as close to her as I can in the shortest amount of time. Out of habit, I start to cross the yard but something pinned to the door catches my attention.

It's a note, stuck onto the weathered wood with some kind of putty.

Stalker,

I thought I'd make your life easier and leave the door unlocked. You know, maybe save these old windows from all the abuse they've been getting lately.

See you inside.

If I wasn't so paranoid about her leaving the door unlocked, I'd laugh. It's a cute note, but tradition is tradition. I pull it off the door, pocket it and go directly to her bedroom window.

She's lying prone on her bed with her feet in the air and two different colored highlighters in her hand. Music drifts through the glass panes, a female singer I don't recognize. I watch her flip through a spiral-bound notebook, underlining hand written notes. Times like this, when she's in the zone studying, is when she looks most comfortable. Her dark eyes bounce around the page, soaking up information. Her nose scrunches when she reads over something tricky. Sometimes she'll even narrow her brows and bite her lip. My brilliant, sexy doctor. I could watch her like this all night. But I'd rather do more than that.

I'm about to pull the window open when luck strikes and she leaves the room. I work quickly to climb through the window, kick off my boots, and settle myself on her bed.

"Shit," I say, rubbing a spot of blood I missed on the edge of my shirt. This is one of my favorite shirts too. I'm so engrossed in what I'm doing that I don't notice Blake coming into the room until she gasps and spews a barrage of curses.

"Where the hell did you come from?" My eyes zero in on the way her hand clutches her chest.

"Here and there. We moved around a lot when I was a kid." I lean back casually and grin.

"You know that's not what I mean."

I nod my head toward the window and say, "I'm a creature of habit, plus an unlocked door... too easy. Come here."

She climbs next to me, making a point of brushing her body against mine as she moves her notebooks aside. "Creature of habit? Try creature of the night."

"Your creature of the night." This makes her laugh and I instantly relax. "You know that, right?"

"What?"

I pull her against my chest. "That I'm yours. All jokes aside, I know I've been busy and I'll let you in on more of that soon, but I'll be around now. Every day. I made some changes so we can spend more time together."

She traces lines across my chest with her fingers. Her touch feels incredible, just simple things like the scrape of her nails against my T-shirt, that's all it takes for me to melt. She's thinking hard, her nose scrunched. I hope I'm not coming on too strong, although that is kind of my thing.

"Look—I'd rather be honest with you from the start about who I am and what I do. I—"

Her finger brushes my lips. "Shh. I don't need to know about what you do. The less I know the better, I'm sure. But yes, I'd like that. Spending more time together, I mean. It's been an interesting start to whatever this is... but as much as it pains me to admit it, I'm drawn to you. You're absolutely unhinged and a little scary and... Anyway, I know you won't hurt me."

As she pulls her hand away I circle her wrist and kiss her palm. "I'm fucking infatuated with you, Blake. You couldn't get rid of me if you tried."

Her palm rests on my cheek while our eyes lock. I look my fill, not that I'll ever tire of her gorgeous face. Her smooth skin dotted with freckles, her short, rounded nose, her plump lips. Perfection. My chest aches and a physical need to be inside her takes over. Before I realize what I'm doing, I grip either side of her face and devour her lips with an intensity I've never felt before.

When her lips part and she slides her tongue against mine, I'm done for. Fuck, she tastes amazing. A moan slips out of her mouth and I can't help but smile as we kiss.

I bring my hand lower and gently wrap it around her throat, giving a small amount of pressure as I suck her lower lip and bite down. She's so responsive to every kiss, every touch. The way she arches toward me, her chest heaving like she's just as desperate for me as I am for her. I need to bury myself inside her more than I need air to breathe.

I pull back and sit up on my knees. "Blake, I need you to give me permission to do what I want with you."

She's breathless as she scoots back onto the bed. Seconds go by where I feel like I'll combust. Finally, she nods.

"I need you to tell me, baby. Tell me I can have *every inch* of you." I drag my hands over the curve of her breasts, stopping when I reach her tight nipple. She gasps and it's music to my ears. "These tits that I've been dying to fuck."

"Damon, please."

Dragging my hand lower, I watch her eyes glaze over as I reach her pussy. "This mouthwatering cunt that was made to take me."

She opens her mouth to speak but I grip her hips and flip her over. Her nightshirt rides up and I have the perfect view of her round ass. I slap it, not too hard, but hard enough that a pretty little red mark shows up and her breath hitches. "This ass too, Blake. I'll fuck you here and you'll love it."

Wrapping my fist in her hair, I lean in and crash my lips against hers. Our tongues tangle as she angles her ass against me. "This mouth, so warm and perfect and all mine. Give me permission, Blake, because once I'm inside you, I'm going to be a changed man. A man who's lost all control. Once I can take every inch of you, I'll never stop."

She rocks against my crotch, and I grip her hips to halt her movement. "God, just—"

"You want my cock, Angel? Say it. Say, Damon, fuck me."

CHAPTER NINETEEN

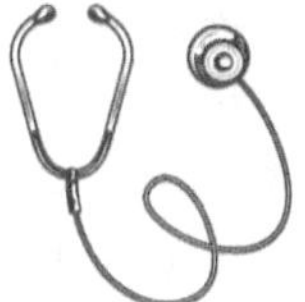

I've never felt so out of control before. So ready to shut my brain off and give in to every second of pleasure Damon will give me. My pussy aches and his dirty mouth only makes me want him more. Am I ready to give him everything? Every inch of my skin. Unfiltered, unhinged Damon. I meant what I said. Somehow, I trust him. But am I ready for his intensity?

My ass has a mind of its own as I grind against his length. He's still fully dressed and I'm in undies and a nightshirt but already the friction is too good. And damn, the way he kisses. Like he wants to crawl under my skin and live there.

"Blake, what do you want?" His voice is deep and commanding, just like every other aspect of him. Maybe I'll regret this later, but now I have to listen to my body and my heart. Mostly my body.

"I want you inside me. Fuck me, Damon. Use me like your good little whore." My face is red hot as the words leave my lips. I've never talked that way before but I love it. I'm desperate for relief from this heavy ache. Relief that I know Damon will be happy to provide.

He climbs off the bed and stands before me like a god. A dark god, but a god nonetheless. I take him in, his lean tattooed body cut with just the right amount of muscle, his thick thighs in those tight black pants. My eyes rake over his impressive bulge, ready to break free. He beckons me with his finger as his dark eyes devour me. "Come here, Angel. Take my cock out like the good little slut you are."

I crawl to the edge of the bed and kneel to undo his button. He smells so incredible, I want to burrow my face against him. Carefully, I slide his zipper down and wrap my fist around his hard length. I hold him there, awaiting his next command. He pulls his pants down until they hit his knees, giving me a peek at his inked thighs and legs.

"Get it nice and wet." He tangles his hands in my hair, tugging gently as he brings his dripping cock to my lips. I moan and lick the beads of pre-cum from his tip. "Fuck, yes. That's my good girl. Suck it, Blake."

Opening wide, I take him to the back of my throat until I can't fit anymore, then bring him back out with a pop. I get him nice and wet, sliding my tongue along his length and letting saliva drip onto him. With each thrust, I close my eyes and picture him sinking into me. My body rocks, harder and faster, while he fucks my open mouth.

"You suck it so good, baby. Fuck, I'm gonna come if you keep going." I open my eyes as he pulls out, feeling dazed. I'm so turned on I can't think.

He pulls his shirt off and tosses it to the floor, then yanks mine off too. His chest is covered in tattoos but he moves so quickly, I can't take them in, other than the skeletal spider and webbing across his neck. While he steps out of his pants he motions to my underwear and says, "Off."

I push away the quick wave of vulnerability and focus on the way this man wants to worship at my feet. He can give two shits about my belly rolls, or my heavy natural tits. I can see it in the way he looks at me. He loves what he sees.

Reaching out to feel his chest, rubbing my palms over the ridges of his abs, I pull him closer. His voice shakes slightly as he says my name. "Blake, you're the most beautiful thing I've ever seen."

He slides his hands from my waist up to cup my tits and brush my nipples with the pads of his thumbs. They're so sensitive to his touch that it almost hurts. My head falls back as I offer him more. My body is his to do what he pleases.

He drags his hand up past my collarbone to grip my neck. "I love the way your pulse races for me."

Our lips meet again, this time slower, like we're savoring every second. My skin's electric with every pass of our tongues. I can't take it. He's denied me before. I'm worried that he's doing it again. "Please, Damon. I need you."

"Come to the edge of the bed and turn around." I back up so I'm on my hands and knees, against the edge of the bed. My nipples brush the bedding and I swear I'm so wet I'm dripping.

Damon surprises me by spreading my cheeks and devouring my pussy. He slides his tongue through my folds and sucks my clit until I'm so close to exploding, I could scream. His tongue flicks and circles me, bringing me higher and higher, and just when I'm about to come he pulls away and slams his cock inside me.

"You'll come around my cock. Now be a good girl and take every inch I give you." His hand grips my hair and pulls while I adjust my position. He slides out, leaving me desperately empty, before slamming back in. It feels like sweet agony. He's so thick, I'm being split in two.

"It's too big," I say as he yanks my hair back, forcing me to arch. "Oh God, I can't."

"You can and you will." He slaps my ass cheek hard and pushes deeper. With each inch, I adjust to his size and we start to move together. "Just like that, take it. Such a perfect slut."

The sound of our skin slapping together and the groans slipping from our lips is nothing short of erotic. I'm so wet, I can hear his cock sliding in and out as he massages my ass cheeks and slaps them together. The fullness and pleasure is like nothing I've ever felt before.

He moves his hand to my throat and adds pressure, squeezing the sides with each pump. "Oh, my God."

"Rub your clit, baby. Come around my cock." I'm already so close, one touch will bring me to the edge. I reach underneath my body and gasp against the blanket when my finger finds my clit. A few circles on the swollen bud and I feel my pussy spasm. "That's it. Come for me, Blake."

As soon as the words leave Damon's lips, I lose myself, shuddering while he pounds into me. I think I scream his name, but I can't be sure because I nearly black out. As I'm riding out my orgasm, Damon grabs my waist and lifts me, flipping me onto my back. My eyes are half closed, but I watch him—the way he moves, how he commands my body. He's everything I've ever wanted.

I spread my legs wide, as he grabs each of them, resting them on his shoulders. "Keep playing with your clit."

I can't. I'm too sensitive.

He's waiting for me to listen, though. His cock lined up at my entrance. And I want him. Need him inside me again. I reach down and rub myself, instantly moaning, and he finally pushes into me. The stretch of him with this angle is... I have no words. "That's my girl. Just like that. Make yourself come again."

It's hard to keep my eyes open but I want to watch him. His concentrated look, the pure bliss in his eyes. It's so hot. But I'm climbing again, chasing another orgasm I didn't even realize I could have.

Damon's thrusts are erratic, slower then faster. He pulls out to slam back in. "Shit, Blake... I'm coming. Come with me."

He starts to pull out and I don't know what comes over me, but I grab his ass and hold him inside me. Not only that, but I rock against him, fast and hard. "Come inside me. Fill me up."

"Fuck," he groans and I see a moment of doubt cross his face, before he grips my thighs and meets me thrust for thrust. "You want my cum, Blake? Such a good little slut. Oh... fuuuck."

"Oh, my God," I moan, completely breathless. His fingertips bite into me so hard they'll bruise as he pumps again. He grazes his teeth along the skin of my thigh and groans.

"That's right, milk my cock." We shudder as we come together, Damon calling my name while he spills inside me.

I'm completely out of breath and hypersensitive. Like I've just been transported to another planet. Damon collapses against me, and I hold him inside me. "That was... Christ, Blake. I'm a fucking goner."

I laugh, as he trembles against me. "I feel the same way." He pushes onto his elbows and pins me with an intense look. "What?" I say, when the silence becomes too loud.

"Nothing... I just can't believe you're real."

An overwhelming sense of warmth flows through me. Like I'm finally cared for by someone. Contentment and peace and... I don't know what to do with these feelings.

He closes the space between us and kisses me softly, then rubs his cheek against mine with a sigh. Maybe we're both just two extremely love-starved people who finally found each other.

"I assure you, I'm very real." I smile against his cheek and plant kisses along his scratchy jaw. "Do you want something from the kitchen? Some water?"

He pulls up and I feel him shift inside me. With a smirk, he says, "Oh, did you think we were done?"

"What? I—uh, yeah? Isn't that how it works?"

He chuckles low against my ear, causing me to shiver. I shift beneath him and feel his cock already growing hard inside me. *Oh.*

"Not with me, Angel. I told you, once I'm inside you, I'm never leaving." Then he wraps my wrists in his hand and holds them above my head. "You're coming at least three more times tonight."

"Damon, I can't," I start to argue as he grinds into me. Rolling his hips so I take him deep. Holy hell, he feels so good now that I've adjusted to his size. Okay, maybe I can.

He smiles, dimples popping out. "I see that look on your face. You can, can't you?"

Fucking Freddy. I'll never sleep again but I guess I can't complain.

SUN STREAMS through the window when I open my eyes. I throw my arm over my face to shield myself from the assault of evil light and feel Damon's arm slung over my rib cage. His hand is holding my breast like it's a stuffed animal. I can't help but giggle. And oh, shit. He's still inside me.

I need to get up. Pee. Stretch my legs. I start to roll toward the edge of the bed but he pulls me closer. "Are you serious?" I ask in a voice that sounds like I was screaming at a concert all night. Only half of that was true. "Aren't you tired?"

I meant his cock. That thing had to be spent.

How the hell was there anything left in there? I'm so full of his cum it's going to start coming out of my ears.

He doesn't answer. I half wonder if he's even awake. Twisting my neck, I try to see his face but can't tell. His chest is slowly rising and falling against my back, almost like someone asleep. I test him and rock my hips. He pulls me closer, anchoring me to his chest like a life vest. And damn, he feels so good, I rock again, getting lost in the sensation. "Damon?" I murmur his name and feel him roll my nipple between his fingers. He's awake. I knew it. He pinches and I hiss, rolling my hips again.

Screw it.

I turn over and straddle him without letting his cock slip out of me. His eyes are wide open and he's smirking. "Morning, Angel."

"You're a machine. How—" I'm cut off as he thrusts up, arching his hips to hit deeper. "Oh, my God. So full."

I lean closer and feed him my tit, moaning when he sucks one nipple at a time between his lips. This angle gives me the perfect amount of friction to grind my clit against him. I rock and circle my hips, chasing my release. Damon guides me, his hands wrapped around my hips with a bruising hold. I don't know how I have any strength left in my body but I'm right there with him, thrust for thrust.

"That's it. Use my cock, Blake. Ride me." I'm flush with his chest, unable to hold myself up any longer. He kisses me and I open for him, our tongues are sloppy as we chase our releases. Sucking and nibbling, groaning into each other's mouths. I know what to say to push him over the edge. I learned it fast last night. Damon loves to fill me up. Almost as much as I love him doing it.

"I'm so close," I whisper against his ear. "I want your cum. Finish in me, fill me." He grips my ass and lifts me up and down on his cock so I'm bouncing. "Yes, oh God." He feels so incredible. I'm right there, just one more...

"Oh, fuck," he groans, slamming me down and wrapping his arms around my back as he comes. I reach between our bodies and rub my clit until I'm there with him, milking his cock dry.

After a few minutes of catching my breath, I finally attempt to roll off him. "Nope," he says. "You're not moving."

"Damon, for real. I'm going to pee on you if you don't let me up." He's unrelenting for a few more seconds and I think he's seriously considering that option, but then he releases me from his bear hug grip. I jump off him on wobbly legs and sprint to the bathroom.

The amount of wetness between my legs is unreal. And I'm sore all over, but especially my pussy. I'm not surprised, the guy is huge. My poor kitty will never be the same again.

I flush and start the shower, turning the faucet so it'll get extra hot. My body needs it. Once I can see the steam, I pull the curtain aside and step in, biting back a moan from the blissful feel of water against my skin.

I've barely wet my whole head when the curtain is yanked aside and Damon, in all his naked glory, stands there, arms crossed. "You're not even going to invite me in with you?"

I laugh and shake my head, gesturing to come on in. "By all means, feel free."

He climbs in and closes the space between us so we're both in the stream. "Mmm, you love super hot showers too?"

"It's the only way," I say. I close my eyes and feel my muscles melt. Normally, I'd be freaking out that I'm missing a class. But some time after round two last night, I decided there was no way I was making it.

He reaches behind me and grabs the bottle of body wash, squirting some into his palms. It's surreal watching him like this, with steam surrounding us, in the dim bathroom lighting. With lathered hands, he soaps up my shoulders, giving them a gentle squeeze that feels incredible. Gliding lower, he takes his time washing every part of me until my knees shake.

"Are you sore?" Crowding me against the tile wall with his body, he grabs the shower head and starting at my hair, rinses the suds.

"A little," I say, biting my lip as he lets the stream pound against my clit. I don't know how I'm still turned on. It should be impossible after hours of sex, but maybe I don't know as much about my body as I thought.

I grab onto his shoulders and lean my head against the tile, opening my legs for him. "Remember I told you I'd take you in the shower?"

"Mhm," I say as a moan slips out. He changes the angle of the stream and to hit exactly where I'm most sensitive. I cry out, unable to stop myself. "Oh, God."

As I'm about to fall, Damon drops the showerhead and grabs me, lifting me up against the tile. I wrap my legs around his hips and grind, riding out my orgasm.

I couldn't care less about the cool air hitting my skin. Not while I'm pressed against him. "Breathe in."

I heave a breath as Damon pushes his cock into me, inch by inch until there's no space between us. I'm so sore from his size. But he doesn't move right away, giving me time to adjust. He takes a step, holding me with one hand, and fixes the shower so we're once again in the stream. The hot water helps relax me again and I move my hips.

"That's my good angel," he says. "Hold on to me."

It doesn't take long until I'm biting his shoulder to keep

from screaming. We chase our pleasure and come together again.

Never, in my life, did I think that was possible. But then again, I'm learning to expect the impossible with Damon.

CHAPTER TWENTY

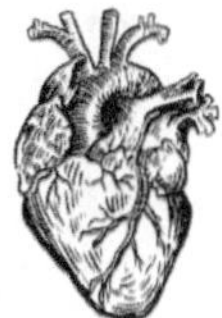

While Blake finishes washing her hair, I dry off, throw my jeans on, and order us some food. There's messages from the guys, because of course they're going to bust my balls for spending time with Blake. What I want is an update.

> Jasper: Hope you're having a good night.

He added a GIF of a round ass getting spanked. I shake my head and laugh. At least he's predictable.

> Leon: It's done. Should be up this morning.

Then time-stamped an hour later, he sent a link. I hope everything went according to plan. I hold my breath as I click it and am immediately relieved.

First, I text Leon back to thank him for coming through for me. This had nothing to do with Bailey or the job. It was entirely personal and he was there for me, no questions asked. Hell, I'm getting choked up.

Next, I copy the link and text it to Jasper, ignoring his ridiculous GIF.

> Me: Not sure if Leon told you, but everything worked out. I know I don't say it enough, but I love you, man. Couldn't have done this without you.

Blake pushes the door open, wearing nothing but a towel. And I thought my morning couldn't get any better.

"You're looking happy this morning," she says, her face lit up with a smile. She glances at my phone. "Good news?"

I toss it on the bed and walk toward her, wrapping her in my arms. "I'm with you. How could I not be happy?"

Feeling her relax against me is everything. She whispers, "Where did you come from?" against my chest.

"I thought I told you last night, we moved around a lot." Grinning against her wet hair, I kiss the top of her head. "I ordered us food while you were in the shower. It should be here in a few minutes."

"Wheat and soy-free?"

"Of course, it's from that place I ordered from before." I knew about the wheat, but not the soy. Good thing I chose a place that was free from all of the top allergens last time. I figured better to be safe.

She throws on a long-sleeve black shirt and some leggings while I enjoy watching her. I notice her absentmindedly touch her neckline a few times, something I've seen her do a lot. Then it hits me. She misses her necklace. I'll have to figure out the right time to give it back, or replace it with a gift of my own.

"I didn't want to bring it up last night, but what you texted me yesterday... about Trevor?" She runs a brush through her hair with her eyes cast down. I wait for her to finish her question. As excited as I am to tell her everything, I'm saving it for the right moment. Her birthday's coming and it's the perfect gift. "What was that all about?"

"Would you listen to me if I told you not to worry?" I rub my hands along my thighs and think of the right words to say. Her raised brow isn't helping. "I'll tell you everything, just not today. Let's enjoy the day together. You're skipping class like a bad girl and I'm ignoring all my responsibilities. Let's not bring him into our bubble."

I know I've got her as her face softens. "Yeah, alright. But you're telling me everything eventually. I'm already anxious enough. I don't need that hanging over my head."

"I know. Come on over here, let me help you with your hair." She hesitates but comes to sit on the edge of the bed. I take the brush and work on detangling some of the monster knots we made. "I was thinking we could have dinner with the guys later? Jasper's worried his shoulder isn't healing right and wants you to take a look."

"I don't know how much help I'll be, but sure. I'd like that." She leans back into my lap, giving me better access. "But I need to get home early. Can't miss any more classes. Actually, shoot, I should text this girl Julie and have her send me her notes."

I hold her in my lap. "You can do that later. Let's get through these knots before the food gets here."

"Fine," she huffs.

"Do I detect a hint of sass in your tone? I thought I'd fucked all the sass out of you last night."

She twists to straddle my lap and I'm instantly hard. With her hands on my chest and her nails digging into my skin, she smiles sweetly. "My snark is woven into my soul and as far as I can tell, you haven't fucked my soul away." She plants a quick kiss on my chin and whispers, "Yet."

"Oh, you're in for it now," I say, grabbing her around the

waist and lifting her up. As I'm about to show her how I can fuck the life right out of her, the damn doorbell rings.

She laughs and taunts me. "There's our food. Guess whatever this is has to wait."

To hell with that. We can warm the food up later.

I shift her so I'm carrying her bridal style and open the front door. As soon as I see what's on the doorstep, I set Blake down and step in front of her. "What's going on?" she asks.

My senses are on high alert as I quickly grab the items and close the door. "Blake, go into your room and lock the door."

"Okay." Her voice is frantic, but she doesn't fight me.

I grab my phone from my pocket and dial Leon. "They're after Blake."

"Whoa, start over. What's going on?"

I pace the length of the hallway. "Get your shit and get over here. Both of you."

"What happened?"

"I just opened the front door to a stack of pictures with a bullet paperweight, man. Just get the fuck over here *now*."

"Fuck. Alright, stay calm. We'll be there soon."

As soon as I hang up, I flip through the photos. Blake walking through campus. Blake at a coffee shop. Blake at her doorstep. "Motherfucker!" It takes everything in me to not punch the wall.

Take deep breaths. First, I'll check on her. She must be terrified. I knock on the door. "It's just me. You can open up."

She rushes into my arms. "I saw photos of me. And was that a bullet? What is going on?"

I don't want her involved any more than she already is, but I guess it's too late. She's in this now, so she may as well know what's going on. "Leon and Jasper are on their way. We're going to check the house and make sure you're safe for the time being. I think this was a message from some very bad people."

She rolls her lip between her teeth before meeting my gaze. "Does this have to do with Jasper getting shot? Are those people the ones who left the photos?"

"I believe so." I huff and pull at my hair. "I'll tell you everything, but first I need to get dressed and you've gotta pack a bag." I grab my shirt from the floor and pull it over my head before reaching for my belt and boots. Blake hasn't started to move. "Do you need help packing?"

"Where are you taking me?"

"You'll stay with us. There's no way in hell I'm letting you stay here after this." She releases a breath and nods. "I'll be right back. Grab everything you need for classes too."

Once I finish tying my boots, I slowly open the front door, checking every blind spot. When I deem it safe, I jog out to my car and grab my gun from the glove box. I'm such a fool for leaving it in the car. What the fuck would have happened if they broke in? This is what happens when I'm careless. In my world, even the smallest oversight can have deadly consequences.

I'm too impatient to wait for the guys. Gun aimed ahead, I case the property, searching for anything out of place. There are too many places to hide here. I know firsthand how easy it is to watch Blake. Even easier to get inside the house. On my first pass everything looks as it should. I figured they wouldn't hang around, but needed to check anyway.

As I round the corner toward the front door, I catch the back of a body walking away. Aiming my gun, I yell to get his attention. "Who are you and what the hell are you doing here?"

The guy turns and I realize I'm looking at a kid no older than eighteen. His eyes widen and he puts his hands in the air. "Hey man, I'm just here to deliver your food. I'm leaving, it's all good."

Fuck.

I tuck my gun into my pants. "I'm sorry, man. We had an intruder here earlier, just being extra careful." I pull a few extra bucks from my wallet and walk toward him but he's already jogging away. I guess I don't blame him.

As the kid peels out, I hear the growl of Leon's bike flying up the street. Jasper's clutching his back like he'll become a flying projectile.

I jog up the driveway to meet them as Leon turns the engine off. "Thanks for coming."

"Are you safe? Blake?" Leon dismounts and scans the area frantically. Jasper follows, immediately drawing his gun.

"I just walked the property and nothing looks amiss. This was definitely a message." I follow them down the driveway while they spread out and search behind trees and in shadowed spaces. "Listen, I should have asked you guys but I told Blake to pack a bag. Do you mind if she stays with us?"

Jasper grins. "It's fine with me. It'll be nice to have a girl with us. Hey, can she cook?"

I smack him on his good shoulder. "Misogynistic much?"

"Of course she can stay," Leon adds. "I was going to insist she does."

Everything is fucked, but I let myself smile, only for a moment. Because I have to admit I'm one lucky bastard to have these two as brothers.

"Come on inside, let's grab her stuff."

I show them through the door, and Jasper walks in like he owns the place. "Fond memories here," he says wistfully. "Speaking of, where's my blonde friend?"

"She hasn't been around. Blake's been here alone for over a week. You think it's something to worry about?" I lead them to Blake's bedroom and knock on the door.

Jasper cuts in front of me and squeezes Blake in a giant bone-crushing hug. "Doc, I'm so glad you're okay."

"Thanks?" she wheezes, until he gets the hint and lets go.

Leon holds his hand out to shake hers, giving her one of his mysterious, quiet guy smolders. "Blake, we weren't properly introduced last time. I'm Leon Colter."

My girl's cheeks tinge pink as she takes his hand.

"Alright, well now that you've all officially met, time to go. Got everything, Angel?"

"Aw, Angel... How adorable," Jasper singsongs. I make a mental note to kick him in the sack later.

Blake's smiling though, so at least Jasper's good for easing tense situations. "Yeah, I'm good. You guys have basic stuff, right? Toothpaste, soap, towels?"

I close my eyes and sigh at the mention of towels, knowing exactly what Jasper will say. Three, two, one...

"Damon and I have this sort of communal towel thing going. I'm happy to share with you too. Right, buddy?" Jas slings his good arm over my shoulder. Yup, a kick in the balls it is.

"You're going to get your ass beat," Leon says, holding back a laugh. "I'll answer for them, Blake. If I were you, I'd grab a towel or two and some extra toiletries. Some of us in the apartment are better at hygiene than others."

"What's that supposed to mean?" I scowl and follow them out of Blake's room. "I'm extremely clean. Some might say I shower too much."

Leon turns to me. "What makes you think I'm talking about you then?"

We both stare at Jasper until he realizes what we're doing and gives us the finger. He's too busy staring at the pile of photos on the counter. "These what they left?"

"Yeah... and that bullet," I answer.

"Grab all that, we'll bring it back with us," Leon adds. Jasper takes the pile and heads outside. Once Blake's ready, I open my car door to find Jasper already in the back seat.

"What are you doing?" He moves to the side as I toss Blake's bag next to him.

Maybe it's the lighting but I swear his face pales. "No way in hell am I getting back on that bike with him today. I almost pissed myself."

"He rode that fast?" I ask.

"Yup, fucking scary. He was worried. Well, we both were."

Damn. For someone who does as much illegal shit as we do, Leon always obeys traffic laws. Jasper isn't joking.

Blake climbs into the passenger seat, carrying the bag from DoorDash. Everything's cold by now, but at least it's edible.

"Hey, what's in the bag?" Jasper reaches over the seat and grabs it before Blake can answer. "Ohh, looks good."

"Don't even—" I say but it's too late. He's already biting into a pancake. "What the hell? That's Blake's food."

"It's fine. I'm too nervous to eat." She turns to look at Jasper. "Have at it."

"I'll order you more when we get home." I scowl at Jasper in the rearview. He can be such a dumbass.

While I drive, I rest my hand on her thigh. The connection is the only thing keeping me grounded. Keeping me from driving to that fucking club and shooting empty walls and open spaces.

"You okay over there?" Blake covers my hand with her palm and squeezes gently. It's like she can read my silence or even the spaces between my words. I swallow and nod, tracing circles on her thigh.

"I'll feel better once we get home."

I park down the street and call Leon. "Hey, can you check the place out before we come in?"

"Already on it," he says. "Stay on the phone. I'll give you the okay when I take a peek around."

Jasper taps my shoulder. "Let me out. I'll go too."

After I let him out, I stay outside the car and take a few cleansing breaths. Then I text the investigator, Ray.

> Me: I have another address I need you to watch. And stay armed.

From now on, Blake won't breathe without me right beside her. No one will hurt my girl.

CHAPTER TWENTY-ONE

BLAKE

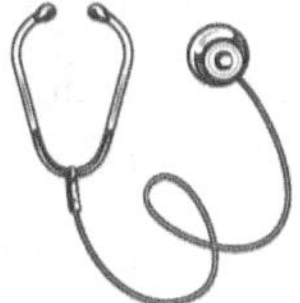

I don't know how I haven't fallen asleep during my professor's monologue. Ethics isn't normally this boring, but if I have to hear him repeat the same story about the time his colleague asked him to violate HIPAA, I might die.

I peek toward the front of the class, where Ethan would normally sit, and find the spot taken by someone else. Damon would lose his shit if I called Ethan, but even so, I'm considering it. There's something weird about how we left things. It's like he disappeared off the face of the earth. And this is a guy who's stumbled into class on more meds than most post-op patients get.

Maybe it's more of my self doubt creeping in. I'm very much done with Ethan, but closure is good.

"Your next case discussion is posted. I'll be at a conference but my aid is available to answer any questions you may have." While he's still rambling on, I click on my list of open assignments and read the topic.

Balancing Professional Ethics and Public Safety.

The case describes a young doctor who happens to treat a

patient with multiple gunshot wounds. The patient admits to the doctor that he was involved in criminal activity, though no specific details are given. My heart pounds as I read the questions that follow, one in particular.

At what point, if any, would the doctor be ethically obligated to report their suspicions?

"That's all for today. I look forward to lively discussion on this topic when I return from my trip." I'm so caught up rereading the assignment that I don't realize class has ended until Julie taps me on the shoulder.

She looks down at me with a grin that's far too bright for someone who just finished an ethics lecture. "Hey girl, want to grab lunch?"

Is it already lunch time? I stand and pack my stuff while trying to think of an excuse. "Hey. Long class, huh?"

We walk out together and stop outside the entrance. It's a sunny autumn day, my favorite kind of weather. I shrug off my sweater and tie it at my waist to get some sun on my arms. "So long, but I don't know, this kind of stuff interests me. You know the whole 'would you steal a loaf of bread to feed your starving family type thing.'" She bumps my shoulder. "How's it going? Haven't seen Ethan around."

And there's the main reason I need an excuse to get out of lunch.

Julie's eyes flutter upward as I feel a strong pair of arms encircle my shoulders, pulling me into a hug. "Ready for lunch?"

His voice wraps around me like a comforting blanket and I turn to give him a kiss. "Yeah, and coffee. An extra large."

Julie clears her throat. "Hi, I don't think we've met."

"Oh, I'm sorry, I'm being rude." Gesturing to Damon, I say, "Julie, this is Damon. Damon, Julie."

"Her boyfriend," he says and holds out his hand.

Julie looks like she's about to fall over but she takes his hand and shakes politely. "Let's catch up soon, Blake. Good luck with the assignment."

Damon whispers in my ear as we watch her walk away. "You're welcome."

"That's mean. She's not that bad." If she'd give up on all the Ethan gossip, maybe we could actually be friends. He twists me around so I'm staring up at his arrogant smirk. "What?"

"It's not mean. She's not good enough for you. I know her type. She's all about what she can get out of you. Gossip, notes, social cred. Better to let her down easy."

If my eyes roll back any farther they might get stuck. "If it were up to you I'd have no friends."

He dips his head so our brows touch and plants a kiss to the tip of my nose. "You don't need friends when you have me."

Shaking my head, I pull away and walk a few paces ahead of him toward the campus coffee shop. He catches up easily and snags my hand, pulling me against his chest. "You're the absolute worst and I'm hungry and grumpy and I need caffeine and—"

He stops my rant with a kiss. "What I meant to say was you have me and the guys now. But of course you need friends. Just not toxic, fake, gossip queens."

It kills me to admit it, but he's not wrong. "Lucky for me, my number one bestie is coming to visit for my birthday." As the words leave my lips I realize the problem. "Shoot. Falin's coming and she's supposed to stay with me."

"We have plenty of room. She can stay with us." He's so nonchalant, like me asking my best friend to stay in an apartment with three random guys is no issue at all. Then I realize this is Falin I'm talking about. She'll probably love the idea.

"I haven't told her about you," I admit. "She's been traveling a lot and we don't get much time to catch up. That's what her visit is for."

We stop outside the crowded cafe, where the smell of coffee instantly perks my mood. Damon's lips curve in a smirk. "What are you going to say about me?"

I tug on his hand and twist one of his rings. "Oh, I don't know. That you're just this weird guy who won't leave me alone."

"Oh, really?" he asks. "How weird are we talking? Because, Angel, you haven't seen me go full freak yet."

"I don't think I can handle whatever *that* is." We move up in line, getting closer to the counter. The mouthwatering smells make my stomach rumble.

"I noticed you didn't correct me earlier when I introduced myself as your boyfriend." He raises a brow and wraps his arm around my waist. I'm speechless for a second. I can't even remember registering those words out of his lips. "I guess I'm more than just some weird guy, huh?"

"I—uh," I stammer.

"Wish I'd said I'm your future husband." He taps his temple and adds, "Won't make that mistake again."

Not long ago, I would have been surprised and maybe even laughed in his face. But now, I just shake my head and pull him along to the front of the counter where I let him pay for my lunch. He's on another level in the land of delusion but I'm too happy right now to knock him down.

IT'S after nine at night and I'm trying to study, but even with Damon's bedroom door closed and my AirPods in, I can hear the three of them bickering. As I pause my playlist, classical versions of my favorite rock songs, I overhear one of them suggest a fight club night.

I can't deal.

I never thought I'd miss that old, lonely house, but right now, I'd take that over this chaos, no questions asked. I pick up my phone and text Brennan. When I first left the house, I'd sent him a quick text explaining that I'd be staying with some fellow students while we worked on a big research paper. It was the first thing I could think of in the moment. He replied with a quick, "okay" and "talk soon."

That boss of his is working him to the bone. Since his response came days ago, I figure I'll try again. Might as well while Damon is occupied.

> Me: Heyyy, miss you! Just checking in. I forgot to mention, I haven't seen Mischa around. Everything okay with you guys? Anyway, call me when you can.

He usually doesn't stay out of the country this long. I can't help but worry.

A thump and groan from the living room has me springing up and out the door. Leon has Damon's head sandwiched between his thighs while Damon swings his arms, attempting to land a gut punch. Motionless in White is playing from someone's phone, loud enough that it's distracting.

"Tap out already," Leon groans, adjusting his position. "You know I won, just say it."

"And let you lord it over my head? Fuck no." Damon squirms, bucking his legs.

With my hands on my hips, I stand there observing like I'm at a zoo enclosure. "What's going on out here?" I finally ask.

Jasper strolls in from his bedroom in nothing but a pair of

boxer briefs. Maybe it's wrong, but I can't help but ogle him for a few seconds. Damn, he's buff. Like jumped off the pages of a magazine buff. Those abs, that Adonis belt… I need to look away.

"Blake, you wanna judge?" he asks, stretching his arms out in front of him.

"Oh, I'm already judging… You didn't have to ask." Leon loosens his grip and Damon mounts him, landing a punch to his face. "What the—"

"Nice hit," Jasper says through a burst of laughter. Then he turns to me, "It's fight club night. Someone's gotta keep score."

Is he serious?

"I'm not going to sit here and watch you guys beat the shit out of each other." But as the words leave my lips, Leon calls time. They break apart, panting heavily, strip off their shirts and grab sips of beer. They're sweaty and tattooed and there's abs… So many abs.

Okay, maybe I can watch for a few minutes.

"Right now they're in a time-out but anything goes. Except biting… Leon has a hard limit against that. Oh, and we can only use knives that are less than three inches long. Keeps us from hitting anything important."

They're all crazy. Every one of them.

"Wait? You're not going to fight, are you? Your shoulder isn't fully healed," I ask Jasper, glancing behind him at the other two, who've started grappling again.

"Of course I am. I always fight the winner." He leans in and whispers, "Because I'm the undisputed champion of fight night. Except for this one time… Actually, I'll save that story." He ruffles my hair and chugs his beer, swiping his hand over his wet lips. "Come on D, finish him," he yells.

Leon groans. "Hey, fucker, why are you rooting for him?"

"Gotta keep things interesting," he answers, shrugging. "Plus, I want to kick his ass in front of his girlfriend."

I open a window to air out the pungent scent of sweat that's now filled the apartment and suck a deep breath in.

"Jesus fuck," Damon yells as Leon gets a hit in.

Jasper's laughing like a hyena, Leon's making suggestive groaning noises, and Damon's cursing while dabbing at his busted lip.

Do I let this continue? On one hand it is mildly entertaining. But on the other these man children will most definitely injure themselves. And I don't have time to stitch them up. I have assignments to finish.

Seems like I should intervene.

Damon's straddling Leon, choking him out with Jasper to their side, yelling, "Tap out! I need in."

Bending over, I whisper in Damon's ear. "I need you inside me." Then I brush a kiss along his lobe and walk slowly toward his bedroom, looking over my shoulder when I reach the door.

He jumps off Leon and pats Jasper on the shoulder. "He's all yours, brother. My girl needs me."

"Fuck yeah," Jasper yells while Leon starfishes, groaning. "But who's gonna keep score?"

"Couldn't care less. I have better things to do." Damon comes up behind me and wraps me in his arms. He bends to whisper in my ear. "I'm going to rinse off. Get on that bed on your hands and knees. I'm hungry for dessert."

He swats my ass, leaving me standing at the doorway, breathing like I just conquered a flight of stairs.

"If Blake needs some warming up, I volunteer," Jasper yells to Damon's retreating frame. He flashes me a salacious grin and adds, "Just say the word, and I'm in."

I let loose an awkward laugh. "Damon would cut your penis off."

"Nah, we've shared before. Many times, actually. Tell her, buddy?" Jasper nudges a still slumped Leon in the shoulder.

"Not getting involved," Leon answers.

"That's because you know I'm right." Jaspers grabs a hair tie from his wrist and grimaces as he tries to pull his hair back. He flashes his bright blue eyes my way and asks, "Can you help me out? My shoulder's bothering me."

"And yet you're about to get into a physical fight with Leon?" I scoff and bend down to where he's kneeling on the floor. "Give me the hair tie."

I try to be methodical as I gather his hair into my palm. Those aren't butterflies in my stomach. Yeah, Jasper is insanely hot. All three of them are. But I'm with Damon and I have to live here. Whatever Jasper's insinuating will only cause trouble.

"That feels good, Blake. Your hands are magic. Fuck, even when you stitched me up you made me feel good."

"I don't know what to say to that. Thanks?" I finish pulling his hair back into a bun at the crown of his head. Being this close, I notice he has a dagger tattoo on the side of his head, partially hidden by his shaved undercut. Without thinking, I run my nails over the coarse hair to get a better look. Jasper hisses a breath and I jump back a step. "Sorry, I saw your tattoo."

"Don't be. Like I said, magic hands.You can touch me whenever and wherever you want." His eyes lock onto mine, icy blue and so intense I can't look away. "Come on over here. I never got to properly thank you for saving my life."

Leon sits up, leaning back on his elbows. His keen eyes rake me over, quietly watching and waiting to see what I do next. I bounce my gaze back and forth between them while the fluttering in my stomach ramps up.

"I-I didn't. It's fine, I just did what anyone would do." I fidget with the hem of my shirt, my fingertips feeling like ice against my flushed skin.

"You're not just anyone, Blake. You're Damon's girl. And that makes you special. Right, Lee? Leon nods and stretches his neck from side to side. "Do you know what that means, sweetheart?"

"What—what does that mean?"

"It means you're our girl too. You're ours to protect." My breaths come in uneven pants as I look to Leon for some kind of confirmation.

"That's right," Leon adds.

"Ours to care for." Leon swallows audibly as Jasper continues. "Ours to play with."

My mind is swimming. There's at least a dozen beer bottles lying around, and I know Jasper's on meds. Leon's way too quiet right now and Damon... He's taking the world's longest shower.

"You're just drunk and on an adrenaline high. You don't mean that."

I startle as Damon speaks up behind me. "What doesn't he mean?"

"Nothing," I say. "We were chatting about fight club night."

Damon scrutinizes both guys and pulls a hand through his wet hair. He looks directly at Jasper. "You want her, don't you? You want to fuck my girl?"

Jasper tilts his head to the side and raises his shoulder, the picture of nonchalance. Meanwhile I'm over here soaking my underwear and freaking the hell out. Damon messes with the towel wrapped around his waist, while he and the guys have some sort of silent conversation.

"I'm going to bed," I say. Whatever's going on with the three of them, I can't get involved. It's late and I'm turned on and tired and a mess.

"Blake," Damon says, making me pause. "Get on your hands and knees."

CHAPTER TWENTY-TWO

BLAKE

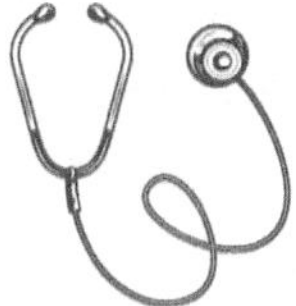

"What? Out here?" He can't be serious. Although nothing about the set of his brow or the intensity in his gaze makes me think he's joking.

"Yes, out here." He drops his towel and I inhale sharply, roaming my eyes over his hard length. He closes the space between us.

"But, the guys," I whisper. "They're watching."

Jasper's behind him, eyeing us with wide eyes and parted lips. While Leon still looks unbothered. Bored, even.

Damon tips my chin up, dripping water onto my chest from his damp hair. "Does that bother you? Or does it turn you on? I won't let them fuck you. You're all mine."

I swallow, attempting to moisten my dry mouth. His voice alone makes my body react. I try to wrap my head around what he's asking of me. "But you want them to watch?"

He raises his voice so the guys can hear him clearly. "Yes, and I think you do too. Your face is flushed and I bet your pussy is soaking wet."

Closing my eyes, I let that fantasy play out in my mind for a moment. The guys watching Damon pound into me from behind. Did I want that? Knowing Damon, he'd kill them for laying eyes on me.

"You'd let this happen?"

"They're my brothers. We take care of our own. So yes, I'd let them watch. But *only* them and only when they earn it. Anyone else so much as looks at you and they'd have all three of us after them. Now be a good girl, Blake, and let Jasper undress you." He nods at Jasper, and Jasper closes the distance between us.

"Come here, sweetheart. Let me help you out of those clothes."

Adrenaline pulses through my veins but instead of cowering to the rush of fear, I embrace it. This isn't the first time Damon's influence caused my body to react with nervous excitement, and I'm sure it won't be the last.

I turn to Jasper on trembling legs. Damon watches from the couch, urging me. "That's it, baby. Lift your arms for him."

I can't meet Jasper's gaze as he softly pulls my oversized T-shirt up but I hear his sharp intake of breath clearly. The cool air hits my exposed skin and my nipples pebble immediately beneath my lace bralette. Jasper's fingers skim my collarbone and I bite back a moan.

"No touching, Jas," Damon says, his voice strained. "Her pants now."

I keep my eyes trained at Jasper's chest so I'm not tempted to look at him. I know if I do I won't stop him from touching me. Doing whatever it is he wants.

He tugs the drawstring of my lounge pants and pulls them loose. They fall to the ground easily. Jasper ghosts his fingers down my legs, urging me to step out of the pants. I know my underwear are soaked. I'm just waiting for him to notice so I can swallow down my embarrassment.

"Look at you. You're a fucking snack, Blake," Jasper says as he floats his fingers over the straps of my bra. "Has anyone ever told you that? How truly pretty you are?"

"Of course I have," Damon chimes in. "I tell her every fucking day."

Tears prick at the corner of my eyes. It's hard to hear their words, to accept their compliments and praise. But I hold it together. I'm strong and I want this.

"You can take off my bra," I say, feeling bold. I glance back at Damon. He's breathing heavily and nodding in approval. "My underwear too."

"Goddamn sweetheart, if you could feel how fucking hard I am right now." Jasper groans and slips his fingers beneath the straps, pulling my bra over my head. He doesn't waste time or linger, just moves right to my underwear, sliding them down my damp thighs.

"Isn't she incredible, boys?" Damon asks, a rasp to his voice. "Our girl."

Leon, who's been quiet up until now, says, "Perfect."

"Come here, baby," Damon says. "Let's show them how pretty you are when you come for me."

Damon's hand falls to his erection and he gives it a slow pull as he stands from the couch. I'm throbbing everywhere. Needing touch, release. And God, I want him inside me, filling me. He pushes the coffee table to the side, scattering piles of paper on the floor, so there's nothing between the guys and the couch where we stand.

His kiss is rough, like he's claiming me. Sucking my bottom lip between his teeth and nibbling. I part my lips, letting him delve inside me, steal my breath.

I wrap my arms around his neck, grinding against him, as he bites his way down to my collarbone. I'm barely able to stand from the intensity. "Oh God, Damon."

"She likes that," he says to the guys. "My angel can handle it rough."

I almost forgot the guys were watching but the reminder has me tense, holding him tighter.

His teeth graze the swell of my breasts and I lean my head back to give him better access. He sucks and bites my nipples, marking me. I know I'll have bruises tomorrow. And when he finally slides his hand between my legs, I almost lose my grip on him. He toys with me, barely brushing my clit. Again and again, until I'm shamelessly grinding against his hand.

Damon sucks my earlobe, making me shiver. He whispers, "Imagine how it would feel to have Jasper eating your pussy right now, baby. Devouring that cunt while I fuck you from behind. Mm, maybe one day, but not tonight. Tonight you're all mine."

He bends me over the arm of the couch and slaps my ass until I cry out. I keep my head turned, facing the back of the couch. I'm not ready to see Jasper or Leon's faces as they watch.

"She's soaking wet. Do you like being watched? Should my boys fuck their fists while I pound into this sweet cunt? What do you think, baby?" Damon sounds crazed, his words tumbling from him in a rushed whisper. He plunges a finger inside me and slaps my ass again and holy crap, I'm so close to coming. "Answer me, Blake."

He lifts my hips and spreads me wide, so I'm on display for them, circling my clit with the exact pressure I crave. I know he wants an answer, but I don't know what to say. Do I care what they do? We're well past any kind of normal friendship now, so what does it matter?

"Yes," I murmur. "Yes to it all."

"That's my perfect slut," he says with another spank that has me biting back a moan. "Don't disappoint her, boys. She wants us to come together."

He pushes into me, inch by inch, filling and stretching me. Thrusting with the same turbulent energy as his words. God, it feels so good. Like I'm being worshiped and punished at the same time. I love every second.

"Feels so good," I say against the cushion.

"Speak up, Angel. Get that beautiful face out of the couch and watch them. Look what you do to them." He reaches for my hair and tugs, lifting my head a few inches from the couch until I cry out. "Tell her."

"I'm so close, Blake," Jasper says, breathless. "You take him so well."

The sounds that fill the air are utterly erotic. Groans and wet slaps of skin. Finally, I open my eyes and force myself to watch them as they stroke themselves. The looks of painful pleasure in their eyes set my skin on fire.

Leon bites his lip, fisting himself rough and fast. I catch glints of metal along his shaft and imagine what he would feel like inside me. What they'd all feel like together. Their eyes devour me while Damon pumps harder and faster and, I can't take anymore. It's too good.

"Y-yes, I'm gonna come."

"You can come when I say so, Blake." He slows his thrusts, pulling all the way out and bringing his hand around my neck. "Watch them, baby. We all come together, remember?"

I nod, panting. "Please."

He lines himself up against me as his palm tightens. "Please, what? Tell me."

"Don't stop," I wheeze.

"Good girl," he says, palming my ass and spreading me wide. I gulp in a breath, as much as I can with the pressure on my neck. I should be scared but I'm not. If anything, I'm more turned on than I've ever been. He's careful with me, controlled, especially now that he's slowed his movements.

He pushes back into me and the room fills with frenzied groans and hissed curses. Some of them come from me, sounds I never knew I could make. I'm overwhelmed with sensation.

Jasper and Leon's eyes are on me, holding me captive. Damon's hands are everywhere, his cock deep inside me. My body slams against the couch, knocking against the wall. I've never felt so alive.

Leon groans and Jasper says, "D, I'm close."

"Me too," he says as he reaches down and rubs my clit. "Squeeze my cock, Blake. Come on me."

He presses in and I cry out as my orgasm hits me hard. So hard that I'm shaking all over, my stomach clenching and hands gripping the cushion. I force my eyes to stay open and watch as both guys finish on their stomachs. It's so hot, it takes me a second to notice Damon still behind me, panting and massaging my ass cheek.

"Fucking hell. That was incredible. You're—"

Leon cuts in, out of breath but clear. "Ours."

"That's right," Jasper says. "You belong with us."

Tired laughter slips through my lips as Damon pulls out and gathers me against his chest. His lips meet mine in a gentle kiss. Nothing like the fervor he had five minutes ago. "Don't forget it."

AFTER AN HOUR of pleading with the guys to let me go alone, I'm waiting at the train station for Falin. She took a flight into the city, then a train here, arguing that she didn't want to inconvenience me for an airport pickup on my birthday week. I'm not a child. I don't need a whole week for my birthday, but according to Falin, "that's utter bullshit."

As the train squeals to a stop I jump up from the bench and

search the crowd exiting onto the platform. It's been so long, I don't even know what color her hair is now. She's notorious for dying it every other month—growing it out and chopping it off too. I wonder if her big shot tech job lets her keep all her bright colors.

Feeling nervous that she missed her flight, I check my phone for a missed call. I'm swiping through notifications from everyone but Falin, when a pair of hands cover my eyes from behind. "Guess who?"

Screeching, I twist around to face my best friend and wrap her in the biggest bear hug I can muster. "You brat, I was getting worried."

"Nah, never worry about me. I'm like Gandalf, I arrive precisely when I mean to." She plants a wet kiss on my cheek, most definitely leaving an imprint of her dark red lipstick behind and holds me at arms length. "Look at you, Bee. You're literally glowing."

I hold back a grin. "Really? I'm stressed the hell out, but I'm happy you're here."

She narrows her eyes and says in a mock-stern tone. "You've been fucked recently. I can tell."

I clutch my chest and feign shock. "What? There's no way you can tell that from one look."

"I can. It's a skill. I call it my fuck-dar. You know, like radar, but for fucking." She shrugs and pulls her duffle bag higher on her shoulder. "You should already know this. Remember how I knew about your first time with Ethan? Speaking of, does he know I'm here? I'd prefer as little time with mommy's boy as possible."

We walk side by side toward my car, the sound of crunching leaves filling the silence as I think of what to say. "I'm not with him anymore. I didn't want to tell you because I know you'd flip out and cut your work trip short to come here, but I caught him cheating on me at the end of the summer."

She freezes and drops her bag. "You're shitting me? That asshole cheated on *you*? Ethan? Mama's boy who wears shirts with sailboats on them?"

A soft laugh bursts from me. "Oh God, I forgot about that shirt."

"Take me to him. I'm cutting his dick off." She clenches her fists and lets out a harsh breath. "No, that's taking it too far. I'll kick him in the balls instead. Let me just change into my combat boots."

"It's really okay, love. I'm over him. Seriously, him cheating was the kick in the butt I needed to move on. Plus, I've met someone else." I can't help the grin that spreads across my face.

"Oh my God, my fuck-dar is never wrong. You better tell me everything." We reach the car and she tosses her stuff in the back before getting in. "Who is he? How did you meet? Dick size? Can he use it?"

I shake my head and turn the car on. "I'll tell you everything. Let's get lunch. I'm starving and you must be too."

"I don't like this new coy Blakey. Yes, you may feed me, but I require answers or I'll tickle torture you into telling me."

"No way, I'll tie you up first." I hate being tickled and she knows it, hence why she uses it as a last resort to get information out of me when I'm being tight-lipped. Evil demon that she is.

"Oh, that sounds like a good time. Torture and ropes. My kind of night." We erupt into laughter as I pull onto the street. Through my rearview, I catch a glimpse of a black muscle car and roll my eyes. Not that I expected anything less from Damon. He was already overbearing and that was before we found out about me being a target.

"So how's Brennan? Are you liking living with him again?"

Falin opens the window and rests her palm against the outside of the car.

"He's good. Super busy, like you. I think he's somewhere in Asia as we speak. I miss him. As much as I love how far he's come with his job, he never gets any downtime." As all of this tumbles out, I realize how I've been avoiding thinking about Brennan lately. It hurts too much to know I have one blood relative left and he's just out of reach. After losing everyone else, I wish I could keep him close.

"Why does he work so much? I guess that's a dumb question coming from me, but we're at different places in life. Doesn't he want to settle down? Start a family with what's her name?"

"Mischa," I say.

"Yeah, her. Miss Friendly." She's not wrong.

"He wants to pay my tuition even though I've told him again and again that I'm fine taking out loans. He won't hear it. And I have no idea what's up with him and Mischa. To be honest, I'm pretty sure she's cheating on him. Or maybe they have an open relationship, I don't know." I shrug and turn onto Main street.

"Can't wait to meet her," she says sarcastically.

I find a spot right in front of the restaurant and dig through my purse for some spare change for the meter. "About that. There's a slight change of plans for sleeping arrangements."

Falin tilts her head, eyes questioning. "What do you mean?"

"We can't stay at Brennan's. It's not safe there. I'll get into all the details but yeah, I highly doubt you'll meet Mischa." Plopping a few quarters into the meter, I reach for Falin's hand and pull her forward. She's staying put like a stubborn toddler in a toy aisle.

"Where will we stay then? Should I call and book us a hotel room?" Her voice is laced with concern.

"Well, that's entirely up to you," I say, feeling nauseated all the sudden. "Depends on if you're okay with staying at my boyfriend's place with his two hot roommates?"

"Blake Alexandra Hyland, you're telling me you've been living with this new boyfriend and his two roommates, my fuck-dar is going wild, and this is the first time I'm hearing about it?"

"Did I tell you how much I love your hair color? Platinum really suits you," I say sweetly.

"Don't change the subject, brat. Once your ass is firmly planted in a chair in that restaurant, you're telling me everything or said ass will have an imprint of my size nine combat boot."

I hold up my hands in surrender. "Okay, no need to get dramatic. I'll tell you everything. But first, should we book a hotel room?"

She rolls her bottom lip between her teeth and says, "That depends on a few things. What did you say they looked like?"

"I can't with you," I say, laughing and pulling out my phone. "I'll text Damon, my boyfriend, and have him send me pics of the guys, Jasper and Leon. But Fal, you gotta promise not to mess around with them. Things are..." I hesitate. "Complicated."

"I'm about to full name you again." She narrows her eyes. "Come on, let's go eat before I beat your round ass."

"Remember it's my birthday week." Smiling, I bat my lashes at her.

"How could I forget?" she says with a smirk. We're seated at a table in the back and out of habit, I scan the place for anyone I recognize. Not two minutes after we're seated, the door opens, and all three guys walk inside.

I guess I don't need pics now.

CHAPTER TWENTY-THREE

DAMON

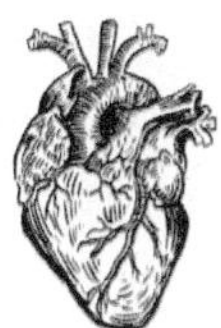

BLAKE'S GLARING AT ME FROM ACROSS THE RESTAURANT like I knew she would. Too bad, though. I'm not going to take any chances. Not after our cameras picked up the same car outside Blake's house multiple times in the past two days.

I won't tell her. There's no reason to get her more stressed and upset. It's her birthday week and I want to make it the best one she's ever had.

"Are we going to pull up some chairs and join them?" Leon asks. "Or is this a covert thing?"

"She already saw us come in, so we may as well join them," I answer.

"Sweet, I'm starving. What do you think's good here?" Jasper grabs a menu from a table occupied by some young college kids and flashes them a shit eating grin. "Besides Blake."

I punch his arm, not caring that it's his "bad" arm. At this point, I'm convinced he's milking it for all it's worth. Either that or those painkillers he's still popping work too well. We reach the table and Blake's friend, Falin, slowly turns her head to look us over.

"What are you guys doing here?" Blake asks, irritation in her tone.

"Don't be rude, Blake. Introduce us to your friend," Jasper cuts in. There's nothing discreet about the way he checks Falin out.

"Do you mind if we grab some chairs and join you?" Leon asks, laying on the charm.

Falin and Blake exchange a silent conversation—all wide eyes and raised brows. Finally Blake relents. "Fine, I was just telling Falin about you guys actually, so I guess the timing isn't terrible."

"All good things, I hope?" I grab a chair from a vacant table and squeeze it in as close to Blake as it can get, resting my palm on her thigh. She tilts her head onto my shoulder so I can brush a kiss on her cheek.

"We haven't gotten to the good parts yet. I'm Falin Sinclair, by the way." She scrutinizes each of us with smoky gray eyes. "You're obviously Damon," she says to me. "And I'm guessing the huge blond is Jasper." She turns to her side where Leon's just pulled a chair beside her. "And you're Leon?"

"Good guesses," I say.

She shrugs. "I've always had a way of reading people. Grew up with a family of cops, even the ones who aren't blood related. The chief is my godfather, the entire department showed up to my college graduation. Some things are just second nature."

"Intimidating... I like it." I glance at Leon and can already see the wheels in his head spinning. Falin could be a huge asset in finding Bailey.

"Can you handle a weapon?" Jasper asks.

She rests her chin in her palm and smirks at Jas. "Of course I can. Big, small. I can and have handled them all."

The server stops at our table to take our order and in the

distraction, Jasper leans and whispers loud enough that both Blake and I can hear. "I think I'm in love."

"Absolutely not," Blake scolds through closed lips. "Hands off my best friend."

"Aww, sweetheart, are you jealous? Don't worry, you're still our best girl." I raise a brow in warning just as Blake kicks him in the shin under the table. "Ow, Christ! What are those, steel-toed boots?"

"No, but thanks for the idea," she says with a mischievous smile.

We order lunch and right away Leon and Falin fall into conversation about the tech world. It's nice to see Leon being talkative. He's been so reserved lately. Jasper and I can barely get a few words out of him that aren't about work.

I whisper to Jasper, "You may have some competition, buddy." He scoffs but throws Leon a dirty look. Damn, I love stirring the pot.

"I was thinking, maybe it would be okay if Falin and I stay at Brennan's. I won't be alone there, and you guys can keep an eye on things," Blake suggests.

"No way. It's not safe for either of you," I say. Jasper chimes in his agreement beside me.

"What's going on? Why wouldn't it be safe at Brennan's?" Falin asks.

Blake answers before any of us have the chance to. "There's these people, bad people, who might be after me. They left a stack of photos outside my door the other day."

Falin's tone grows solemn. "Why the hell would people be after you?"

Blake meets my gaze and I nod. "They're targeting her because of us. This group must have figured out that Blake and I were growing close, so they're trying to intimidate us, but don't worry, nothing will happen to either of you."

"Do I want to ask why they're after you guys?" Falin doesn't beat around the bush. I like that in a person.

Leon nods my way and Jasper says, "Tell them."

"I can't tell you everything, not here, but long story short... Jasper's sister, Bailey, was taken about a year ago. She was out with some friends and left for the night but never made it home. Once the police did everything they could, which was absolutely nothing, we left school and now we spend our days trying to find her." I pull my hand through my hair and release a breath. It's been a while since I've talked about Bailey, not unless I was pulling information from someone strapped to a chair with my gun to their temple.

Blake squeezes my hand and murmurs an apology. This is news to her as well. I let her in on aspects of what we do, but not the full story.

"Let me guess... Your methods aren't exactly on the up and up?" Falin asks.

"It's nothing you need to worry about," Leon answers. "We have everything under control and we're closer to finding her than we've ever been."

Falin locks eyes with Blake, conveying messages silently. "I'm sorry for your loss. I can't imagine how difficult it must be. If Blake's good with it, I don't mind staying at your place."

The tension in my chest lessens and I rub circles with my thumb over Blake's thigh. "What do you think?"

"If we can steal your room then I'm good," she says with a smile. "And you guys gotta give us some space to breathe. I have a long weekend off from classes and my best friend is here. This might be the only chance I get to enjoy myself until the holiday break. Even then I'll be studying."

The server drops our plates in front of us one by one and we thank her before digging in. Falin takes a sip of soda between bites and says, "That's why I'm here. All work and no play makes Blakey a dull girl."

"*The Shining*. I love that one," I say.

"I prefer *A Nightmare on Elm Street*," Blake adds, winking at me.

I smirk at her. "Keep it up. One of these days, you're going to regret saying that."

"Why do I feel like we're talking about more than movies?" Jasper says, darting his eyes between us.

"No reason," Blake says as she tucks a strand of hair behind her ear. She's too damn cute and she knows it.

Falin watches our exchange with a grin. "This weekend is going to be so much fun."

MY ARM IS slung around Blake's shoulder as we head out to our cars. The hardest part of my days are being apart from her, but I know she wants to settle in with Falin, and we have some shit to do.

"We have to check on a few things. Go right to the apartment and lock up when you get there." Wrapping my palm around the back of her neck, I bring her in for a kiss. "Be good and if you see anything at all or even get a weird feeling, call me."

I walk them to Blake's car and open up my app that detects GPS trackers, releasing a breath when I find her car clear, with the exception of my own device. I've been checking it multiple times a day. Can't be too careful. Once I buckle her in safely and watch them pull away, I turn to the guys.

"One of you can drive. I'm too fucking anxious." My sweaty palms would slide off the steering wheel.

"Fuck, you never let us drive your car. You wanna talk

about it?" Jasper asks. I toss him the keys and he hops in the driver's side. Leon climbs in the backseat and I sit passenger.

"Blake will be okay," Leon says. "I have cameras all over the place. I'll get alerts if a leaf falls within their boundaries." He pats my shoulder but I shrug him off.

"I'm fine. Let's just go and get this over with." Leon shakes his head and leans back in his seat. I know I sound like a dick. Like finding Bailey isn't important to me anymore. And fuck, maybe that's partly true. It's been over a year of this and I'm worn the fuck out. Blake's brought me back to life and there's no way in hell I'll lose her. Not for Bailey, or anyone. If that makes me a shitty friend then I don't care.

The rest of the car ride to Blake's house is silent, each of us stewing on our own thoughts. We hop out and start a perimeter check, although everything looks clear from the driveway. I pay extra attention to Blake's bedroom window, testing it to make sure it's still secure.

"Is Ray meeting us here?" I ask Leon. He texted us earlier saying he has an update.

Leon checks his phone. "Girls just got to the apartment." He smirks and adds, "And apparently they bought out the liquor store."

"Lemme see," I say, grabbing his phone. There they are, getting out of the car with bags on their shoulders and bottles of wine clutched in each hand. "Should be an interesting weekend."

Leon chuckles. "Interesting is an understatement. I have a feeling Falin brings out a side of Blake we haven't seen yet."

He might be right. If so, I can't wait to see. Every side of my girl is perfect—her shy side, her feisty side, her nerdy side. She's got me by the balls.

"About Ray? Is he showing up?" I remind him.

"I'll text him now and tell him to meet us inside." He types the message out and leans against the house. "I fucking hope he has good news. It didn't sound like it though."

I brace myself for the worst, but that doesn't stop the pit from sinking deeper into my gut.

Jasper finishes his side of the property and finds nothing out of place. We head inside and do the same. There's a musty smell in the main spaces, like it's clear the house has been empty for a while. It's lifeless without Blake's presence. Where the hell is her brother and his girlfriend?

Ray texts Leon that he's outside, so we finish up and gather around the kitchen island. Ray looks nothing like the middle-aged, washed-up, off-duty cop that I thought he'd look like. He's taller than Jasper and built like a linebacker, maybe only in his thirties or early forties. He's got a heavy New York accent, clear as day from the first words out of his mouth.

"Nice office you got here," Ray says, looking around the place. "You know why it's been empty for so long?"

"Blake, the one that they're targeting, is staying with us. This is her brother's house. He and his girlfriend are traveling for work."

Ray nods and scratches the stubble on his chin. "Something don't seem right about that. Your girl... she say that's normal behavior for her brother?"

"Yeah, as far as I know," I answer.

"Well, try to get more outta her. Not like these rich folks to leave and not even hire a gardener or cleaner." He swipes his index finger along the baseboard and rubs it between his thumb.

"What do you have for us?" Leon asks. Jasper quits fucking around on his phone and locks in.

Ray pulls out his phone and zooms in on a photo of a car. The same one we caught on camera. Only this time, he has a clear shot of the plate number. "Followed this car when I saw them poking around. They took me on quite the scenic journey." He swipes through a few photos of Blake's campus, Main Street, and finally the front of our house.

My heart beats out of my chest as Leon holds his hand out to stop him from scrolling. "When was this?"

"Yesterday," he says. "That's your place, ain't it?"

"Fuck!" I kick the cabinet under the island. "We need to get back."

"Wait, there's one more thing. You know this girl?" Ray swipes to the next photo and it's an image of a woman, long, straight brown hair, dressed in scrubs. I narrow my eyes, and it hits me. "Shit. Yeah, she's friends with Blake. Her name's Julie."

"Well, I'd check in on her. She had a few followers yesterday, nothing nefarious looking but I don't trust 'em."

I lock eyes with Jasper and he nods. "Ray, we're going to need all the addresses from yesterday and anything you can get on that plate number."

"Sorry man, I checked and the plate's a dead end. One of them fakes that are popular in the racing community."

My jaw is clenched so tightly it's beginning to throb. "We gotta go back to that club. I know it's been a ghost town but we should see if the car matches anything around there."

"I can do that," Leon says. "Why don't you and Jasper go check on the friend?"

"What about Blake and Falin?" Jasper asks. "I don't feel right leaving them unprotected."

"They can come with us," I say. "I'll text her now."

"Anything else you need from me today?" Ray asks. "I got a hot date in a few hours, and I need to get myself ready. Jerk off a few times so I last."

I spy a wedding band on his left finger. Poor lady doesn't

even know what she's in for... or maybe she does. She did marry the guy. "Taking the wife out?"

He catches me eyeing his ring and chuckles. "Nah, she's at home with the kids. This one's young and hot. Just turned twenty-one." He rubs his hands together and smirks. "If you need me tonight, you don't. If you catch my drift."

My fists are balled at my sides as Leon places a firm hand on my shoulder. "Have a good night, mate. Thanks. I'll call you when we find something."

Ray leaves and we settle on a plan before heading out. Leon will scout the club again. Now that he has a solid photo of the car, maybe we can make a match. Bonus points if we see the asshole who drives it. Blake and Falin aren't thrilled about having to come with us, but I used my powers of persuasion.

Before long, we're heading to Julie's apartment a few blocks from campus. I notice how close it is to Ethan's. "Is this campus housing?" I ask Blake.

"Sort of. It's mostly grad students that live over here," she says. "What exactly are we looking for?"

"You're gonna go check on her," I say. "Tell her you need notes or something."

"You really think this girl could be in danger?" Falin asks. "I never expected to be living a shitty episode of *Law and Order* on this trip."

Jasper cackles beside her. "Good one."

"Should I call her first?" Blake asks. "It feels weird showing up unannounced."

I think it over but decide on the element of surprise. If she's in danger, they'll be watching her phone. "Nah, we can play it off like you forgot your phone at home." She nods as we park a block away. "Alright, I'll go with Blake and you two hang out around the corner of the building. Check for any cars matching the description."

I slide my gun into my jeans and go around to open Blake's door. She's chewing her bottom lip, but otherwise staying strong. I lean in and whisper, "If we see anything in there, you run like hell, okay, baby? Run to Jasper and he'll take care of you."

"Yeah, okay." Her voice is a worried whisper. I pull her into my arms and kiss her forehead.

Julie's apartment is on the ground level, easy enough to access. Blake squeezes my hand before ringing the bell. "I don't even know if she's here."

"We'll see in a second," I say.

When there's no answer, I knock hard a few times and Blake calls her name. The pain in my jaw draws its way down my neck and into my shoulders. Blake turns the handle but it's locked. "What should we do?"

"Step aside," I say and give the door one more pound with my fist. When I don't hear footsteps, I take a step back and kick the door in as hard as I can. It flies open with a bang. "Julie!"

"Julie, it's Blake."

Music plays from a room down the hallway, and I lock eyes with Blake, mouthing for her to get behind me. Pulling out my gun, we stick to the sides of the wall and follow the sound. The door's closed, but I recognize the music... It's Nickelback. Fucking weird choice. I put up my fingers and count down from three with Blake's wide eyes watching my every move.

At one, I twist the handle and peek inside before busting the door wide open. There's Julie, ass naked on her back, with none other than mama's boy Ethan, fucking her with a dildo from the bottom of the bed. They jump out of their skin, the dildo flies out of Ethan's hand and smacks the wall, and Julie screams louder than a cat in heat.

"What the fuck is this?" Ethan yells, throwing a blanket

over Julie. Then his eyes widen as he spots Blake behind me. "Bee?"

"Oh my God, Ethan? What's going on? Julie, you're with him now?" Blake swivels her gaze from each of their guilty faces and then around the room. There's a camera set up on a tripod facing the bed.

"What the hell are you doing in my apartment?" Julie screeches. "Get out!"

I cross my arms and look Ethan over. He's still in his boxers... Too bad, I would have liked to see my handiwork. I can tell the second he recognizes me. His jaw drops and his eyes pop out of his head. "You?" He points an accusatory finger. "You're the asshole from the bathroom!"

I smile and alter my tone so I come across as playful. "I don't know what you're talking about. I've never seen you in my life."

"Bee, are you with this psycho?" Ethan's voice trembles.

Blake flashes me a smile and I sling my arm around her shoulder. "Yup. And this psycho treats me like a queen. Better than you ever did."

"Why are you still here?" Julie yells. "Ethan, make them leave."

"Enjoy him, Julie," Blake says. "He's all yours."

"What's left of him," I say, leading Blake out of the apartment. Once we're outside, I hold her close. "You okay?"

She releases a deep breath and attempts a smile. "I really am. I think I needed that. Now I don't have to feel an ounce of guilt about him."

"You never did. He's the scum of the earth, Angel. And he'll never bother you again." I wrap my fingers into her hair and pull her in for a kiss. Her lips are so fucking sweet and so is the way she melts against me.

"Sucks about Julie," she says as we walk toward where

Jasper and Falin are waiting. "You were right about her, I guess."

"You're making me hard. Say it again," I tease.

She rolls her eyes. "You were right."

I moan suggestively and she breaks into laughter. "Come on, let's go do something about this boner."

"You're absolutely insane," she says.

I stop and press her against the wall of Julie's building, letting her feel what she does to me. "Insane and all yours."

CHAPTER TWENTY-FOUR

BLAKE

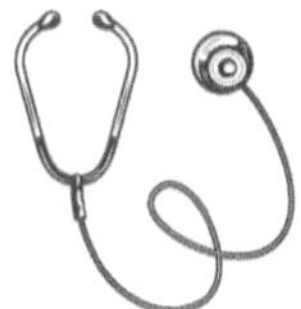

My laptop calls to me from across the room. I haven't taken this much time off from studying in years, but Falin's keeping a watchful eye and has threatened to bludgeon me if I try to work.

Speaking of Falin, her and Jasper are in the kitchen fighting over the correct way to make gluten-free pancakes. They've been at each other's throats over one thing or another since we got back last night. I seriously need to get her out of the house.

Damon slips into the bedroom, holding something behind his back. He's so damn cute when he's being mischievous. "Happy birthday. Falin told me you were up."

I rub my eyes and feel a slow smile spread across my cheeks. "Thank you. Come snuggle, I missed sleeping with you last night."

He holds out a bouquet of the most beautiful flowers I've ever seen. They're a deep purple color, so dark that from far away they look black. In his other hand is a black box. "These are just the first of your gifts," he says with a grin as he settles onto the bed beside me.

"These are gorgeous. I've never seen flowers like this before. What are they?" He sets the vase down on the side table and pulls out a single stem.

"They're called black beauty peonies. The color reminded me of your hair." He sets it on the pillow beside my head and leans down, brushing a kiss across my lips.

As he sits up, he studies me, like I'm the subject of a painting. I feel warm and exposed all at the same time. My voice is hoarse as I thank him, but I hold the wave of emotion back. It's my birthday, a day to celebrate, not to get all choked up.

"Open the box." I scoot up and take the box from his shaky hands. I've never been great at receiving gifts or compliments. It's something that I'm working on, especially since the guys came into my life. "I hope you like it."

"It's from you. I know I will." My face flushes as I open the lid of the box revealing a gorgeous silver anatomical heart necklace. Carefully, I remove it from the velvet pad insert and take a closer look. "It's beautiful, I love it."

"It's a locket. Let me show you." He holds his hand out and I place the heart carefully in his palm. "There's a vial inside, filled with my blood."

He hands it back to me so I can take a better look. It's a bit morbid, but that's Damon. "Does it mean something?"

"It means everything. I wanted you to have a part of my life force so I'm always with you. Wearing someone's blood means you share a spiritual bond. There's a magical quality to it. Back in the day people would carry locks of their loved one's hair in jewelry or sew it into clothing, but this is better." He gestures for me to turn around, gathers my hair to the side, then fastens the necklace around my neck. It hangs in the exact spot Bryan's thumbprint would. I force myself to stay in the moment, thinking about Bryan or Mom would get me upset and that's the last thing I need when Damon's being so sweet. "There," he says. "I'd gladly spill more blood for you, Angel. Every part of me is yours."

I inhale a ragged breath and pull him close. "Thank you. This is the most thoughtful gift I've ever received."

He holds either side of my face as our lips brush together, gentler than normal. My eyelids drift closed as our tongues tangle and explore. He touches his tongue to my lips, tasting me before delving deeper, capturing my breath.

Everything fades away—the noises from the kitchen, the stress of studying, the chaos of whoever is after us. There's only Damon and me. He tugs my lip between his teeth. I hiss a breath and match his energy, sucking his bottom lip and nipping.

"I want you," I murmur between kisses while sliding my hand under his shirt. "Please."

Damon pulls back. I notice his blown pupils and heavy breathing. Seeing what I do to him makes me bold, like I can take what I want. He tugs his shirt over his head and I splay my hands across his chest, tracing over his tattoos. I'm aching for him, and I know he feels the same way from the bulge in his sweatpants.

I wrap my palm around his length, making him groan. "Lay back. I haven't had breakfast yet."

He palms my stomach and pushes me against the mattress, settling his legs on either side of my body. I reach for him, but he holds my hands together, pinning them above my head. "Please," I beg, lifting my hips against him, searching for relief.

"Shh, baby," Damon whispers. "Just lay back and let me take care of you."

I let my hands drop onto my pillow as Damon slides down my body and slips his hand into the waistband of my under-wear. I raise my hips and let him pull them all the way down and off my legs. I'm shaking with anticipation... literally dying for him to touch me, taste me, anything.

His finger glides along my slit, stopping and circling my clit until I buck my hips. "You're so wet." He pops his finger into his mouth and sucks. "I've been thinking about your delicious cunt every damn day."

"Oh, God," I moan. My entire body's attuned to his touch. Alive and on fire.

"Be a good girl and spread wide for me." He groans as he buries his face in my pussy and presses his tongue against my clit. "Fuck, Blake, you taste so fucking good."

He sucks my clit and flicks with his tongue, starting slow and matching the rhythm of my hips as I grind against him. I know I'm completely drenching his face, but I don't care. It feels too good to care about anything else.

He slips a finger inside, pumping like he's fucking me. "Damon, I'm close... Please, don't stop." He clamps down, sucking my clit and my orgasms barrels through me. I hold his head in place, my nails digging into his scalp as I ride it out. "Oh my God... That was—that was... I don't even know," I say, panting hard.

When I release his hair, he stays put, tasting every last drip of my juices. "Fucking incredible," he says, kissing up my body. "I could live my entire life between your legs."

My eyes grow heavy as he climbs beside me, laying on his back. He pulls me into him, and I rest my head against his beating heart. "I don't know if I could handle that. I'd probably black out."

"Should we test that theory today?"

I kiss his chest and sit up slightly. "I think Falin would break the door down."

She most definitely would. Nothing will get between her and executing her birthday plans. Not even Damon.

I trail my hand along his torso and slip it under the waistband of his pants, teasing the base of his cock. "Blake."

With a smile, I nuzzle and kiss the crook of his neck, basking in the way his body tightens and voice cracks. "Damon."

I tighten my palm around his length and stroke slowly from base to tip, drinking in the sharp intake of breath from his lips. "Baby, you don't have to—" My thumb circles his tip, gathering the moisture and spreading it lower. His arms tighten around me and he raises his hips into my hand. "Fuck... come here."

Smiling, I pull my shirt up and off and straddle him. I love getting my way. He pulls his pants down and shifts me, lining his cock up with my entrance. The way his fingers dig into my hips, moving me exactly where he wants me, like he's a desperate man. God, I can't take another second without him inside me.

"Use my cock. Ride me until you come." He guides his cock inside me, and I get adjusted to his size, inch by full inch, until I'm fully seated on him. "That's it. Fuck, you feel so good like this."

I roll my hips, angling my pelvis so my clit rubs against him. "Yes... feels so good." He sucks my breast, nibbling my nipple until it aches. I feed him the other one, loving the delicious sting of his teeth while I shamelessly ride his cock. I use him, just like he told me to, chasing my orgasm fast and rough. There's nothing sweet about it. It's raw and primal. Our skin sliding against each other, the groans that escape our lips, the bite of fingers and teeth.

I think I hear banging on the door, but it sounds far away. We're a vacuum, a bubble. There's only us and the pleasure we chase. "I'm close... Oh, God."

Damon pushes his hips up, pumping into me. He's so deep, I swear I can feel him in my chest. "You're gonna be so full of my cum that it'll drip out of you all damn day. You want that, baby?"

"Yes, please. Come in me." The image of his cum dripping down my legs fills my mind and I lose control. My entire body shudders and squeezes as I come, screaming his name. Damon's grip on my hips tightens and he lifts me up and down on his cock before groaning and holding me down.

His jaw tenses and his eyes clamp shut as he comes inside me. "Fuck, Blake... Jesus Christ."

Collapsing against his chest, with my ear to his racing heart, I'm so damn elated I could burst. I'm drunk on him. I'll never get enough of the way he looks when he comes. Or how he responds to my touch, to being inside me. It's addictive and I'm afraid that he's changing me. I've never felt this out of control before but I'm too far gone.

"Same." I let out a laugh against him and toy with the locket around my neck. "This is the best birthday I've ever had and it's only 10 AM."

"I'm glad. You deserve the best always." Warmth spreads through my chest as we lay in peaceful silence. That is, until Falin bangs on the door again.

"Are you two done? It sounds like you are. We made breakfast and it's getting cold."

"We should probably go out there," I say. My cheeks heat knowing they all heard exactly what was going on in here. Falin's going to tease the crap out of me.

"You sure? You only came twice. I think you have one more in you." He slides his hand across my chest and between my legs where I'm dripping wet, pushing a finger inside. "I'm keeping this cum in there as long as possible."

That's so damn hot.

"Blake Alexandra, get your sexy ass out here!" Falin yells.

Damon sighs and brushes a kiss across my lips. "Is she always like this?"

With a wide grin I say, "Yup. Unless she's drunk, then she's even louder."

"Fun." He gets up to grab our clothes. "You want to eat in here? Breakfast in bed?"

The thought is so sweet, but I'd much rather be with everyone. "No, it's okay. I'm ready to get up."

We eat the rubbery pancakes and bacon, while Jasper and Falin continue to argue. It's wildly entertaining. If Jasper think's he's going to get to Falin, he has another thing coming. Leon's in a good mood too, smiling more than I've seen since I met him. When I look at the guys, I still get flushed thinking about them watching us the other night. They haven't said anything about it, so I've felt weird bringing it up. I'd have to know what I want anyway, which I don't. So it's best to leave it be, a hot memory that makes me clench my thighs from time to time.

"What do you want to do today?" Damon asks as he swallows a bite of pancake. "Anything you want, it's yours."

"We're going shopping this afternoon," Falin cuts in. "We need to find the perfect outfits for the show later."

"Show?" Damon asks.

"Yeah, I forgot to tell you. Falin got us tickets for this haunted burlesque show tonight. It looks fun. Maybe there's still tickets available if you guys want to come."

Falin raises her brows. "Nope, no way. This is girls night. I know it's your birthday, Blakey, but tonight is all ours."

I shrug and mouth *sorry* to the guys.

Damon narrows his gaze at her. "What exactly goes on at a haunted burlesque show?"

"No idea. That's part of the fun. There's a dress code though, thus the need for costumes. You think you can give us one day, lover boy? If it makes you feel better, give me your gun. I can keep Blake safe." Falin leans back in her chair, making direct eye contact with Damon. Long enough that even I start to get uncomfortable.

Then again, I'm not one for confrontation.

Damon rubs his chin and we share a look. "Enjoy girls day." He goes into his wallet and pulls out a few bills, handing them to Falin. "Whatever Blake wants, she gets."

I almost spit my water across the table. "Damon, you don't—"

"Blake." From the way his eyes blaze, I know there's no arguing with him.

Falin stands and brings her plate to the kitchen. "Alright bitch, let's go shopping."

WE HAVE the best time hitting the Halloween store in town, then heading to the mall nearby for some finishing touches. Once we were shopped out, we stopped for lunch at Leaf and Ladle and Falin surprised me by having them bring out chocolate cake the size of my head. When the server told her they don't usually sing happy birthday there, she proceeded to sing her own loud, out of tune rendition that included amazing additions like "you smell like a skank and you act like one too." I think her love language is embarrassing me.

The unexpected part of the day was that Damon actually gave me space. Not one text, call, or random appearance. At least not that I saw. I was having too much fun with Falin to be hypervigilant. But maybe I was used to his clinginess, because all day I kept touching my locket and wishing he was there with me. I wondered which costume he'd like best, and when I saw a

Freddy glove, my heart flipped. I bought it, of course, excited to hear his sarcastic remark when I give it to him.

While I was out, Brennan texted me to wish me a happy birthday. It was a quick back and forth but he promised he'd call me tomorrow. At least I know he's alive and kicking. That's all I could ask for on my birthday.

Back at the apartment, the guys are playing some first person shooter game in Jasper's room while Falin and I get ready. We're blasting My Chemical Romance and singing the lyrics at the top of our lungs. She pulls some of my hair back into a teased half pony and adds some volume to the rest. I feel like we're back in college, dancing around our room to emo music while she forces me to abandon my studies and go out for a few hours.

With my hair and makeup done, I slip into my outfit—a black lace corset and gothic burgundy and black skirt. I slide on some fishnets, and my combat boots, and accessorize with a choker and some bracelets, along with Damon's necklace.

"Last but not least," Falin says, handing me the box of real-istic-looking fangs we bought earlier. "Let me know if you need help."

She puts on her own at the same time and then we finish off the look with a few well placed drips of fake blood. I finally take a look in the mirror and can't believe that I'm the person staring back at me. I look hot—like holy shit, I'd bang myself, hot. And so does Falin, but that's nothing new, she always looks amazing.

I guess the stress of school has really gotten to me lately. Other than the gala, I haven't seen myself in anything other than comfy clothes or scrubs and definitely haven't worn makeup like this in all the years I dated Ethan. He hated when I'd dress too provocatively, or wore unnatural looking makeup, even on Halloween. That was one of the things that turned Falin off of him right away.

"You look hot as hell, Blakey. We're going to get so many free drinks tonight." She sprays a light mist of hairspray over her head and touches up her black lipstick.

"Don't we have a bunch of money left from what Damon gave us?" I ask.

Falin tilts her head and smirks. "So? That doesn't mean we can't accept free drinks. Come on, I've got you. Just have fun tonight and don't worry about a thing."

Right. Pretty sure those are her famous last words.

Damon knocks and comes into the bedroom holding a cake. When he sees me, he freezes in place. His eyes flare in surprise and I get the knee-jerk reaction to grab something to cover myself. Bracing for the harsh words that I'm certain will come, I look at my feet and wrap my arms around my chest.

He closes the space between us in two steps and tips my chin up. "Let me look at you." His slow perusal of my body has my skin tingling and when he flashes a hungry smile, my stomach flutters.

"Isn't she fucking hot?" Falin says, turning from the mirror to watch Damon's reaction.

"Hot doesn't even begin to cover it. Holy hell, Angel. You're a walking wet dream." I smile, showing off my fangs and he reaches out to feel the tip with his index finger. "You're keeping these on later."

His hand trails down my neck and over the swell of my barely contained breasts. "And this... all of it."

"That can be arranged," I say, standing as tall as I feel. "What do you have there?"

He hands me the gorgeous cake on what looks like a vintage stand. "Mrs. Langston dropped it off for you earlier. It's allergen friendly, she made sure of it."

"That was so sweet of her. I'll have to go thank her later. How did she know it was my birthday and about the allergies?"

He smirks. "I obviously talk about you to everyone I can. Poor women's probably sick of my gushing."

I laugh and put the cake stand on the dresser for now. "Oh, I almost forgot. I got you a present."

"What? But it's your birthday," he says, bewildered. I pull the Freddy Krueger glove out of the bag and hand it to him with a grin. As soon as he sees it, he shakes his head and lets out a short chuckle.

"I had to," I say. "Try it on!"

Falin's watching this exchange with her hands on her hips, looking at us like we're crazy. Which we are, so it's fine.

He slides the glove on, and clicks it together in front of my face until I'm laughing and pushing him away. "You're so in for it now. Just wait."

"Okay, well, whatever weirdness this is unfortunately needs to end. We've gotta get going or we'll be late," Falin says.

I brush a light kiss on Damon's cheek, leaving a smudge of my dark red lipstick as Falin grabs my hand and pulls me out of the room.

"I'll walk you guys out," he says. "I don't mind driving you there. What's the address?"

"We're good," Falin answers. "If we drink too much we'll just Uber back."

Damon meets my gaze and I interrupt Falin before he has a chance to argue. "I'll call you if we need a ride."

I had to park down the street since parking is limited with all of us in the house, so it's a few minutes walk to the car. Damon's hand is in mine, keeping me tethered to the present. The crisp night breeze chills my skin but I feel alive, like the whispers of the wind hum with possibility. Dry leaves scatter across the road in front of us as we reach my car. Damon's grip tightens and he pulls me behind him.

"What's wrong?" I ask before I see what he's already noticed. My car is completely wrecked.

CHAPTER TWENTY-FIVE

DAMON

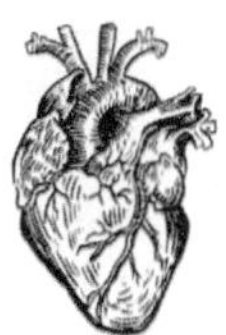

"Absolutely not. You're not going." I've been arguing with Falin for ten fucking minutes about her and Blake still going to their show.

"Unless we're calling the cops, I don't see what sitting around is going to do. I'm sure you guys will have everything under control. It's still Blake's birthday. I don't want this to ruin her day." She's hugging Blake, who's still staring at her car in shock.

Sure, we have everything under control... If she means we have absolutely no fucking clue who's screwing with us. Anger rises to the surface but I tamp it down before I do something I'll regret, like punching the other fucking rearview mirror out.

Whoever did this, made it look like nothing more than a hit and run. The entire driver's side was sideswiped with enough force that the door was crushed in. I called the guys right away and they're heading over to help me get it off the road.

"Do you really still want to go out?" I ask Blake. The last thing I want to do is let this ruin her day, coincidence or not.

Falin holds Blake at arms length and whispers something

low enough that I can't hear. Blake nods. "Falin's right. Unless we're going to call this into the police, there's no reason for us to sit and wallow all night. We got all dressed up and I still want to enjoy my birthday."

Of fucking course she'd say that. I lean against the car. My leg vibrates while I think. "Fine, but I'm coming with you." I see Falin start to open her mouth so I cut in. "That's the only option. I tried to tell you earlier, Blake's not safe right now. So it's either I go or she stays."

The whoosh of a car driving by startles Blake enough that she gasps. Whether she wants to admit it or not, she's rattled and that's not okay. Our eyes lock and she nods, finally agreeing with me. Not that her insistence on a girls shopping trip stopped me earlier. Blake was never out of my sight today, not for a minute.

Once the guys show up and we move the car into Leon's spot, I grab my keys, open the door and watch the girls get settled while I smoke a quick cigarette.

Leon heads over, Blake's keys in his hand. "Meet you there?"

"Yeah, but be discreet. I don't want them getting pissed. But you're with me, right? There's no way this was an accident."

He shrugs and glances back at Blake's car. "Hard to tell, but given the circumstances, we shouldn't take any risks."

"Jasper went back upstairs?" I ask.

"Yeah, I think he needed to grab his meds or some shit but don't worry, we've got your back."

I pat him on the shoulder and crush my cigarette under my boot. I'm anxious as hell but have to keep my shit together for Blake. We'll go to this show, come home, and I can finally give Blake her real gift. Nothing else better fuck that up.

WE ARRIVE AT THE VENUE, a large tent set up on the local fairgrounds. It's packed with people, all dressed in costumes. Some went all out in full makeup or masks, one dude is walking around on stilts. Nervous laughter and screeches from guests waiting in line fill the air, along with an ominous music track coming from hidden speakers.

Falin pulls Blake ahead, both giddy with anticipation. "This looks so fun! Oh my God, look at that guy's costume." She's pointing at someone dressed as the headless horseman. Even I admit the costume is pretty sick.

Flickering jack-o'-lanterns and fake cobwebs decorate the space while scare actors walk around tapping unsuspecting guests on the shoulder. They better not touch Blake. I'm in no mood for that shit.

"Let's take some selfies," Falin says, pulling out her phone. Her and Blake mush together and take a few pics with the tent as their background. "Damon, want one with Blake?"

I clear my throat. We haven't taken any photos together as a couple. Blake has no idea how many I have of just her. "Of course."

I pull her in, and we smile for the camera. Then she turns to kiss my cheek, but I move in time to capture her lips. Tasting her has my stomach muscles relaxing, my body feeling relieved. I'm trying my best to give her space to be with Falin, but it's so fucking hard.

When we break apart, I hear someone whistling behind us in line. "I luuuv a pre-showww," the guy slurs. He's about six feet tall, dressed in a pirate costume and swaying on his feet, clearly drunk. "Kissss 'er again... thisss time facin' meee."

"Lay off the rum, Jack Sparrow," I say through gritted teeth. Falin still has her phone out, most likely recording.

"Myyy baaad." He holds his hands up unsteadily and stumbles a step closer, knocking into the group of people directly behind us in line. "But if ya don' wan' people ta look... then do tha' shit at... at home, ya know?"

Blake grabs my hand and squeezes. "It's not worth it." She's right, of course, and I need to be here for her. If I punch this prick in the face, I'll get kicked out. "I think I smell cider. Can you grab us some?"

I huff and glance behind us, checking that the drunk pirate is done running his mouth. He stumbled back to his spot in line, thankfully. He's lucky he backed off. I nod and ask if they want anything else, before ducking under the ropes and walking in the direction of the food stands. I fill my lungs with the scent of smoke and spices that linger in the air, letting them calm my nerves. I could use another cigarette but I don't want to let Blake out of my sight.

I reach the stand and order three spiked hot ciders and some kettle corn, paying with cash. While I wait, I check my phone.

Leon: We're here. Jas is pretty messed up from his meds. Don't know how much help he'll be, but I'll hang out around the line. I got us tickets too.

Me: Perfect, thanks. Keep an eye on a pirate behind us. Guy's fucking wasted and shooting off his mouth.

Leon: Got it.

The line's moving by the time I make it back to them with our drinks. Once inside, we find seats close to the front. It's set up like a circus, with a large stage in the middle and seating all around. The entire tent is bathed in red light, while fog machines spew mist that creeps heavy along the ground. That eerie music is louder in here, even over the chatter of at least a hundred people. Blake's legs vibrate with excited energy as she drinks her cider.

"This is so good," she says. "A few of these and I'll be buzzed for sure."

I drink some of mine and feel the warm burn slide down my throat. She's right, they didn't skimp on the booze. This many people in such a crowded space makes me uneasy. It was different when we were outside, but in here, it's like the tent is swallowing us whole. A couple dressed as zombies squeezes past us and slides in next to Blake, so close that their thighs touch. I grab her hand and gently tighten my hold, taking another long chug of my cider.

"You okay?" she whispers against my ear.

"Yeah, fine. It's just crowded in here." She wraps her hands around the back of my neck and pulls me in for a soft kiss. I breathe in the scent of her hair, and savor the taste of her lips, feeling my pulse calm.

"'Nother freee showww," a slurring voice says behind us. *Fucking perfect.* I don't need to turn to know it's that pirate asshole again. He makes obnoxious kissing noises and moans, "Kissssyyy... *hic*... kissshyyy."

All the things I'd like to do to him play through my mind like a slow motion montage. How I'd drag him out of this tent by his throat and throw him down in the dirt. I'd pluck his eyes out one by one for daring to look at Blake. The sounds of his screams would be my own personal symphony. I'd let the notes float in the air until I cut his pathetic tongue out and shove it down his throat.

Blake runs her fingers through my hair, scratching my scalp with her nails and I blink, coming back to the present. "Look, I think it's starting."

A spotlight shines on a guy dressed in full skeleton paint as he takes center stage. "Creatures of the night, welcome to *Nightmare Manor*, where vampire vixens and sinister sirens will bewitch and entrap you with their unholy appeal. Where ghoulish glamor and macabre masks will awaken your deepest and darkest fantasies. Our spectral performers and phantom entertainers will titillate your senses and chill your bones. Witness acts that defy both gravity and mortality, as our dangerously alluring cast blurs the line between ecstasy and terror. Exciting, isn't it? But heed my warning: those with the blackest of hearts will find themselves a permanent home inside these walls. If your soul remains pure, untainted by the seductive darkness that permeates this place, you'll find the exit to your right. For the rest of you... well, we hope you'll enjoy your stay in eternity."

Blake and Falin clap along with the rest of the crowd, but I'm still seeing red. That fucking pirate is hollering behind me, yelling obscenities.

"Our first performer is the lovely Mistress of Shadows with her act, The Vampire's Embrace." Skeletor leaves the stage and the lights blink then turn to a low blood red hue.

Images are projected onto the canvas walls, creeping shadows and flickering lights while a haunting melody begins to play. A gorgeous woman with thick flowing black hair, wearing a long gothic dress, not unlike what Blake has on, glides across the stage. She moves in slow, hypnotic motions, swaying her hips and drifting her arms in come hither gestures.

"Holy shit, she's hot," Blake whispers, squeezing my hand. I can't help but smile.

"Not as hot as you," I say, resting our entwined hands on her thigh.

As the music builds her movements follow. She crawls along the floor, stalking her prey, and removes a layer of skirt.

"Taaaake it offff baaabyyyy!" the pirate yells, before whistling with two fingers in his mouth.

"What a fucking tool," Falin says, loud enough that the couple to our left snickers.

The show continues, the dancer unbothered. But I'm fucking seething. Pricks like him shouldn't share space with people like Blake. The dancer leaps and lands in a seductive split, tossing her hair for added effect. The music rises to a crescendo and she pulls a bewildered man from the front row, placing him in a wooden chair on the middle of the stage. She dances around him, toying with him, pretending to bite his arm before backing away. Removing another layer, now in nothing but a corset and panties, she glides to him and as the music ends she bites his neck seductively, pulling back to show herself covered in blood.

The crowd roars; even I clap. But I'm distracted by the pirate, grabbing onto the head of the person in front of him and using them as leverage to stand. I watch him sway through the row, toward the exit.

Without another thought, I lean in to Blake. "I'm going to go grab some more drinks. Be right back."

She nods and focuses her gaze ahead, clapping as the skeleton man enters the stage. I make my way out of our row slowly, not drawing attention to myself. I know I should leave it alone. He's nothing but a drunk asshole who doesn't deserve my time or energy, but I'm wound so tightly, my skin prickling for the release that only comes from violence.

With my fists clenched at my side, I shuffle by a few patrons, heading outside, my eyes trained on one figure alone. I see him, heading to the food and drink area and the tingle of anticipation rises in my chest. Keeping close behind him, I get in line at the small booth selling booze. It's nothing more than two costumed young women behind a few folding tables, with coolers and canteens filled with cider.

"Neeeed a whis... key... dub-ble. An' a beeeer... none a' that im-por-ted shiiiit. Gimme... gimme a Coorsss." The two women make eyes at each other and one of them, dressed as a sexy witch, speaks.

"Sir, I'm going to need to get our manager. We're not allowed to overserve here. Please step to the side and we'll be with you in a moment." She gestures to the person in front of me but the pirate isn't having it.

"T' fuuuck izz thisss shiiiit!! I'm a payin' cuss-tomer an' I wan' my god... goddamn driiiink!" He leaks spittle from the corner of his lips and bangs his fist on the table. The women step back, one of them making a call on her phone.

I've had enough. With my sweetest smile, I cut in line and speak to the witch. "Hey, I'll take care of him. So sorry about that. He's my uncle, not all there in the head. Can I get a beer and I'll keep him out of your hair all night?" I pull out a few twenties and lay them on the table. "For your trouble."

She nods, glancing back at the pirate, who's uttering curses and stumbling around, before handing me a can of Bud. I thank her and step beside the pirate. "T' fuuuck you wan'? Ohhh... it's luvvver boyyy... where'sss yer preeetty girlfrienddd?"

I sling an arm around his shoulder and show him the beer. "Look what I got you. You want this beer?" He grabs for it, but I tsk at him. "Come on over here, let's find a nice quiet place to cool off."

I lead him away from the booths, toward the darkened part of the fairgrounds, using the beer as a lure. Once we're far enough away that the noise of the show and the hushed voices of the patrons outside fade away, I crack the can and hand it to him. I grab a smoke out of my pocket and light one up, taking a long drag.

"Got 'nother?" he asks, pointing to my cigarette.

I hold it in front of him. "You want a smoke?" I ask, slowly enunciating each word. The pressure in my chest is ready to erupt, I can't hold back anymore. When I look at him I see his leering gaze all over Blake. I hear the wet, sloppy kissing sounds he made while looking at her.

I reach into my pocket like I'm grabbing my smokes but pull out my switchblade. I move faster than he can comprehend in his drunken state, jamming my knife into the front of his hand and through his can of beer. He opens his mouth to scream but I cover it with my free hand, my cigarette burning close to his nostril. "Listen closely, you piece of shit. You're going to leave this place, go to whatever shithole you call home, and take a good hard look at your life. If I find out you're disrespecting women again, I'll show up when you least expect it, and next time, I won't be so forgiving."

His gurgled moans slip through the cracks of my fingers as I yank my blade out. Blood spills from his wound mixed with beer from the leaking can. I release my hand and he immediately squeals, wrapping his injured hand with the other. "Shii-it... you... you fuckin' stabbed meee. Heeeelp! Heeelp!"

He gives me no choice; what a dumb fuck. I push my cigarette against his uninjured hand, putting it out before knocking him upside the head with the handle of my blade. He goes down easily, face in the dirt where he belongs.

My shoulders relax instantly but my limbs vibrate with released adrenaline. I need to get back to Blake and Falin. They've already been alone for too long. With one last look at him, I pop a mint into my mouth and head back to the tent.

CHAPTER TWENTY-SIX

BLAKE

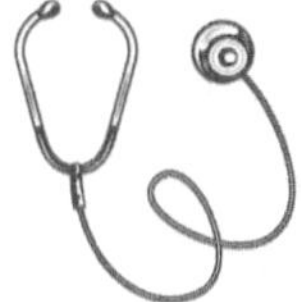

I have to hand it to Falin, she picked a winner this time. "That was incredible," I tell Damon, lowering my voice to add, "I'm super turned on."

"Yeah? Let's get out of here and take care of that." He circles my waist and pulls me in close. "Where's Falin?"

"No idea, she was just hitting the bathroom quickly before we leave. Let me call her." As I pull out my phone, I spot Falin in the crowd of people. "There she is, she's headed this way."

"And she's not alone," he says.

She's arm in arm with the skeleton man himself, while Jasper and Leon follow closely behind.

"Did you know they were coming?" I ask Damon. He bites his lower lip and gives me a guilty look. "You did! Were they here the whole time? Honestly, I don't mind. It's Falin who was all... *this is girls night*. Apparently she's changed her tune from the looks of it."

They close the distance between us and Falin pulls me from Damon's arms. "This is Blake, it's her birthday." She spins me around for the skeleton guy. "Blakey, this is Ian. He invited us to their after-party and I said we'd love to go."

"Um, hi," I say. "Great show... Especially loved The Haunted Marionette. Creepy." I shuffle my feet and try to think of a way to gracefully turn Falin's offer down.

"That's my sister, Meg. She's crazy good, right?" Ian asks. "You're all welcome. We usually hang out in the tent, party for a few hours after each show."

Damon meets my eyes and I silently convey my desire to do anything but that. "Thanks for the offer man, but I have some plans for my girl's birthday."

Falin opens her mouth to argue but I stop her with a hand to her chest. "You had me all day. Why don't you stay and have some fun?" I turn to Jasper and Leon with wide eyes. "The guys can stay and look out for you, right?"

I can see the miniscule changes in Falin's face that tell me she's relenting. She huffs and squeezes my hand. "Okay, you two have a good night. I'll need details in the morning."

Laughing, I hug her goodbye and thank the guys for staying. Jasper shoots daggers at Ian but follows him and Falin back into the tent.

"You good?" Damon asks Leon.

He nods, one hand in his jeans pocket. "I'll keep an eye on those two. Get home safely, and Blake, I forgot to give this to you earlier."

Handing me a piece of paper, he turns and strides away before I can thank him. Damon's smiling down at me, like I was just given a rare gem. He turns his phone's light on and points it at the paper. "Open it."

I unfold it and reveal a gorgeous drawing of me done in black ink. The likeness is incredible... I've never looked so beautiful before. I swallow the lump in my throat. "He drew this?"

"Looks like you've won Leon's heart." He plants a kiss on my forehead and takes my hand. "Not an easy feat."

"I love it. We'll have to buy a frame tomorrow." I'm overcome with a wave of joy. To have so many people care about me and shower me with love isn't something I'm used to.

"Anything you want," he says. "Come on, I have a surprise."

We drive with the windows down, my exposed skin bathed in cool night air. Damon's hand rests on my thigh and mine is tangled in the hair at the nape of his neck. Warmth blooms in my chest despite the goosebumps pebbling my arms. I have no idea where we're going, but I know there's no one else I'd rather be with.

We turn onto a dark, dirt road. Loose rocks ping underneath the car as Damon expertly avoids mounds of dirt in random spots. I watch the stark trees blur from my window as the car jostles me from side to side. The headlights illuminate a clearing in the distance, set up with a fold out table and a few camping chairs.

Damon parks and opens my door, leading me by the hand to the set up. "I found this place when we first moved here. It was a fluke, really. I needed some space from the guys, too much shit going through my head, so I took a long drive and somehow ended up here. Come sit, I'll go grab some stuff from the trunk."

I let my head hang back to admire the scattering of stars in the clear sky. Moonlight shifts through bare branches, providing the perfect amount of light. Damon comes up behind me and wraps a warm blanket over my shoulders. "Mmm, thank you."

"I'll start a fire," he says, plopping some logs down next to a ring of rocks. Within a few minutes crackling embers burst to life, throwing delicious heat against my chilled limbs.

Damon's quieter than usual as he watches the sparks pop in the fire's glow. I wish I could read his mind. See what's causing the lines etched in between his brows. Is he worried about me? Or Jasper's sister? What kind of plans is he making deep in the recesses of his brain?

"Ready for your present?" He rolls a branch between his palms and pokes the burning logs.

"You really didn't have to get me anything else." Although my curiosity is piqued.

"I know, but this is special. Hold on, I'll get it from the car." Standing, he drops the branch at his feet and passes me, wringing his hands together like he's nervous. This is a different side of Damon. It's endearing. Seeing his vulnerability makes him feel less all encompassing somehow. Like he's an actual human, with actual feelings.

He kneels in front of me, so we're eye to eye and I can't help but reach out, laying my hand on his cheek. "Are you nervous?"

His tongue darts out to wet his lips. "Yeah, I guess I am. I'm worried you're going to run when you see this side of me—my shadowed edges and broken pieces. But I want you to know every twisted, dark inch of my soul, Blake. With this gift, I'm showing you exactly who I am and what I'll do for the people I love. I just—I can't lose you. I won't."

I pull his head into my lap and gently stroke his hair. My heart's a thunderstorm rolling in my chest. I have no idea what he's about to show me, but I know it'll be something we can't come back from. "Freddy," I say to lighten the mood. "Look at me." His eyes meet mine, like burned copper in the fire's light. "I'm not going anywhere. As much as I've wanted to deny it, you've awakened something in me that I've kept hidden behind a wall of busy. I've used my packed schedule as a shield because I'm too damn scared to open my heart. It's been easier to hide my grief, keep going and going, a wave of constant motion. Every commitment, every task, every unnecessary hour of studying are just more ways to drown out what's deep inside.

Loneliness.

Heartache.

Insecurity.

But when I met you, saw the darkest parts of you, I knew I wasn't the only soul who felt the same ache and pain. We may be different on so many levels, but in here, we're the same." I rest my palm against his heart, feeling its steady rhythm. "I'm not going anywhere, okay? But this isn't me pressuring you to do anything differently. I'm happy like this, right now, under the stars with you."

He cups my cheek as he inches forward, claiming my lips with a searing kiss. He pulls back, brushing kisses down the slope of my neck. "We were made for each other. I've never known something more than I know that. You and me, we're it. We're forever, Blake."

"Yes," I murmur as an ache grows in my core. "Forever."

"Remember you said that," he says, planting one more kiss along my collarbone, and brushing my hard nipple with the pad of his thumb. He sits back on his knees and pulls his phone from his pocket. "When I asked you about Trevor," he begins, causing the blood in my veins to run cold. I focus on his lips moving, forcing myself to stay present. "Blake, I found him. I-I couldn't let him go on living a normal life after what he did to you."

"What did you do?" I ask, my voice trembling.

"We ruined him, baby. He was working at your old high school, day to day around kids the same age that you were. We made sure he'll never work around kids again. Here, take a look."

My stomach churns, but I take his phone with shaking

hands and can't believe what I'm looking at. It's Trevor, much older and thinner than I last saw him, propped up against a gym locker. He has a sign settled in his lap that reads: *My name is Trevor Matlin and I'm a pedophile. An abuser who preys on young kids.* I blink and read it again while tears form in the corner of my eyes. "I don't understand."

"Leon posted this to all the social media accounts in the school district and sent it to every email account in their database. He's cooked. There's no way that man will get away with what he's done. And if that's not enough, I have something else. Your real gift." He stands and pulls me by the hand. "I set this up last night while you and Falin were asleep. Didn't want you to see it and ruin the surprise."

We walk deeper into the clearing, the only light guiding our way comes from Damon's phone and the slivers of moonlight cutting between branches. He stops and points ahead about ten feet in front of us. I narrow my eyes and make out a human torso. "Is that a dummy? Like the kind they use in karate classes?"

"Something like that," he says, taking both my hands in his. "I wanted you to have some closure. A way to channel some of that festering pain and when you said the thing about the tattoo, I knew what I wanted to do."

He leads me forward, closer to the dummy. I can hardly hear my footsteps crushing dried leaves over my harsh, rapid breaths. "Oh, my God," I choke out. Stretched and pinned like some kind of twisted canvas, is Trevor's flayed skin. His barbed wire heart that's haunted my dreams since I was fourteen hangs dead center on the dummy's chest. "That's—that's what I think it is?"

"Yes. Don't worry, we didn't kill him, although I wanted to. If I could have carved out a pound of flesh for every year of peace he stole from you I would have, but Jasper made sure I kept my cool."

This is what he calls keeping his cool?

"I don't know what to say," I whisper through chattering teeth. Seeing that photo, the flesh of the man who took everything from me, it's too much. I turn my back and bury my face in my palms, forcing slow, deep breaths in through my nose. Damon rushes to me, pulling me into his warm embrace. I draw in his scent through my nostrils—mint and wood smoke. It helps to quiet my unsettled thoughts.

"Shh, it's alright, baby. I'm here, I've got you. I'll never let anything happen to you again." We stay cloaked in the comfort of each other's bodies, rocking side by side for a long time. Long enough for my breathing to slow and the storm clouds in my head to dissipate. He steps back, his hand still firm on my shoulders. "Do you trust me?"

It only takes a moment for me to think that question over before I nod slowly. How I've come to trust the man who first kidnapped me at gunpoint is something I'll one day ponder on a therapist's couch, but right now, tonight, he's one of the only people I trust.

He reaches behind his back and pulls out his pistol, keeping it aimed at the ground. "Have you ever handled a weapon before?"

I shake my head. "Never."

"Would you like to? I also have this." He pulls out a switchblade from his pocket. "I think it would be freeing for you to get it out. If you want to?"

My eyes dart between Damon's hands and the dummy. I force myself to look at that tattoo, feel the pain and remember the tears shed. Rage boils deep inside me like a powder keg ready to erupt and with a shaking hand, I grab the switchblade from Damon.

My eyes are fixed straight ahead, as my feet travel the distance like disembodied parts. My muscles shake with barely contained energy, one small out of place motion and I'll combust. I clench my fist around the knife's handle as the skin of the monster who ruined me comes into focus. All sights and sounds around me dull, and I let loose a scream from the recesses of my chest. My arm flies up and slams its way down, piercing the dummy again and again. "You piece of shit! Don't you know the word no? Why? Why me? Why did you do it? I loved you! I fucking loved you!" I scream and sob, impaling the knife into his skin until I can't see through the tears in my eyes.

Damon catches me as I'm about to collapse, wrapping his hand around the knife and tossing it aside. He cradles me in his arms and carries me back to the fire, murmuring words of praise with each step. "You're incredible. I'm so proud of you, Angel. Shh, it's okay."

Time passes in his arms until I'm finally calm enough to speak. "That was cathartic," I say, lifting my head from his shoulder. "Thank you."

"I didn't want to force you to do it, but I was hoping you would." He glances toward the clearing. "You did a number on the dummy over there. Doc stabs like a champ."

Wiping my eyes, I manage a small smile. "I guess I'll be able to cut it as a surgeon."

"Nice pun," he says. His long fingers stroke the escaped pieces of my hair.

"I just hope Bryan wouldn't be disappointed in me," I say, glancing up at the night sky. "I never told my family when it was happening. Bryan loved Trevor too much. They were together all the time, even had plans to get a place. All that changed when Bryan started using. I'm not even sure if Trevor stuck around. I kept myself away from home as much as I could. Extracurriculars, babysitting jobs, volunteering on the weekends. Anything to keep me from facing him or seeing the disappointment in their eyes. It's funny how you can be infatuated with a person one day and the next..." I trail off. I've said more than enough already.

"You can talk to me about it anytime, okay? All of it. Bryan, your mom. You don't have to carry your grief alone anymore." I imagine chipping off pieces of my grief like peeling wallpaper and pasting the pieces onto Damon like a collage.

"It's been a heavy burden," I say, releasing a breath.

"I understand. I lost my mother when I was in high school. Jasper and his family were there for me, helped me through it, but I don't think I've ever fully processed her death."

"You were so young. I'm sorry." The quiet is thick between us. "What about your father? Was he around?"

Damon chuckles. "Nope... I'm just another sad bastard with daddy issues. It's fine, really. My mother left me with the Shea's for over two years before I got the news of her passing. It was bound to happen. I think deep down I was always waiting to find out."

"And then not long after, Jasper's sister was taken?"

I watch the shift in his features, the wrinkle in his brow, the worry in his eyes. Losing Bailey has hit him harder than losing his own mother. From what I've learned about his relationship with Jasper's family, I can understand why.

"Yeah, she just started college as a freshman. She went out with friends one night to a party and never came back." He swallows hard, and continues to wrap his fingers in my hair. "I try to have hope that she's still alive out there somewhere but every day it's harder and harder to hold on. And fuck, I thought we had a solid lead when we came here. But clearly we're not cut out for this detective shit."

"Don't lose faith," I say. "I don't know what I believe in, whether there is a God, or universal being, or a giant unicorn dictator up in the sky." Damon smirks and some of the tension leaves his face. "I know you were brought here for a reason."

"Maybe that reason was you."

He fixes his gaze on my lips as he shifts me against his lap. I already feel his hard length pressed against me. My eyes drift closed and anticipation fills my veins.

But our moment is cut short by Damon's phone ringing like a jarring alarm in the quiet of the night.

"Ignore it," I say, bringing my hand down to cup his erection. He hisses and pulls me in for a kiss.

Finally the ringing stops as our kisses grow hungry. I tug my fingers through his hair, eliciting a moan.

Again, the phone rings, causing me to jump back.

"Fuck, let me see who it is." Damon sucks in a breath and pulls the phone from his pocket. "It's Leon. I'll just be a second."

"Go ahead," I say, about to push to stand until he circles my hips and keeps me firmly planted on his lap.

"Leon, what's up?" He leans his head back and groans. "Are you sure?" "Okay, we'll head over now."

"What's going on?" I ask.

"Leon got an alert from the cameras and it's going to take him a while to get out of there. They need a ride or an Uber. He wants us to go check it out. I'm sorry, we can continue this at home."

He walks me to the car and goes back to extinguish the fire and gather all our things, including the decimated Trevor dummy. Something about the urgency in Leon's request has me on edge.

"You think everything's okay?" I ask, once we start driving.

I can't help but notice Damon's tight grip on the wheel and sharp, focused gaze.

"Yeah, I'm sure it's fine."

The tightness of my chest says otherwise. I rest my hand on Damon's thigh and tell myself not to worry.

CHAPTER TWENTY-SEVEN

DAMON

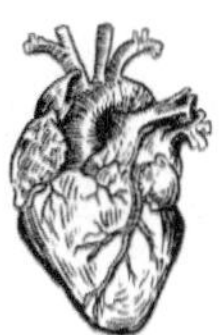

I block Blake with my body as we get out of the car. Something doesn't feel right. There's a stillness in the air that has my hairs standing on end. "Stay behind me."

With a trembling lip, she nods, following my quiet footsteps. I keep to the edges of the property, doing a quick sweep around. Finding it clear, I gesture toward the stairs, gripping my pistol as we round the corner.

"Wait here," I whisper, once we're standing outside our door. I let all thought leave my head and focus on the here and now, steeling myself for the worst. Slowly turning the knob, I peer into the apartment. "Hello! Anyone there?"

At first glance, the place looks exactly as we left it. Energy drink cans lining the counter. Breakfast dishes in the sink. Shoes left by the door. The place is dead quiet, more so than it's ever been.

I do a walk-through, checking each room thoroughly and finding nothing out of place. "Blake, you can come in."

"Everything's okay?" she asks, worrying her lip with her sharp canines.

"It looks like it." I peer out into the hallway again before closing the door. Something's off, I feel it in my gut. The way Leon called to interrupt my time with Blake was so unlike him. "I feel bad that we had to cut our night short."

"Don't feel bad. We have the place to ourselves. It's never this quiet in here." She arches her brow. "And I'm still wearing my vampire fangs."

"Does that mean I have you all to myself until sunrise?"

"Maybe," she teases. "But first..." She dips out of the room and comes back with her cake. "We owe it to Mrs. Langston to try her cake."

While Blake sets it on the counter and pulls out a knife, my gaze is fixed on the cake. I realize what feels so off. I felt it earlier but now it's like a neon sign in my face—the silence. Our nightly soundtrack of Mrs. Langston's soap operas blaring at full volume is missing.

"This looks amazing. Does she bake for you guys a lot?" Blake chats, while she cuts into the dessert.

"Stay here, I'll be right back." Without another word of explanation, I grab my pistol and hurry downstairs. She runs out the door to follow me. I should have known she would.

"What's wrong?" she asks frantically.

I bring a finger to my lips, gesturing that she stay quiet. If she's going to follow me down, there's no way I'm letting her get hurt.

We head outside and around to Mrs. Langston's entrance. I knock on the door with a heavy hand. "Dolores? Are you up?"

After a few seconds of silence, I twist the knob, finding it unlocked. Ushering Blake inside, I gesture to the corner of the living room, near her well-loved recliner. "Can you call Leon while I check the place?" She nods, her eyes full of fear. I don't let my gaze linger. The pull to comfort her is too strong. "Dolores?" I call again.

At first glance the place looks the same as always, until I reach the bedroom. Dolores is laid out on her back with a bullet hole through her skull. Bile threatens its way up my throat. "Fuck... Blake, don't come in here!"

I double over, letting loose a stream of curses. This is all our fault. We weren't here to protect her. We did this. I don't know what to do, but I can't leave her like this. With blurred vision, I glance around the room and find a hastily scribbled note on Dolores' side table.

I'll take what I'm owed with bullets and flesh.

Your move.

Blake's gasp pulls me to the present. "Oh, my God. Should I start CPR?" Her voice wavers but I can tell she's channeling her med school training. She rushes to Dolores' side to check for a pulse. "Sh—she's gone. Someone killed her?"

There's no sense in confirming what we both already know. "What did Leon say?"

She stands over her, holding her hand while tears stream down her cheeks. I don't have time for this, I need to take action. Pulling out my phone, I call Leon. He answers on the first ring.

"I'm trying to get out of here but Falin's somewhere with that skeleton guy and Jasper is nowhere to be found." Music filters through the speaker along with the incessant chatter of drunk partiers. "Should I leave them? What's going on?"

I step into the hallway and lower my voice. "Dolores is dead. They left a note. Just leave them, I need you here."

"Fuck," he draws out the word. "Alright, mate. Hang tight, I'll be there soon. In the meantime, I'll call Ray."

"Ray?" I ask. What the hell will he do to help us?

"Unless you think we should get the cops involved, we need him. He has a crew that handles this kind of thing."

"He's a fucking cleaner too?" I'm shocked. I guess our ex-detective isn't so by the book after all.

"Whatever you want to call him. It'll cost us though." He curses under his breath. "I'll need to call my father and get a wire transfer."

"No, I'm sure we can handle it." There's no way I want to involve Leon's sperm donor. We've gone this far without much direct contact with him. Leon gets his monthly stipend and that's been enough to keep us comfortable, along with the side jobs we take on.

"You got an extra hundred grand laying around that I'm unaware of? This isn't like the asshole in Palm Cove. Mrs. Langston needs a proper cremation. She deserves that."

Not only that, but New York lacks the necessary amount of gator-filled lakes. Florida was good for a few things.

"You're right." I blow out a breath. "Maybe we call this in? I'll take the note and we can claim we have no idea what happened?"

"What does the note say?"

I lean against the wall, desperately wanting to slide down and rest my head in my hands. "You can read it when you get here. Just move your ass."

THE NEXT FEW hours are chaos. Leon and I, along with Ray and his team, make sure every ounce of evidence from Dolores' place is secured. Ray has an in with a cremation worker at a funeral home a few towns over. He's promised to make sure she's well taken care of. After I say my goodbyes and watch Ray's guys drive away, I slump on her couch and rub my eyes. Leon joins me a few minutes later.

"Jasper's going to lose it," Leon says.

"I know." I light a smoke, inhaling with my head hung low. "You talk to your father?"

"Nah, I got his assistant, but she said he'll get back to me. I gave Ray a big chunk to keep him happy. He knows we're good for it."

As I watch the cherry burn, I say what I've been thinking for a while. "What if we just get the fuck out of town? I could try and get Blake to transfer schools. We could start a security business somewhere or pick up more of whatever the hell it is that you do. Fuck, we can even open a gym. I didn't hate that idea when we were playing around with it in Florida. Start fresh. Live our lives."

Leon stares at a framed photo of the Langston's when they were young for what feels like an hour. When he faces me, his eyes are rimmed in red. "You want to give up on Bailey? Just fucking pick up and start a new life with Blake? Go buy a house in a gated community, join a country club, play some golf? Well, fuck off. Bailey's out there and I refuse to give up on her. So go ahead, leave. If Blake will even go with you." He stands and makes his way to the front door but I jump up and block his path.

"What do you mean *if* she'll go with me? She will. This isn't just some hookup for me. I love her, man. You've gotta know how it feels to do anything to protect the one you love?" Leon's eyes simmer with unspoken rage. I realize what I've said and wish I could punch myself in the face. "Shit, sorry man. That's not what I meant. Listen, we're tired. It's been a long fucking day. The sun's about to come out already. Let's go get some sleep and talk about shit when we're rested."

"Does she even know what you've been up to? How she's not the first woman you've gone mental over? Does she know about the cameras and the pictures and your special secret box?" He scoffs. "Don't fucking tell me shit about love. You haven't got a clue."

He storms out the door and a few seconds later I hear the sudden roar of his bike coming to life. By the time I make it outside, the only trace of him is the distant buzz of his engine from down the street.

I stare after him, hoping with everything in me that he doesn't make a dumb mistake. We all can be reckless, that much has been proven time and again, but the Leon that I've known for years is slipping away. With Bailey being gone this long and whatever shit he's been dealing with from his father, he's different. Short-tempered. Withdrawn. I know I struck a nerve and I feel like shit, but he threw some low blows and now I'm in my head.

Maybe I haven't been as open with Blake as I should? Would she stay if she knew all the shit I've done?

Fuck.

I can't deal with this now. Not with Dolores' body still imprinted on the mattress and the fucks who did it still out there. I should be working with my brothers to figure this out, not fighting. That's on me.

Before I go upstairs, I pull out my phone to text Leon.

Me: I'm sorry, brother. I don't know what I was thinking. Be careful, alright?

Blake looks so serene asleep in my bed. Exactly where she should be. Her dark hair lay like a satin sheet beside her head. Her parted lips, still stained in fake blood, expel slow and steady breaths. In these still moments, when she's vulnerable and free from the mask we wear for the world, I'm drawn to her more than ever.

I quickly strip down and rinse off, letting the water beat on my tired shoulders. When I come back into the bedroom, I find the blanket shifted, revealing Blake's gorgeous bare skin.

After everything we went through today, my need to be inside her is overwhelming. To erase any distance between us, eliminate every molecule separating our bodies, so there's no telling where I end and she begins. The desire coursing through me is more important than breathing. At this point I'd rather asphyxiate than spend another second without her.

I pull the blanket down and climb in beside her, tracing her curves with a feather light touch. She murmurs and shifts closer, pressing her full ass against my cock. I was already hard from watching her sleep, but feeling her soft skin against me, I'm fucking done for.

I reach around and slide my hand into her panties, suppressing a groan when I find her wet for me. Spitting into my palm, I fist my cock and stroke, making sure I'm wet enough to slide into her with ease. My patience has all but run out. Pulling her panties to the side, I line my aching cock against her slit and push inside, staying still while her walls tighten around me. My muscles tense with the urge to pump my hips, but I sit with that need, letting our bodies relax before plunging all the way inside her, not leaving an inch between our skin.

I breathe through the urge to move but it's all-consuming. Seeing how quickly Mrs. Langston's life was snuffed out was the gut punch that I needed to wake the fuck up. We're not guaranteed a single second on this earth, and I'll be damned if I waste one night hiding who I am.

Blake is mine.

My fixation.

My singular reason for existing.

I'm fucking drowning and she's the air I breathe.

She has no choice but to accept who I am. I'll hold onto her with every fiber of my being. Keep her safe from the monsters of this world. I'd rather die, than live without her.

I wrap my arm around her waist and cup her breast, circling her nipple until it hardens into a perfect bud. She reacts to my touch with a murmur and slight shift. I brush the pad of my thumb over her nipple again and ever so slowly grind my hips. She feels too damn good.

I need to move.

To fill her.

To mark her as mine.

Biting my lips to keep from groaning, I hold her hips steady and slowly pull out to the tip. As she starts to stir, I push back in, using my grip on her hips to guide the movement. Her hand finds mine, and she squeezes.

"There's my angel. Waking up for my cock like a good slut." She arches her back and gasps as I grind into her.

Now that she's awake, I don't hold back. I can't. My thrusts are rough. Erratic. My hands are everywhere. Biting into her hips, molding her body to mine. Incoherent moans mix with the sound of skin slapping against skin. It's music to my ears.

"I need to fill you, baby. You're mine, you know that right?" I drive into her as I let spill every one of my obsessive thoughts. "I'll fucking watch you wherever you are. Have cameras on you. Kill anyone who looks at you."

She hums in response, sending me into a damn frenzy. Releasing those thoughts into the open air feels almost as good as coming. It's a release I desperately needed, only I didn't know it until this moment.

Unable to suppress my madness, I pull out, flip her onto her stomach and spread her wide, burying my face in her slick pussy. Her taste and the way she responds drives me wild. I lap at her entrance, gliding my tongue to her swollen clit.

"Oh my God, right there." She juts her hips higher, shamelessly grinding her greedy pussy against my lips until she's shaking and moaning my name.

I slide up her body and plunge into her again, hissing at the way she chokes my cock. "Your pussy is so fucking tight, Blake. Feel what you do to me. How you drive me crazy."

Ragged exhales leave my lips as I relentlessly pound into her. My eyes are half-lidded, clouded by ecstasy, but watching the way her body takes me, stretches for my thickness, demanding to be filled, is an out of body experience.

Hoarse moans fill the room, I'm so fucking gone, I don't know if they're coming from me or Blake. "Fuck, baby, rub your clit. Come for me."

Tingles run the length of my spine and my balls draw in tight. I'm so fucking close to shooting every drop inside Blake. I push her body into the mattress, locking onto the back of her neck as she quivers beneath me, pushing me over the edge. With a guttural moan, I still, coming inside her while her walls pulse around me.

I'm so goddamn spent that my vision blurs at the edges.

Keeping my cock inside, I roll us both back to our sides and crush Blake against my chest. She's trembling and breathing heavily but manages a hushed laugh. "What the hell was that?"

"I think you know what that was." I trail my fingers over the curve of her waist, tucking in closer.

"Damon?" Her hand covers mine and she brings it to her lips, kissing the center of my palm. "Are you going to stay inside me again?"

"You're asking questions you already know the answer to, Angel."

It's the only way I'll get any sleep tonight. Our breathing slows, and I feel myself drifting as Blake whispers, "Did you mean what you said?"

"Remember when we first met? What's one of the first things I told you?" I shift, feeling myself grow stiff again.

"That's a loaded question."

Brat.

"I told you I always keep my word. I choose my words carefully and always mean what I say." She's quiet again, so I add, "Why do you ask?"

"I'm trying to decide who's more messed up: you for all the things you said or me for loving it."

I let out a slow, sleepy laugh. "We're cut from the same mold, baby. Your light dances with my darkness to create the perfect shade of gray. There's nothing messed up about residing there in the in-between. The difference between us and all the other miserable souls out there is that we're not afraid."

"I guess when you put it that way, you're not wrong," she says, sounding as drowsy as I feel. "But I don't know if you're right either."

"I'll show you how right I am," I say, brushing a kiss below her earlobe. As tired as I feel, I'm not done with Blake this morning, not that I'll ever be.

By the time we crash, it's mid-afternoon and I've almost forgotten about the tragedy of the previous day. *Almost.*

CHAPTER TWENTY-EIGHT

BLAKE

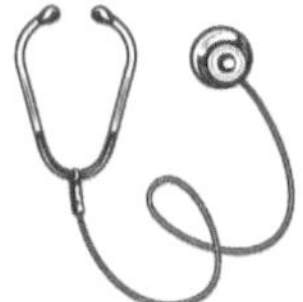

I wake and find Falin passed out, ass up on the couch with Jasper on the floor beside her. There's a story here... One that I'll need copious amounts of coffee and carbs to pry out of her. They look so peaceful. One conversation when they wake up will change all that. I'm sick to my stomach thinking about sweet Mrs. Langston. Sicker still, knowing how poorly Jasper will take the news.

"Leon's still asleep," Damon says, coming from Leon's room. "I'm going to shower then run out and grab some food. You want to try waking these jokers up? I don't want to leave you here without protection."

He pulls me in for a kiss and I nod against him. "I'll do my best."

It takes some coercing but Falin and Jasper wake up, groaning and shuffling to the bathroom. I meet Falin outside the door with a mug of hot coffee. "I always knew you were my favorite person."

Jasper passes us in the hallway and grabs for Falin's cup. "Coffee, I need."

She scowls and smacks his hand away. "Hell, no. Go make your own cup, you meathead."

"But yours will taste better." He smirks and pulls the cup from her hand, taking a long sip. "So good."

"I hope you know, you just started the apocalypse," I warn Jasper. Falin shoots daggers at him as she stomps out of the hallway.

"She's such a peach," he says, scratching his wild head of hair.

"What happened last night?" Falin's in the kitchen aggressively opening cabinets in search of another mug. She's going to hate finding out the guys only own two.

"Too much to talk about when I just woke up." I follow him into his room, trying to fish something out of him. He grabs an unlabeled pill bottle from his dresser drawer and turns, realizing I'm behind him. "You want something, sweetheart?"

I wrap my arms around him, squeezing tight. "No, just this." His bear paw hands glide up and down my back, soothing me as I suppress a sob.

"Interrupting something?" Falin says, leaning against the doorframe with a hand on her hip. I pull away and run my palm over my face.

"We need to talk when Damon gets back." I try to keep my tone neutral but am afraid I'm failing miserably.

"What happened?" Falin asks, her entire demeanor shifting.

I focus my gaze on the floor. There's a tiny groove in the weathered hardwood that through my veiled gaze almost looks like a face.

"Did something happen last night?" Jasper asks, all hints of jest gone from his voice.

"Mrs. Langston is dead."

FALIN and I have been laying in Damon's bed for over an hour, watching a movie on my laptop. I've only digested a few minutes of it. The rest has been nothing but background noise. Even so, the guys needed space, and I needed quiet time with Falin just as much.

"I can't believe she's gone," I say, picturing the lively woman who, just a few nights ago, grabbed Jasper's butt on the way out of the house. Seeing her on her back like that, in the same position my mother was in, brought my grief to the surface. If I close my eyes, it's not Mrs. Langston's face that I see, it's hers. The pain is as fresh today as it was all those years ago.

"I'm so sorry. She seemed great." Falin pulls me into a side hug and twirls a strand of my hair. "I know you had a rough few days, but while we have some space, I wanted to talk."

"Okay," I say, drawing out the word. "What's on your mind?"

She sighs and gathers her thoughts, which means she's about to deliver a whopper. If there's one thing I know to be true about my best friend, it's that she says what she wants, unfiltered as a hand-rolled cigarette. That's her, and I love it... most of the time.

"Come to San Francisco with me. Take a semester off, relax a little, visit some schools. I have plenty of space in my place now and plenty of money to spoil my best friend. I don't know about these guys, Blakey. They seem alright, but their life and yours are headed in opposite directions. And don't get me wrong, I love a man who goes after what he wants but Damon... He's not just one red flag, he's an entire field of them."

I sit up, worrying my bottom lip with my teeth. The skin there is red and raw from how often I've chewed the same spot.

"Trust me, I know he's not perfect, but neither am I. He's passionate and loyal and he hasn't said it but I'm pretty sure he loves me. And I know what we have going is intense, but maybe that's what I've needed."

I haven't felt like Blake the Bore since Damon and the guys came into my life. The insecurity that's been a constant whisper in the back of my mind has quieted.

"Ethan was an ass who treated you like shit and I know your luck with guys hasn't been great before him, but Blakey, you're worthy of love, of a healthy relationship. I get it, the unhinged ones are wild in bed, and they scratch this itch somewhere deep inside us, that little nagging feeling that says we're not enough." She plays with a silver ring on her finger, looking at me with genuine concern. "I'm just worried about you. With Brennan gone all the time you're alone so much. And now, what? People are dying around you, your car is getting wrecked. You won't hear me say this often, but I'm scared."

I hate to admit it, but she's not wrong. The pit in my stomach has made itself a permanent home, even planted a garden and put up a picket fence. But what Falin doesn't know, what no one else knows, is that the pit's been there for as long as I can remember. It has nothing to do with Ethan, or losing Bryan or my mom, or any of this that's happening now. It's been a part of me for so long that I don't know how to live without it.

I scoot closer for a hug. "I know you're scared, I am too, but I don't want to uproot my life. I need to see if this thing with Damon can work out."

With a sign and a nod against my shoulder, she says, "If you're going to stay, have you at least peeked through all his stuff? You need a full picture of who this guy is and there's only a few ways to accomplish that."

Pretty sure he showed his true colors when he gifted me

Trevor's skin, but there's no way I'm telling Falin that information. She'll cuff me and drag me back with her whether I like it or not.

"Not really. I've had no reason to."

She climbs off the bed and turns the lock on the door. "Oh, honey, we have work to do."

I didn't want to take part in it, but once Falin started opening drawers and lifting the edge of the mattress, I got sucked in. It gave me a small thrill to know that I was doing something that Damon would disapprove of. I'd take any feeling other than grief at this point.

A few jackets hang in his closet. I shift them over to one side, finding the rest of the space completely empty. Falin's finishing up the dresser but so far she's found nothing but an abundance of black clothing.

"I feel like this is a waste of time and total invasion of privacy," I finally say, plopping on the bed.

"You'll thank me if we find something creepy," she says, pushing another drawer closed. "Did you check under the bed?"

"I'd hate to be your kid one day. They won't get away with anything." To appease her I get down on my knees and peer under the bed. At first I only spot a few dust bunnies, but I pull my phone out of my pocket and shine my flashlight on a shoebox.

"Of course, they won't. I've already used every trick in the book," she says, combing through the last drawer.

"I found something." Shimmying onto my stomach, I stretch my arm to reach it. "It's a shoebox."

"Oh my God, I knew it. Quick, bring it up here on the bed." She sounds absolutely giddy. I sit back on the bed with the box in front of me. "Come on, open it."

My hand is suddenly weighed down. I know what I'm

about to do is wrong on so many levels. If Damon went through my stuff, I'd be pissed. Couples need a reasonable amount of privacy. It's healthy, normal—which are two things we need more of in this relationship.

"No. I'm not going to invade his privacy like that." The second I make the decision, a weight is lifted off my chest.

Falin grabs the box before I can stop her. "I'm not dating the guy. I'll look in it."

"Falin, no. Let's put it back." I plead with her but it's no use. She yanks the lid off and her eyes bug out.

"Oh, shit. Blake, you're going to want to look in here."

I grab it and realize I'm looking at a box full of my stuff. My bottle of perfume, some of my underwear, and a photo of me and Falin that was in my bedroom at Brennan's. I pull that stuff out, scared of what else I'll find. My stomach drops. Bryan's thumbprint necklace is sitting tangled up at the bottom of the box, along with a few other random pieces of jewelry.

Holding it in my palm, I try to control my breathing.

"Oh, fuck, is that Bryan's necklace?" Falin asks, concern lining her face.

I nod, biting my lip to keep from crying. "Why would he have this? I thought I lost it. I've been so upset."

His locket hangs heavy on my neck and I'm reminded of how he knew I was missing the necklace the entire time. He probably felt threatened in some sick way and had to make sure I was wearing a piece of him instead of my brother. *What a monster.*

"Blake, let's put all this back how we found it and make an excuse to leave." Falin starts arranging the box how it was before. She holds her hand out for the necklace, but I refuse.

"Absolutely not. He's not getting this back. It's the only thing I have left of Bryan. Here, put this in there." I undo the clasp on the locket he gave me and pass it to Falin. "I don't want it."

I know she has something to say by the way she's looking at me, but I'm grateful she's holding back. I can't right now. I'm pissed at her for making me look through his stuff, pissed at him for stealing from me. All of it. He says he's nothing like Ethan, yet this feels like worse of a betrayal than cheating.

"Should I call an Uber?"

"I don't know." I grab the box and shove it back under the bed, hesitating for a long moment before answering. "Yeah, I need some space." And time to process why he'd even have a box like this. Should I really be surprised after everything else he's done?

"Let me go out there. I'll make something up."

I nod and blink the moisture from my eyes. My things are scattered around the room and toiletries are in the bathroom, but at this point I don't care enough about anything other than my laptop, chargers, and other school stuff. Falin leaves tomorrow and then it's back to real life. I have goals and I can't let Damon come in and derail everything I've worked for. I'll get back to my schedule and everything will be fine. I've always gotten by that way, and I'll get through this too.

I feel Damon's energy like a prickle on the back of my neck, and sure enough when I turn, he's in the doorway watching me. I kick my bag under the bed where he won't spot it. "Falin said you guys want to go out tonight? Any idea where you'd like to go?"

Meeting his gaze with a neutral expression takes every ounce of resolve I have left. "Probably just dinner and a movie. It's loud here and we need some time to decompress after everything that's happened."

He nods and runs a hand down his face. "That's a good idea. I was going to come in and tell you that the guys want to go check out a few places tonight, so I'd feel better knowing you're in a public space."

"That's true. I hadn't thought of it that way." He tilts his head an inch to the side, narrowing his gaze.

"Come here, Angel. You look terrified." With his arms wide open, he gestures for me to come to him. I'm so torn between my growing feelings for this man, and the spiral of doubt and fear snaking around my mind. The farther I can get from him, the better, but for now I need to play it cool.

Stepping into his embrace is like sipping sweet poison; I'm lured in by the taste, but by the time I've drunk, the cyanide ends me.

"It's going to be okay. I'll never let anyone hurt you." His deep murmurs settle in my core as he slides his palm up and down my back.

I fake a smile and step away, planting a kiss on his lips. "I know you'll never let anyone hurt me."

The irony of his words. It's him that will hurt me.

"Be safe. I'm going to make sure Falin is armed."

Before I can argue, he's out the door.

Releasing a breath, I wait until I hear them leave the house, then finish gathering what I need. Falin hurries back in. "Okay, they're gone and the Uber's on its way."

I peer around the apartment, unsure if this is the last time I'll be seeing it. We've made so many memories here in such a short amount of time—memories that will be ingrained in my mind forever.

Falin slings her arm over my shoulder. "Let's go. It'll be here soon."

I hold back tears as we pass Mrs. Langston's door, silently hoping she's in a better place. My wrecked car still sits forgotten in the driveway, reminding me of the phone calls I need to make in the morning. Maybe I should just say screw it all and go with Falin to San Francisco. My life is in the same state as my car and I can't see it getting better any time soon. I doubt Brennan would mind. He knows he's not around anyway.

"It says it'll be here in two minutes," Falin says, checking her phone. "Shit, I think I forgot my charger up there. What's the code? I'll run up and grab it. If the Uber gets here, just hold it for me."

I tell her the code to the door and stare off at a yellow falling leaf across the street. Whether we go back to Brennan's or to a hotel room, I don't care. I just want to rest.

A black sedan pulls up, so I grab my bag and hoist it over my shoulder. The passenger window rolls down and the driver smiles wide.

"You're our Uber driver?" I ask, stepping toward the back door.

Before I know what's happening, the door opens and I'm yanked inside the backseat by a huge man wearing a black mask, similar to the one Damon wore the first night. In my struggle, I drop my bags, but I can't overpower him. His grip on me is too strong.

I open my mouth to scream, but he slams a covered hand over my lips. "Shh, little doll. It'll all be over soon."

I feel a pinch and my vision begins to darken at the edges like burning paper. I try to swing my arms or kick my legs, but my body is too heavy. I'm weighed down and falling through space. The last thing I see is the leather seat before my world fades to black.

CHAPTER TWENTY-NINE

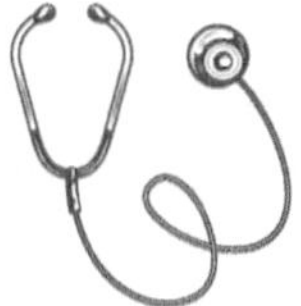

I'm hit with a wave of nausea so powerful that I empty my stomach before even opening my eyes. Realization crashes into me—I was taken. Flashes of those moments before I went under cross my mind. The car, the man in the black mask, the leather seats. It all happened so quickly, I can barely make out the blurred edges in my own mind.

My head throbs as I lift my bound hands to wipe my mouth. With my eyes fully open, I blink to adjust them to the fluorescent lighting above. I'm in some kind of store closet, tossed on the floor with my feet bound by plastic zip ties that bite into my skin.

I don't know if I should scream or keep quiet. Screaming could bring the wrong person's attention and that's the last thing I need. At least I'm alone and can take a few minutes to get my bearings.

I know it's only a matter of time before the guys find me. So I need to figure out how to stay alive until then.

I scoot toward one of the industrial shelves, holding cleaning supplies and sealed boxes. One of the shelf edges may be sharp enough to cut through the zip ties on my wrists. If I can get my hands free, my feet will be much easier.

With my heart pounding out of my chest and residual dizziness, I do the best I can rubbing the zip ties in a sawing motion against the edge of the metal shelf. I keep glancing over my shoulder, terrified that they'll be back, but I need to stay strong. I've gone through more than enough crap in my life to surrender now.

Sweat beads on my forehead, dripping into my eyes. I wipe it away and check my work. I've been at it for minutes by now and nothing. It's probably a complete waste of my energy, but I can't just sit here, paralyzed by fear.

Voices sound from outside the door and I freeze, straining to hear what they're saying. "I'm waiting for the green light from him. He wants to make sure the boyfriend follows."

Dread squeezes my insides like a clenching fist. They're baiting Damon and the guys. Shit. I've got to get out of here; I can't let them get hurt.

"Well, that doesn't mean we can't have a little fun with her first. That one's got an ass on her like I've never seen."

Oh, no. Their voices are getting closer.

I scoot against the only sliver of open wall, plant my feet and push against it. Once I'm standing, I frantically search the space for something, *anything*, to help me.

"Bro, I wouldn't do that if I were you. If he finds out..."

There's a mop. I could try to hit him with it. Or maybe I can pull some of these boxes down on him.

Think, Blake.

There's a thump and then raised voices. It sounds like whoever's out there is fighting. Holding onto the shelves, I make it to the back of the closet and peer into an open box. *Yes.* A packing tape dispenser.

I grab it, being extra careful to not knock the box over and get to work, flipping it in my palm so the serrated edge lines up with my binding.

Drops of blood smear my fingers, but I barely feel the sting from where the blade nicked me. I'm too focused on getting free. It's close. When I pull, I can feel a small amount of give in the ties.

"Shit!" The dispenser slips from my fingers and lands a few feet away. I'll have to get low and crawl.

Sliding down the wall, I freeze as the door swings wide, revealing two towering figures dressed in black. They look as if they're related. Brothers, maybe. The one on the right looks older with graying hair and harsh lines etched into his face. It's the one on the left that makes my hair stand on edge. He's smiling at me with crooked teeth like I'm his next meal.

"Little doll is awake," the younger brother says. From his tone, I know he's the same man who grabbed me. He peers down at my bloody hands. "Looks like you started the fun without me." I'm trembling and trying to control my breathing while the space closes in around me. He bends to pick up the tape dispenser and chuckles. "Bruce, look at this."

He shoves the bloodied object at his brother. Bruce's face is immobile—hard as stone. I'm not sure which man frightens me more. He runs his fingertip over my damp blood and brings it to his nose, inhaling deeply, before fixing his expressionless gaze on me.

"You see what I'm saying now?" the younger brother says. "I've been watching this one. She's feisty when she wants to be."

"Lock the door," Bruce says as he steps closer. One hand reaches down to undo his belt.

"Please," I plead. "You don't want to do this. Please." Tears stream down my face as I back as far away from them as I can.

"Shh," the younger one says as he turns for the door. "It'll be over soon. Be a good little doll." My vision fades again, but not because of any drug. I've been here before, when I've needed a place to go, to protect my mind from what was happening to my body. A shadowed recess of my psyche to escape the darkness.

The sound of the lock clicking echoes in my mind. This is it. It's the moment before the end. I suck in a choked breath, forcing it down into my chest, while the man hovers over me. I could fight—kick and scream. But I know it'll only make things worse in the end.

The younger brother's taunts are mixed with the labored grunts of the man above me. Fisting my bound and bloodied wrists, he slams me onto the cold concrete, the impact sending shockwaves of pain through my skull.

"Cut her ties," he grunts, pawing at my leggings. I squirm, trying to free my arms from his grip.

His phone rings just as his switchblade makes contact with my binding. *Please.* I'm not the praying type but I'll pray to any deity for this to be someone that gets them far away from me.

The ringing rumbles off the walls like a fire alarm, and the two men pause their assault to look at each other. "Who is it?" Bruce asks.

He replaces the switchblade with his phone. "Ah, fuck. It's him." His voice drops to a hardened tone and his sneer is replaced with a deep frown as he looks down at me. "Hey, boss... Uh, huh... Yeah... No. We'll bring her."

Once he hangs up and puts the phone back in his pocket, he has a silent conversation with his brother. Bruce lets my arms drop and stands with flared nostrils and narrowed eyes.

The younger brother's back to sneering at me. "It's your lucky day, doll. Well, maybe not... Once you see what he's going to do with you, you're gonna wish you were still in here with us."

I'M ALONE, strapped to a metal chair, in another storage room filled with boxes. Have I truly been saved from one horror only to endure another? The feeling of foreboding fills me... like each breath I take brings me closer to death.

The squeal of door hinges pulls my attention, and in walks a man so familiar to me, I should feel a sense of relief. But the cold expression in his stare sends a chill down my spine. His right hand rests on the grip of his holstered gun, ready to draw and fire at a moment's notice.

"Blake... I hope my men have been treating you well. Did you have a nice nap?" His slight Russian accent adds an unsettling facade to his fake politeness.

I steel myself and speak as calmly as I can. "Alexander, this must be a misunderstanding. If you bring me home, I won't tell anyone what happened. Let's just talk about this."

He drags another chair across the concrete floor. The grind of the metal reverberates across the room. "No mistake, Blake. You have two choices. Would you like to hear them?"

I need to keep him talking for as long as I can so I nod, keeping my gaze trained on his cold blue eyes.

"Mind you, these choices are special... I've always had something of a soft spot for you, Blake. Losing your mother and brother so close together... What a pity. Then again, sorrow looks good on you." I don't realize I've looked down until he's reaching to tip my chin up with the barrel of his gun. "Such sad, beautiful eyes... I could get good money for a girl like you. The men I work for have a taste for the broken ones. But you..." He strokes my cheek with the gun. "You're not quite there yet, but you will be soon."

"Please," I beg. "I-I'll be with you. Isn't that what you've wanted? I'm sorry I turned you down, it's just I had a boyfriend and I—"

A menacing chuckle leaves his lips. "It's too late for that, doll. Now your choices: you come with me—after I kill your little boyfriends, of course—and you make me a lot of money."

"Why do you want them? What have they done to you to deserve this? You're a shipping heir, not some kind of mobster."

Again, that laugh echoes through the room. "You're entertaining, Blake. I've needed a laugh since I put a bullet between that old woman's eyes."

Mrs. Langston. Oh, God.

"Since we're having a nice chat, I'll tell you. Your boyfriends killed my best men, had the nerve to come into my club unannounced and shoot them dead. My cousin, Peter, was among them. I cannot let that go."

Pieces of the puzzle form in my mind. The night Jasper got shot, they were here... or wherever it happened. It was Alexander and his men. Do they think he's the one that kidnapped Bailey? I never would have imagined that, not in a million years, but now everything I thought I knew is caving in on itself.

"I'm sorry for your loss, but please, more death isn't the answer." If I can plead with him, maybe get him to see reason, there could be a chance, however small.

"Ready for choice number two? Choice one, if you remember, is coming with me. Choice two is I kill you while your boyfriends watch." He sighs and pulls a hand through his closely cut blond hair. "Now that would be a real shame. Like I said, you'll make me good money. Maybe I'm tired. I don't have it in me to fight you the whole way, so you must come willingly. What will it be, Blake?"

He averts his gaze for a moment as his phone vibrates. I watch his expression as he reads. Whatever message he received changes his face from an annoyed grimace to a gleeful smile.

"Hold that thought. We're about to have an audience." He stands, gripping his gun tightly. My pulse roars in my ears. I have no idea who will walk through that door, but I can't bear it if Damon or the guys get hurt or worse.

The door swings open and Brennan takes in the room—me tied to a chair with blood smeared up my arms, his best friend holding a gun at the ready. It hits me in that moment. We're at one of MechExpresses warehouses.

"Alex, why the fuck is my sister tied to a chair?" Brennan approaches slowly, his hands out in front of him.

"Unfortunately, good buddy, she got herself caught up in a mess. That's what happens to whores who fuck criminals. Think of it as a two for one deal. I get to piss you and her boyfriends off in one go."

Brennan's eyes are wide as he looks me over. "Bee, are you okay?"

I nod, and let loose a sob from somewhere in my chest. Brennan must be as shocked as I am... This has been his best friend for the last ten years. The man who got him the job that changed his life. Introduced him to his long-term girlfriend. I can't imagine the pain he must be feeling. Why would Alex do this to us?

"Let's go in the other room and talk. I'm sure we can come to an agreement," Brennan says, his voice steady and hands held open in an appeasing gesture.

"Too late for that. The boyfriends are on their way. Lukas just spotted them on the cameras." He turns to me. "You should pick smarter criminals, Blake. Someone more like your brother."

"Alex," Brennan warns. "Come on, let's be reasonable."

Criminal? What is he talking about?

"Brennan?" I ask, barely able to look at him.

Alex laughs, pacing the length of the room. "She has no idea, does she? Oh, this is gold. Thank you, Brennan, for the entertainment of the night." Alexander sits across from me again, as giddy as a kid at a party. "You think Brennan is going to save you? What's that nickname he calls you again?" He scratches his chin. "Little Bee. That's it. Little Bee, would you like to know what your big brother does for a living?"

Brennan steps closer until Alex pulls out his gun and aims it at his head. "What will Ivan think? Come on, this doesn't have to go down right now," Brennan pleads.

Alex ignores him, bringing his attention back to me. "Big brother traffics women and children. Don't you, Brennan? Go on, tell Little Bee how you drug them. How you take them from their homes or find them on the streets. Sometimes, he gets extra bonuses for the fresh ones... pretty college girls or teens walking home from school. So young and pure. You have no idea how much money people pay for a piece of them."

"That's enough!" Brennan yells. "Stop being a dick and tell me what you want so we can all go home."

"You already used up your favors for Mischa the Whore. She almost gave us away, spreading her legs for anyone with a pulse. Now don't make me tie you up too."

Brennan steps closer while Alexander pulls out his vibrating phone. I shift my gaze to the floor, my stomach churning from what I just learned. He's not my brother, he's a monster.

"Bee, look at me," he whispers while Alex argues over the phone in Russian. "I'm going to get you out of here, you have to trust me."

"Get me out of here and then we're done. I never want to see you again," I seethe.

He closes his eyes for a moment before dipping his chin.

"I'll explain everything, but we need to move while he's distracted."

Brennan works on the rope they used to bind me to the chair while I keep my eyes on Alexander, who looks more and more irritated by the second. "Hurry," I say.

"I almost have it." The rope pulls taut against my torso as he works on the knots and I try to control my breathing. "There."

"The zip ties on my feet," I whisper. "I won't be able to run."

"Fuck, okay, I think there's a utility knife somewhere. Can you try to walk?" My head spins as he hauls me to a stand.

"I can try."

The chair squeaks when I bump it with my arm and Alexander's eyes snap toward the sound, his hand drawing his gun in one quick motion. "Shit, Bee, follow my moves."

He puts his hands up in surrender and I do the same, my bound wrists limiting my movements. My vision blurs at the edges as time around me slows.

"What do you think you're doing? You think because you're Sweeper, you're above me? Above my uncle's own flesh and blood? You're wrong."

I'll never forget the look on his face as he pulls the trigger. His wide, bloodshot eyes. The spittle at the corner of his lips. The veins protruding from his neck.

He aims directly at me and in the flash of a second he fires, the room exploding in sound.

My ears ring and I blink, finally seeing straight. Brennan's crumpled on the floor, blood pooling onto his shirt.

"Brennan!" I scream, a guttural sound from deep in my chest. "Oh God, Brennan, no!" I sink to my knees, cradling his head as rasped breaths escape his lips. "It's okay, I've got you. Hang on."

With my bound wrists, I do the best I can to keep pressure on the wound. "Bee," he says through labored breaths. "Go. Get out."

"I'm not going to leave you here to die." I look up through a veil of tears and realize Alex is gone. Then I hear it—all hell breaking loose right outside the door. Rapid gunfire mixed with furious shouting. It has to be Damon. He's found me. "Brennan, Damon's here. We're going to be okay."

I look into his unmoving eyes and cry his name. *No, no, no.* Oh, God, he's not breathing. "Come on. You can't die on me. You're all I have left."

I pump his bloody chest with shaking hands, frantically trying anything in my power to get him breathing again. "I need you... Please, Brennan. This isn't happening. This can't be happening."

A strong pair of arms wrap around me, pulling me back from Brennan's body. I scream through sobs, thrashing my arms to break free. "No! I can't leave him!"

"Blake, it's me. I've got you. You're safe." The voice sounds muffled, like it's coming from broken speakers. "Come here." Gentle hands lift me, and the cold floor is replaced with a warm chest. We move, but my eyes stay pinned on Brennan's motionless body as we're torn apart forever.

CHAPTER THIRTY

DAMON

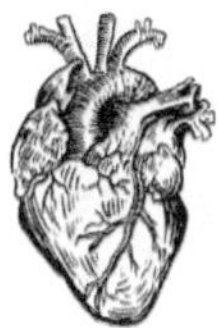

I step over bodies and around pools of blood, away from the violent frenzy near the entrance. Jasper and Leon's lives are on the line, yet the relief I feel to have Blake in my arms is unmeasurable. She's sobbing and trembling, begging me to go back and it kills me to disregard her wishes in favor of her safety. I'd give her the world— but not if it means risking her life.

I'm so close to the exit I can almost feel the crisp dawn air caressing my skin. "Almost there," I tell her. "I've got you."

Pounding footsteps at my back pull my attention and I duck into a crouch as gunfire hits the wall above us. Setting Blake down, I pull out my gun and fire back, staying as low as I can.

Where are you, motherfucker?

If Leon calculated correctly, there should only be a few guys left. I'd love to find the one who grabbed Blake in front of the house and personally drive a blade through his heart, but that would require leaving some of them alive to find out his identity.

More shots come at me from around the corner, pelting the wall inches from my head. I pick up my pace and round the bend, finding the culprit, and fire three rounds into his torso. I want him to feel pain as he bleeds out.

"Damon!" Jasper shouts. "Cops!"

Shit.

I run back to Blake and scoop her into my arms, ignoring the man's gurgled cries filling the air. Once I'm outside, I hear the wail of sirens getting closer.

Blake has gone limp and quiet, with blank eyes and trembling parted lips. I run around my car and gingerly sit her in the passenger seat, buckling her belt before hurrying to my side.

Kicking the car into drive, I peel around the corner, searching for Leon's bike. When I see it missing, I sigh in relief. They must have made it out right before us.

As I turn onto the main road, I spot a black sedan without plates speeding away in the opposite direction. It takes one look at Blake to stop myself from going after them. Those scumbags don't deserve to go free. Fuck, it kills me. But she's more important.

I head in the direction of the prearranged site, a cheap motel near the highway. The apartment is no longer safe, and knowing that some of them left the warehouse alive, I'm even more affirmed in our choice to abandon the place.

It takes about thirty minutes to get to the rundown motel, but the stunned silence in the car makes it feel longer. I know Blake needs to process what's happened, so I don't push her to talk. I just keep a hand on her thigh like an anchor, letting her know I've got her. I won't let her float out to sea.

I breathe a sigh of relief when I see Leon's bike parked near the office entrance. This place should allow us to fade into the background, plus they don't ask for ID and they take cash. Checking my phone, I notice a text from Falin. She checked us into room numbers ten and eleven. Smart of Leon to park away from our doors. I follow his lead and do the same.

With Blake in my arms, I take stock of the surroundings. The cracked concrete walkway is teeming with weeds that have pushed their way to the surface. Crushed broken glass is scattered around like fairy dust, while empty beer bottles lean against the rust-covered siding. There are only two other cars in the lot, an old pickup and a white minivan. Both look like they've been here a while from the layer of dirt on their windows.

I knock twice and Falin swings the door wide, a panicked expression on her face. "Oh shit, is she okay?"

"I think so, but she's in shock."

Leon's sitting at a dilapidated desk in the back of the room, clicking furiously on his laptop while simultaneously checking his phone screen. He turns at our arrival and jumps up. "Fuck, is she alright? Bring her here." He yells toward the bathroom. "Jas, start the hot water."

Blake stares ahead, not meeting their eyes. I continue rubbing calming circles on her back. Leon comes up behind me and runs his palm over her blood-stained cheek. I breathe out. "Thank fuck you guys got out okay."

"It was close, but we took a bunch of them out. They clearly knew we were coming. No idea how." Leon kisses Blake's forehead and backs away. "No idea who called the cops either."

Jasper comes out of the bathroom, rubbing a towel over his damp face. His clothes are covered in brown dried blood. When he spots Blake in my arms, his shoulders slump and his nostrils flare. "Is she—"

"She's alright," I tell him before he has the chance to ask. "Just shocked and exhausted. Let's get her cleaned up and we can catch each other up. Falin, you grabbed the stuff from the apartment, right?"

"Yeah, whatever I could fit in Mrs. Langston's car." She pulls the drape over an inch to peer out the window. "You're sure you weren't followed?"

"As sure as I can be," I say.

"Falin?" Blake says in a hushed tone. Falin's at our side in a second, speaking low to her best friend.

"Why don't you let me take care of Blake while you guys catch up?" My arms tighten around her, but Falin's right. She's better for this and clearly Blake needs her. I nod, and bring Blake into the bathroom, placing her down on the closed toilet lid.

I bend so I'm eye level with Blake but my gaze volleys between the two of them. "If you need anything, I'll be right out there." With a soft kiss on Blake's forehead, I step out, closing the door behind me.

Jasper's pacing the room, clenching his fists, while Leon is back to his screens. I slump down onto the edge of the bed and release a long winded, "Fuck."

"What room did you find her in?" Jasper asks. "Tell us everything that happened once we separated."

I spend the next few minutes recounting how I kept to the edges, searching offices and closets, until I finally found her in a large warehouse storeroom. I filled them in on what I heard in the moments before I found Blake covered in her brother's blood. What that guy said.

"What do you think you're doing? You think because you're Sweeper, you're above me? Above my uncle's own flesh and blood? You're wrong."

Sweeper—the guy we have been looking for this entire time has been right where we thought. The address was correct. He was just better than most at hiding his true nature.

Jasper and Leon are stunned still, taking in this new development.

"So the guy who shot him? Was it the same guy from the club? King?" Leon asks.

I nod. "The same piece of shit. From what he said, his uncle is involved. Seems like that's who we really want."

Jasper goes back to pacing. "What the hell are we going to do?"

I rest my head in my hands and stare down at the thread-bare carpet. "Fuck if I know, but we can't stay here."

"We don't have to make any decisions right now. I'm going to call Ray with an update. Tell him to watch his back. Jas, why don't you go next door and shower?" Leon says.

"Yeah, alright. I'll be back in a few to check on Blake." He grabs the other keycard from the desk and heads out the door.

"I'll go in the other room too, give you all some privacy," Leon adds. I meet his sympathetic gaze and nod. "Call if you need anything."

Before he leaves, I say, "Thanks again. If it weren't for you and Falin tracking that car, we could have been too late."

His lips pull upward but there's no joy in the expression. We're lucky to have gotten out of there intact, yet there's no reason to celebrate. Not with blood still staining our hands.

FALIN and I tuck Blake into one of the full-sized beds, pulling the faded floral comforter up to her chin. By the time I click the bedside lamp off, plunging the room into shadows, her eyelids are already drooping.

Falin brushes a strand of damp hair out of her face before coming around the other side of the bed. "You should go in the other room. I'll stay with her." Her tone is laced with resentment and heartache.

"I'm not leaving her," I say, matter-of-factly. "She needs me right now."

She sighs and rubs her temples. "Look, you're not going to want to hear this, but I don't have it in me to give a shit right now. It's over between you two. We were leaving. As in, getting the fuck away from you and all of this."

The ropes of muscle in my chest pull taut as my eyes dart between Blake's sleeping form and Falin's unforgiving gaze. "No. You have no idea what you're talking about."

"I'm sorry. I can tell you care for her, but she needs better than this. You have to let her go." She reaches out to place a hand on my shoulder but I shrug her off.

"Where is this coming from?" Everything was fine before she was taken—as fine as could be expected with Mrs. Langston getting murdered under our noses.

Falin averts her gaze to Blake and we watch slow steady breaths leave her lips. "We found your creepy little box under the bed. Her brother's necklace, Damon? Really? I'm no expert but you need some serious help."

My heart hammers like it's trying to break free from the confines of my chest. "It was from before... I was going to give it all back."

"I don't think that matters. You need help, Damon, and Blake... She needs support. I was there after Bryan died and then again only weeks later when she lost her mom. I made sure she ate, showered, and slept. I held her when she sobbed, listened to her when she was ready to talk. Are you even capable of being there for her like that?"

Shame and disgust collide in the pit of my stomach. Both emotions take up a permanent residence in my body, but I've never felt them more than I do right now. "I don't know."

I'm shocked by my own admission. But I've always strived to speak truthfully, sometimes brutally so. I've been working toward telling Blake everything, opening up to what Jasper so lovingly calls "my bullshit."

If I could reach into my skull and remove the fucked up pieces, I'd do it in a heartbeat. My relentless drive, my obsessive nature—it's as much a part of me as my own DNA. Unchangeable and intrinsic to who I am deep down. I truly believe Blake loves that part of me, she's just afraid. Who could blame her? I've told her time and again that I'd never hurt her, but I lied. I only hope this isn't the end.

"I'm not leaving unless she asks me to," I finally say. "Please."

She gives me a look full of pity, but nods. I'll take it. Asking for permission like this is different, but it feels right, like trying on a new shirt that's made for my body. I want to show Falin, as much as Blake, that I'm right for her. That I'm here to stay.

The blood crusted under my fingernails catches my eye. "I'm going to get cleaned up. Yell if you need me."

As the water washes away the violent acts of the night, I tell myself, *whatever it takes*. I won't live without Blake. It's me and her to the end, no matter what.

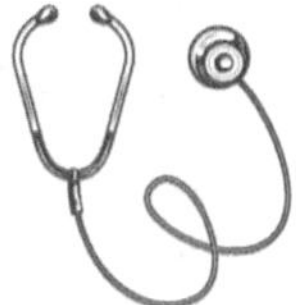

I'M EXPERIENCING ONE OF THOSE MOMENTS WHERE I'M aware I'm awake, yet my eyes refuse to open. Slight sounds catch my attention, but I'm not ready to be fully present. I'm trapped in purgatory, caught between sleep's comfort and the hell of reality. Once my lids finally open, I'll have to succumb to the truth.

Brennan was a monster.

Brennan is gone forever.

Without looking, I know Falin's beside me. I feel the heat of her body, hear her quiet comforting snores. It could be midday or midnight. Time has no meaning, not when the person who's loved me since the day I was born is dead. Not when everything I knew about him was a lie.

I want to stay here on this cheap mattress, with coils poking my back, inhaling the smell of stale cigarettes that's permeated the fabric. Curl into a ball and take up residence until I wake up from this nightmare.

But I can't. I know that. My entire life hangs in the balance and I have shit to do, plans to make. Truths to accept about the man Brennan was.

When I finally open my eyes, adjusting my vision to the sliver of yellow light coming in from the bathroom door, I focus on the brown stain and the peeling paint on the ceiling. I've gotten through a lot by picking one point of focus and clearing my head, even if those sights sometimes come back to haunt me.

"Blake?" Damon calls to me in a hushed whisper. "Are you awake?"

If I close my eyes again and stay perfectly still, maybe he won't talk to me? I try, but an itch on my nose betrays me.

"I see you moving over there. Do you need anything?" His bed creaks and before I can answer, he's crouching beside me, brushing my hair out of my eyes with his warm palm. "I'll be right back."

I grieve the loss of his touch immediately and I hate myself for it. Even with everything that's happened, I still can't forget about his deception, his complete betrayal of my trust. He's the reason Brennan is dead. The reason I'm in this mess. Why do I still want him?

The lock on the door clicks and he's back, once again crouching at my side. "I got you some water and some salted peanuts. They were the only thing in the vending machine that you could eat."

I open my eyes again and take in the concern on his face. My mouth is too dry to turn away water, and it must have been twenty-four hours since I've eaten anything. Scooting up against the headboard, I accept the cold water bottle, and take a long sip.

"Thank you," I say, wiping my palm across my lips. He leans forward and hands me the pouch of peanuts, watching me open the package with raised brows like he's a hovering mother handing her picky toddler a vegetable. To appease him, I shake a few into my palm and pick on them slowly. He seems to sag in relief.

We sit in silence for a few minutes, while I chew and swallow a few peanuts, and he observes me with a tilted head. I can tell he's dying to talk, but I appreciate the time he's taking.

Finally, after I take another sip of water and put the capped bottle on the bed, he takes my hand. His golden eyes shine with moisture in the dim lighting. "I'm so fucking sorry, Blake. About your brother, about everything. Please... tell me what to do to help you? I'll do anything to make this right. I'm sorry, baby. So sorry."

Dipping my head, I suck in a breath to keep my own tears at bay. I need to be strong, to let him know that I know *everything*. That this isn't just about what happened at the warehouse, it's about him and what he's done.

But before we have that conversation, I need to know one thing. Meeting his gaze, I ask, "Where is Brennan's body?"

He's not expecting that question. His brows draw together as he answers. "The police showed up soon after we made it out. I'm assuming they have him. We'd have to go down to the station and ask, or I can call Ray and have him check it out?"

After learning what I have about Brennan and his nefarious deeds, I don't know what I want. But I can't let him rot there in a morgue. We have different last names. I'm not listed on any of the bills. It could take the cops a while to track me down. I need closure if I'm going to move past this.

"I need to see him, to say goodbye." Damon catches a tear from my cheek before holding my face in his hands. His eyes burn into mine. So intense, I want to look away.

"I'll make it happen. Whatever you want, you get." He pulls me against his chest, and kisses my head like he's cherishing this moment. "I'm sorry."

"I believe you."

AFTER A FEW HOURS of broken sleep, each of us woke up, one at a time, antsy to leave this dump. I'm supposed to be at microbiology class this morning, but there's no way that's happening with everything I have to do.

Damon and I leave for the police station. Falin stays to call the airline and change her flight, while the guys look into another place for us to stay. Somewhere safe and preferably without the sound of truck horns blaring at all hours.

Damon's antsy. I'm sure the police station is the last place on earth he'd like to be, but I appreciate him coming with me. With our hands entwined, we ask at the front desk about a missing person, being vague with our words as to not garner suspicion. I'm not naturally gifted when it comes to hiding my expressions, so I let Damon do most of the talking. He gives our assigned officer a physical description of Brennan and then I open my phone and pull up the most recent photo I have of him, biting my lip to hold back the flood of tears.

The officer pauses and studies the photo for a few moments before telling us to have a seat.

"She recognized him," I whisper. "He must be here."

Damon wraps his arm around my shoulder, holding me close. "Yeah, I think so. You're doing great. So fucking strong."

His praise warms the ice in my veins. "Yeah well, I have some practice with this situation."

It was different with Bryan. I had no idea what I was walking into when they called me to identify him. I was sure they'd been mistaken. It wasn't my brother that they found behind an overpass with a needle in his arm. It must have been someone else.

The memory of stepping into that eerily still room, with its cold metal counters and harsh fluorescent lighting, still plays clearly in my mind. The stinging smell of disinfectant, my plodding footsteps on the tile floor, the moment when the attendant pulled the pale sheet back, revealing my brother's lifeless form.

Here I am, about to repeat history, except now I know what I'll be walking into. I've accepted it, but it doesn't make it easy. I don't register the officer's appearance as she guides us through the corridors, but her words ring in my ears. "I'm sorry."

She's sorry. Damon's sorry. Everyone's sorry.

I'm tired of those words... I've heard them so much in my life that hearing them now makes me want to scream.

We're met with icy air and the scent of decay as we step into the morgue. Damon squeezes my hand, his grip like a much needed lifeline.

The next five minutes are a blur. I know the attendant and the officer speak to me but their words are muffled in my ringing ears. Damon answers questions beside me and before I know what's happening, we're back outside.

I stop in front of the car and put my head in my hands, sucking in breaths of cool air. Damon's right there, like he always is, holding me close.

"Slow breaths," he murmurs. "Nice and easy."

I know the signs of a panic attack. Not just from a textbook, but from living with them for years now. It's been a long time but even if it hadn't, each time they come on still feels like death's squeezing my insides with its bony fingers.

"I-I c-can't," I say through rapid breaths.

Oh God, my fingers are numb. My feet will come next. Then the full body shakes that make me feel like I've been plunged into icy water.

Damon reaches under my arms and sits me on the trunk of his car. "Baby, look at me. Focus on my face."

He tips my chin up, but I can't focus. I'm too disorientated. "Ch-choking," I manage to say through desperate inhales.

Random obscenities leave his lips as I close my eyes, lay back on the windshield, and go into a dark space in my mind. A space where Brennan and Bryan and Mom are alive. They're laughing, and not in pain. My chest constricts and limbs tremble. It hurts... Everything hurts.

A sharp sensation has me snapping my eyes open. I vaguely hear Damon say my name followed by more muffled words. "Blake, don't fucking hate me for this."

A slash of metal follows his words and I feel it again. Stinging, sharp pain. My vision clears as I focus on the sensation—the needle-like bite of his blade piercing my arm.

With my head down, I zero in on the crimson dribbles blossoming across my pale skin like soft rose petals. It's a beautiful sight, to see my own life force spilling out of me. Minutes go by with me transfixed on the sight.

"Blake, look at me." Jerking my head up, I'm met by Damon's wide amber eyes. "Are you okay?" I nod slowly, pulling in a lungful of air through my nose. He makes a cut on the edge of his shirt and tears a large piece off. "Let's get you wrapped up."

I watch his deft hands work to secure the fabric along my wounds, tucking the end into itself. Feeling comes back to my extremities by the time he lifts me into his arms.

"W-what was that?" I ask, my voice barely a whisper.

He sets me in the passenger seat, buckles me in, and heads over to his side before answering the question.

"Something I learned a while ago," he says while backing out. "Physical sensations help ground us during a panic attack."

Leaning my head back against the headrest, I concentrate on the throbbing ache. It's unconventional, but it worked. "Thank you. That was a bad one."

"You don't have to thank me." He rests his hand on my thigh, gliding his thumb in a calming circle.

"Can we stop somewhere quiet? We need to talk." As exhausted as I am, I can't do this with him anymore. Not without letting everything out into the open air.

His jaw tenses. "Are you feeling well enough?"

"Yeah, I'm fine," I lie. The truth is, I won't feel any better until I've said what I need to say.

He dips his chin and turns down a scenic road lined with bare trees. Only a few red and yellow stubborn leaves still cling to branches, unable to accept their inevitable death. I roll down the window and breathe in the rich scent of dry leaves and wood smoke.

"Coffee?" he asks, breaking me from daze.

"Uh, yeah, that sounds good." I could use the caffeine, among other things.

After grabbing us some drinks from a coffee shop nearby, he pulls over at a small empty park. He opens my door for me, and leads me to a wooden table under a towering oak tree.

I sip my coffee, feeling the warm liquid slide down my throat, waking my nerve endings. Damon jerks his head around, likely checking that we're actually alone here.

"I don't even know where to start," I say. So much has happened recently that I feel like I'm living in another plane of existence. I close my eyes and focus on here and now, not the plans I had before everything went to shit.

"The necklace," he says. "You found my box."

I wrench my eyes open. "You knew?"

"Falin told me while you were asleep. Blake," he starts. "I could come up with some bullshit excuse for why I did it. I could lie and say I wasn't thinking, or I didn't mean to take the necklace. But I won't. I want to be honest with you."

He stands and paces the length of the bench. "Go on," I say.

"I took the necklace because I was jealous. I needed to possess the object that you cherished above all else. I watched you for a while. I think you already know that. I saw how you always touched it when you were deep in thought, or nervous, or scared. You'd play with that little heart on the chain with a wistful look in your eyes and... I don't know, Blake. I needed to claim a piece of you. I couldn't resist. I didn't know it was your brother's at the time or maybe I would have felt differently. Everything else—the perfume, the underwear, the photos. They were all ways to keep you tethered to me." I stare at my coffee cup, digesting his words. "Say something, please," he pleads.

"I don't know what to say. That's super messed up? You have issues? I'm upset with you? Honestly, I have no idea how to respond."

He sits so we're face to face and wraps his hands around mine. "None of that is news to me. I know what I am. But Blake, I've been showing you who I am from day one. Don't forget that. You told me once you love all the fucked up sides of me, remember? Or did you only say that because my cock was inside you?"

"What the hell?" I whisper. "You can't say stuff like that out here."

He lets out a deep rumbling chuckle and raises his brow. "Why not? We're alone. I could fuck you right here on this picnic table and no one would ever know."

My cheeks heat at the thought of him bending me over this table, the weathered wood splintering my naked skin. "Absolutely not." Rolling my lip between my teeth, I add, "And that's not why I said what I said."

"What? I can't hear you." He knows exactly what I said, he's just being a teasing ass.

"I didn't say I love those parts of you just because we were being intimate," I hiss through gritted teeth.

"Don't be shy now. I've heard your dirty mouth before. You can say fucking, Blake. When we were fucking like two starved animals." He's so damn smug, I could slap him. I would but I bet he'd love it. "Does that turn you on? Your pretty cheeks are pink." He lowers his voice to a deep hum. "The same color as your perfect cunt."

My eyes flutter closed and I force controlled breaths into my nose. *Think of anything else, Blake. Do not let him get to you.* "Back to our conversation. I need to know that I can trust you or we'll never work. I can handle a lot, and I wasn't lying when I said I like the way you are—"

"Like? I believe the correct word was love."

I roll my eyes and huff a breath. "Fine... I love the way you are, but—"

"No buts, you love the way I am. You love how possessive I am. How I make you nervous and excited at the same time. You love how I'll always put you first, even before myself. How I worship every single inch of your body. You love who you are when you're with me. Fuck, Blake, just say it."

"What do you want me to say?" I yell. Once I start, it feels so good, so freeing, I can't stop. I stand on the bench and toss my head back. "You want me to say that I fucking love you, Damon? Is that what you're waiting for? Well, fine! I love you, okay? And maybe I'm scared of what kind of person that makes me."

My chest is heaving as I meet his gaze. I watch a slow smile spread across his lips, his dimples appearing. He reaches for my face with trembling hands, cupping my cheeks. "It makes you mine."

Our lips crash together in a tangle of teeth and tongues, like we're trying to breathe every one of our emotions into each other. The way he sucks my lip and claims my mouth has me weak and shaking.

He pulls back for a moment, nuzzling my neck and kissing his way to my earlobe. "I love you, Blake. I've loved you from the moment I set eyes on you and will love you until I take my last breath on this earth."

Our mouths meet again with matching urgency. His hands climb up my shirt, palming my breasts and ghosting over my hard nipples. My skin is electric under his fingertips, sending bolts of desire straight to my core. I suck his bottom lip, nibbling playfully, before saying, "Close your eyes."

He lets out a hummed chuckle. "I like when you're bossy."

Peppering kisses down his neck, I reach the shell of his ear and whisper. "Count to ten, and then come find me."

"Fuck." He draws out the word in the most delicious way. I plant one last kiss across his lips, and run toward the copse of trees behind us like my life depends on it.

DAMON

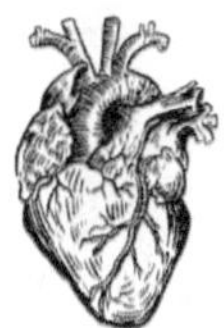

"You better run, Blake!" I yell into the wind. How the hell did I get so lucky? She fucking loves me. I can die a happy man now. To see her being playful like this, after what she just went through is truly something. I'm in awe of her—her strength, her resilience, her spirit. She doesn't even fully grasp the gravity of my infatuation, but I'll make sure she learns.

I count to ten, then grab my mask from the glove compartment, for old times sake. I'm already hard and aching for her as I take slow, steady steps into the woods. Adrenaline courses through my veins, causing my pulse to pound with anticipation.

"I hope you're ready for me," I shout into the shrouded mass of trees. My voice echoes off the bare branches, sending a few birds fleeing.

Shadows dance along the trunks while I make my way deeper into the dense woods. There's countless places to hide, but I know Blake wants to be found as much as I want to find her. My ears perk up as a faint rustling noise comes from a few feet ahead. The air shifts and I still, watching for any slight movement. Any good hunter knows that patience is key.

Waiting for your prey to make their move, letting them get caught in your sight. The thrill is nothing short of euphoric.

A flash of dark hair catches the corner of my eye. I whirl, pulse pounding, and sprint toward Blake's retreating form. Her breathless laughter rides the breeze, mixing with the crunch of fallen leaves beneath her feet. I weave through trees and fallen branches, keeping her an arm's length away. "Did you think I wasn't going to find you, baby? You can't hide from me, I'll always find you."

"Then catch me, Freddy," she taunts, panting for air.

I up my pace and snag her waist, swinging her into my arms. She's giggling between breaths. "Got you, bad girl. Now what should I do with my prize?"

Lifting her higher, I drape her around my neck with her legs dangling to one side and my hand securely holding her ass. "Damon, oh my God. Don't drop me."

I slap her ass with a nice flat palm, reveling in the echo. "Say something like that again and I'll have to punish you." A suggestive groan leaves her lips, so I do it again. "You like that? Does it make you nice and wet for me?"

"Mhm."

Desperate to sink inside her, I lift her from my shoulders and pin her back against the nearest tree. With one hand braced on the rough bark above her head, I tip her chin up, pull my mask so my mouth is visible, and speak softly against her full lips. "I'm giving you two seconds to get out of those clothes or I'll rip them off you."

She releases a breath and tugs her jeans down first, followed by her shirt. I trace her curves with my palm, taking in how fucking good her skin feels against mine. "That's my good girl, ready to get fucked against this tree like a little slut."

"Oh, God," she gasps.

I tear her underwear at the seam, smiling as they fall to the forest floor. Cupping her sopping pussy with my palm, I push her back against the tree. "Tell me again."

"W-what?" she stutters, leaning her head against the rough bark.

I add pressure and nuzzle my face against the slope of her neck. Whispering in her ear, I say, "Tell me you love me." I suck her soft earlobe, toying with her earrings between my teeth until she moans.

"I love you, I love you, please." The words tumble from her lips in a desperate plea.

Yanking my pants down, I stroke my length with my free hand. Blake reaches down, pushing my hand away and taking over the movement. "Not yet, needy girl. You come first."

I get on my knees in front of her, which is exactly where I should be. As I'm about to pull my mask off, she stops me with a hand on my face. "Keep it on." She rolls it up to my nose as I chuckle.

"So demanding." I open her legs wider to accommodate my size, and ghost my lips over her pussy. "I pretty much grew up in forests just like this one. You know what that means?"

"No idea." She juts her hips forward but I hold her still.

"It means I finally get to fuck the woman I love in the place I call home. You want to know the best part about my home, Angel?" I glide a finger through her slick folds, toying with her while I wait for her response.

"What?" she asks, breathless and desperate, making me throb with need.

"You can scream as loud as you want and no one will hear you." I spread her with my fingers and delve my tongue against her clit.

Her legs tremble as she moans into the open air. She tastes so goddamn good, I could come right here and now. I lap her clit, increasing my pressure but keeping the same delicious pace until she's bucking her hips and grinding against my face. "That's it, baby. Take what you want. Ride my face. Come all over it."

I plunge a finger inside her, curling it and matching the pace of her hips as her legs tense and shake. "Oh, God, I'm so close."

Flicking faster, I feel her orgasm building to a beautiful crescendo. Her muscles suck my finger tight as her clit pulses against my tongue. "Scream for me."

Diving back in, I suck her clit between my lips as she comes, screaming my name against the cool breeze. I lap up every drip of her delicious come, fucking her greedy pussy with my finger until she's barely able to stand.

"Please, Damon… I can't." As her legs give out, I scoop her into my arms, pinning her against the tree.

"Wrap your legs around me. I'm not done with you yet." I tease her entrance with my cock, sliding myself between her drenched lips until we're aligned just right. "Does your back hurt?" I ask, remembering her skin is pinned against the grooved bark.

"A little," she answers, still panting.

"Good. I want you to feel it for days and remember how you took my cock like this. I want you to lose your voice from crying out my name. Fuck, Blake… I need my cum dripping from these soaked thighs right now."

I hoist her up and slam into her slick pussy like she was made to take me. She's so damn tight, so perfect. I pump into her, gripping her ass hard enough to leave bruised fingerprints on her skin.

"Damon… Shit, you feel so good."

Sucking her neck and nibbling her earlobe, I drive into her roughly. She feels incredible. "Look how well you take my cock, baby. This tight cunt is all mine."

About to lose control, I pull out and lower us to the ground. Dried leaves and broken branches are strewn around us, but I couldn't care less. Not while Blake is laid out before me like a goddess. In this position I'm free to roll her nipples between my fingers, pinch them, bite them. She yanks my shirt up and pulls me down so our bodies are skin to skin. My cock begs to slip back inside her.

"Fuck me, Damon. Pound my body into this dirt, and fill me with your cum." Her nails dig into my ass, guiding me home.

"Christ, that mouth. Such a dirty little slut for me." My hips move, pressing her harder into the dirt. Every ounce of self control I had left snapped the moment she told me to fill her. We fuck relentlessly, like wild animals. It's primal and chaotic but so fucking perfect.

"I love you so much, baby. Come with me, squeeze my cock with your perfect cunt." My words spill out between groans. I'm so close. Every nerve ending in my body is firing at once as my balls draw up tight, and I thrust harder.

Blake slides her palm between us, rubbing her clit while moaning my name. "That's it, rub yourself. Oh, fuck, Blake. Fuuuck, you feel so good."

A tidal wave of pleasure shoots through me as I empty myself inside her. Her body quivers under me while she squeezes me dry.

Yanking off my mask, I grab her face and claim her lips, sliding my tongue against hers. An unknown feeling grows in my chest, like a warm glow that spreads. Our kisses are slow, savoring each other's taste, sharing each breath. I'm so gone for her, I physically ache.

Pressing up with my palms, I put a few inches of space between us so I can take in how perfect she looks right now. Her flushed cheeks, her plump red lips, her half-lidded eyes.

"Is there something on my face?" she asks with a self-conscious laugh.

I stare deeply into her storm cloud eyes, feeling a connection stronger than any I've known before. It's an intense bond, like finding the one soul in a crowded room who understands my unspoken words and truly sees me.

"Damon, you're freaking me out." She brushes her cheeks with her hand. "What is it?"

"Just memorizing this moment so I can carry it with me forever."

A smile lights up her face. "Look at you being so sweet."

"There's also an entire tree's worth of leaves in your hair, so that's pretty fun to look at." I smirk and plant a kiss on her forehead.

She pushes my shoulder playfully, knocking me off-balance so I land on my bare ass in the dirt. "Serves you right."

Her laughter fills the air around us as I roll onto my back beside her. I'm not ready to get dressed and face reality. Not yet. In the quiet stillness, our breaths sync and hands intertwine. I'm so content, I can almost sleep like this.

"I have to tell you something," Blake utters softly. "It's about Brennan." Rolling to my side, I pull her into my chest. "When they had me tied up, before you got there, I found out some things about him. Things I never knew. I'm ashamed to tell you... I feel so stupid and torn. He's my brother, but I can't let him get away with what he's done. And maybe this has something to do with Bailey."

I continue to listen, running my fingers through her tangled hair. "It's okay, you can tell me. You're so strong, baby. You got this."

"The man who shot him... That was Alexander, Brennan's best friend. It's a long story, but Brennan was always the one to take care of us. He worked two jobs by the time he was out of high school. One of those jobs was for MechExpress. He started as a part-time janitor—sweeping the floors, shoveling snow in the winter. He worked so hard that Alexander noticed him and brought him into his inner circle. Even introduced him to his cousin, Mischa. Alexander's the one who introduced Brennan to Ivan, the CEO of the company, who took Brennan under his wing and promoted him. All this time, I thought my brother worked for a shipping company, traveling the world doing business stuff I never understood, but..."

Her words trail off while she takes a deep breath. "We can talk about this later. It's okay if it's too hard for you."

"No," she says. "I need to." Taking another deep breath she continues. "Brennan got caught up in trafficking. I don't know the details, just that all of them are bad people. MechExpress must be some kind of front and Brennan was heavily involved. What if he's the one that took Bailey?"

Her voice catches on a sob. "There's no way for us to know that. Don't worry about things we'll never find the answers to. Shh, I've got you."

I hold her tight while she relays more of what she heard. "It was so close to being me too. H-he said he'd make loads of money off me."

I clench my jaw and imagine putting a bullet through that prick's skull. "You're safe, baby. I've got you."

"We need to find her, Damon. I-I can't let her get violated by those men. I can't live with myself knowing my brother was a part of that."

"We will, don't worry."

Now that we have names, it's over for them.

"I know this is wrong, but I can't stop thinking that maybe I'm glad Brennan is dead. If it means another monster is off the streets, then I'm glad." She wipes her eyes, coating her face in a mix of dirt and tears. "How messed up is that?"

"Not messed up at all. Nothing is black and white in this world. You're allowed to mourn the brother you loved while also hating the evil man he became. Don't lose yourself in this, Blake. Stay with me."

She nods and buries her head in my chest, sobbing quietly. We stay like that for a long time until her skin pebbles with goosebumps. I quietly dress her and carry her back to the car, despite her insisting that she can walk.

Once we're settled, I check my phone, finding a text from Leon with a new address. Turning to Blake, I ask, "How do you feel about checking the house for information? Maybe Brennan has something in his desk? Plus, this may be the last time we go there. You should have some of his things."

It's risky, but with this new development, we can't just leave potential leads without checking first. The guys will be pissed at me for not including them, but this is as much about Blake getting closure as it is about searching Brennan's belongings.

"I think I'm okay, but I don't want to stay there for long. It's Mischa's house, which means it belongs to her family. It's not safe for us."

My chest swells with pride. "We'll stop in for fifteen minutes, tops." I show her the text from Leon. "It looks like they found us a temporary rental a few towns over. No more motel."

"Thank God, that place gave me the creeps." She turns up the radio and adds, "Let's get this over with."

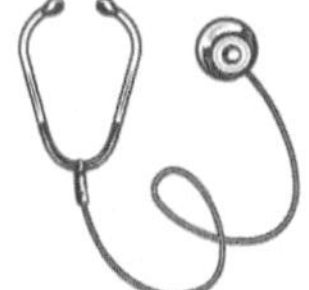

The next week floats by in a fog of restless sleep and blurred hours spent making phone calls and sorting paperwork. In our search of Brennan's house, we found a life insurance policy with my name listed as the sole beneficiary. I struggled for a few days with whether or not I wanted anything to do with that money, but after taking a leave of absence from school and realizing I have nowhere to live and no money to support myself, I caved.

The first thing I'll do with the funds is make a huge donation to a global foundation that fights to end human trafficking, only leaving myself with enough to get by until I figure out a plan.

While I was having a panic attack at the police station last week, Damon was setting up Brennan's transfer to his colleagues' funeral home. Yesterday, we went to pick up his ashes with a mold of his thumbprint in case I wanted to get a necklace made. His thoughtfulness brought me to tears again. Lately, tears seem constant—not just from the deep well of grief

I'm drowning in, but also from the unspoken kindness of Damon, Falin, and the guys.

I thought Brennan was my only family, but I was wrong. I'm surrounded by more love than I could ever hope for. With time, I'll get through this and come out stronger and smarter.

The place we currently call home is a quaint three-bedroom house at least five miles from civilization. Its siding is weathered and porch creaky, but I love the solitude. The interior looks as if it was decorated by an eclectic grandmother, with patchwork quilts and porcelain knickknacks. There's even a faint scent of mothballs in the air. But it's safe, and we're together. That's what matters most.

Sitting outside surrounded by tall grass and wildflowers, I watch a doe and her fawn nibble from a raspberry bush. It's been a long time since I sat in nature this way, not worrying about which test I needed to study for, or when my next class would start. I haven't even recited human anatomy in my head for weeks now. I've always wanted to be a doctor, and I know I will, but this is what I need. Time without planners and schedules. Space to process my feelings. Maybe even a little bit of danger to remind myself I'm alive.

The screen door creaks, scaring the deer away. I turn to find Damon lurking in the doorframe. "Can't be a creepy stalker with a creaky door like that," I tease.

He lets out a low chuckle. "Nothing a can of WD-40 won't fix."

Standing and stretching my arms above my head, I make my way over to him. "Jasper and Falin still arguing in there?"

"Of course. I swear if they're not already fucking, it's going to happen any day now." He wraps his arms around me and kisses the top of my head.

"I don't think he can handle her," I joke.

His chest rumbles with laughter. "You're probably right. He needs a kick in the ass though, so I approve."

Leon's voice calls from inside. "I found something. Get in here!"

Damon and I exchange surprised looks. We've all been pouring over every scrap of paper we found in Brennan's office, plus Leon and Falin have been working to hack into his electronics. Sadly, the only thing he had at the house was an older laptop. I assume most of his personal effects were at an office somewhere.

We hurry inside and find Leon actually grinning. I hadn't seen anything but a scowl on his face since the warehouse. Falin sits beside him and asks, "Did you do what I said?"

He barely moves his head, but she registers the slight nod. "Yeah, and I added this here." He points to his screen, where multiple programs are running at once.

"Well, what is it?" Damon asks, crouching to get a better look at the screen.

"How do you all feel about New York City?" Leon asks.

I glance around the room at each of their faces. Jasper's eyes widen. Falin smirks like she won a medal. Damon tenses his jaw. I'm the first one to speak. "Let's do it. If it brings us closer to taking these monsters down and finding Jasper's sister, then I'm all for it."

Damon turns to me, his brows furrowed. "Are you sure? That's a big change and with everything that's happened..."

"You heard the woman," Falin says, her tone enthusiastic. "We're moving to the city."

My jaw drops and I study my best friend's face. "You're coming? For real?"

"Of course. I'm in this now. Plus," she shoulder bumps Leon, "this bucket of fun over here needs my help. He wouldn't know a buffer overflow from a stack overflow."

Leon grumbles and flips her off. "I'm guessing that was an insult?" I ask, shaking my head.

"How'd you guess?" Falin teases.

Jasper seems to pipe in out of nowhere. "The city, huh? It's been a long time." I raise my brow at his slow, slurred response.

"Yeah, but not long enough. I fucking hate cities, but I guess that's where we're headed." Damon crosses his arms and leans back, almost knocking over a crocheted wall hanging.

"Aww, don't be sad, Freddy. You can chase me through Central Park." I kiss his dimple and squeeze his firm butt.

"On to more important things," Falin says. "What are we doing for Halloween tomorrow?"

"Oh, my God. How did I forget?" It's my favorite day of the year.

Damon slips out of the room, but before I can ask where he's going, Leon adds, "We should be packing and getting things squared away for the move. Every day we stay here is another day of them strengthening their numbers."

"You really think they're gone from this area?" I ask, finding it hard to believe an entire warehouse crew just up and relocated.

"I do. We've been watching. So has Ray and all his guys. They're gone. Once the cops got involved, it was too risky to stay here. They must have connections in the city. Maybe they're regrouping to buy new warehouses. That I don't know. But we can't wait to find out. There's loads to do."

"Jasper, why don't you go lay down? You look dead on your feet," Falin says in a tone laced with snark.

"I'm fine," he says. "Just need to eat."

Damon comes back into the room, holding a DVD and a grocery store shopping bag. "What's all this?" I ask.

"Our Halloween plans." He flashes the box and I laugh. It's

a copy of the original *A Nightmare on Elm Street*. "Complete with an entire bag of allergen-friendly candy."

"Aww," Falin cries out. "Damon wins the green flag boyfriend award of the year. But did you get *Scream* too? What about *Halloween*? I need some Ghostface and Michael on our special day."

I gather Damon into the biggest hug I can muster. "Thank you, that sounds absolutely perfect."

"Maybe I can get you to put on those vampire fangs again," he whispers, brushing his lips over mine.

"I think that can be arranged," I say.

"One more thing. Turn around." He spins me around and moves my hair to the side. "Grabbed this while I was looking for the DVD."

The weight of a pendant settles around my collarbone as he secures the clasp. I reach up to feel the locket he gave me. "I did miss wearing it."

"I missed seeing it on you."

Falin groans. "I'm bored. Isn't there someone we can go question? Or a kidnapped woman to rescue?"

Leon and Damon lock eyes and smirk. "There is something we can do," Damon says. "It's kind of a tradition for us. A boredom buster, some might call it."

She perks up. "I'm down. What are we talking about?"

"Fight club night," Leon croons. Falin's reaction isn't unlike mine when the guys introduced me to their nonsense. "You ladies can take round one."

"Absolutely not," I say. "I'm almost a doctor. I'm not going to beat the crap out of my best friend."

Falin shrugs and stands, stretching her arms from side to side. "Come on, Leon. Let's move the furniture."

"Wait, what's happening?" Jasper asks, finally piping in when he notices Falin stand.

"Fight club night, dummy," she says. "You better be ready. I was trained by a family of cops and I'm going to whoop all three of your asses."

"Oh, it's so on," Jasper drawls.

I wrap my fingers around my locket and watch the shenanigans unfold before me, grateful to know that in this chaotic and dangerous world, I have an anchor as long as we're together.

WANT AN EXTRA SPOOKY & SPICY BONUS SCENE?

Head to https://laurengreenebooks.com/ and check out the bonuses to read!

ACKNOWLEDGMENTS

Writing this book was a wild ride, but I loved every minute with Damon, Blake, and the gang. I'm grateful to so many people who supported me through every step of this project. Whether it was bouncing ideas, hyping me up, reading early drafts, or sharing social media graphics – I cannot thank you all enough.

Havoc, you gave me the nudge I needed and helped me transform a loose idea into an entire world. Thank you for showing me what I was too nervous to see for myself. Getting that thumbs up from you made me so proud.

Leah, I don't know what I'd do without you. Plain and simple, you're my soul sister forever, and I appreciate you beyond words.

To my beta readers – MJ, Veronica, Lizet, and Delaine – thank you for taking the time to read and provide much-needed feedback. I loved all your comments and deeply appreciate everything you've done to help shape this book into its best version.

To my family and friends, your endless support means everything to me. I love you all so much.

And to my readers, I couldn't do this without you. Thank you for everything.

ABOUT THE AUTHOR

Lauren crafts angsty, steamy romances filled with complex characters and witty banter. When she's not writing, she's navigating life in Arizona with her busy family. Lauren's creativity is fueled by spooky season vibes, reruns of The Office, and copious amounts of iced coffee. A devoted animal lover, she surrounds herself with furry companions while dreaming up her next happily ever after.

9 798987 636060